Best wishes
Cindy Bingha

MW00967346

LION'S
Awakening

Cindy Bingham

WESTBOW
PRESS
A DIVISION OF THOMAS NELSON

WestBow Press books may be ordered through booksellers or by contacting:

WestBow Press
A Division of Thomas Nelson
1663 Liberty Drive
Bloomington, IN 47403
www.westbowpress.com
1-(866) 928-1240

Scripture quotations taken from the New American Standard Bible®,
Copyright © 1960, 1962, 1963, 1968, 1971, 1972, 1973, 1975, 1977, 1995 by The
Lockman Foundation. Used by permission." (www.Lockman.org)

Scripture taken from the New King James Version. Copyright 1979, 1980,
1982 by Thomas Nelson, inc. Used by permission. All rights reserved.

ISBN: 978-1-4908-0281-7 (sc)
ISBN: 978-1-4908-0282-4 (hc)
ISBN: 978-1-4908-0280-0 (e)

Library of Congress Control Number: 2013913144

Printed in the United States of America.

WestBow Press rev. date: 8/23/2013

Dedication

This book is dedicated to Josh, whose question to me years ago when he sat in my English class prompted me to admit my desire to someday write a novel,

And to the ladies of my critique group, who helped me take the words I'd written and craft them into a story,

And to my husband Mark, whose love and encouragement never let me give up.

Introduction

Professional football in America is a multi-billion dollar industry fueled by ticket proceeds, advertising dollars, and sales of authorized NFL gear. The football faithful brave the traffic, the weather, and hostile crowds to attend the games of their favorite teams.

Feeding the ranks of the NFL are thousands of college men playing in schools, large and small. These athletes practice long hours, travel great distances, and set aside other facets of their lives for the opportunity of making a name for themselves among the pros. A small number are drafted each year by one of the thirty-two elite teams.

Lion's Awakening focuses on one portion of the college football players who don't make the NFL. Often these athletes are the ones who, because they show great promise, make the starting lineup and lead other members of their team. They are also the players who, despite great talent, never have the opportunity of becoming the next star. These are the men whose careers are forestalled by serious injury.

Christian athletes are not immune to life-altering injuries. Some turn away from God, give up, and become bitter and hopeless. Others "renew their strength" and move on. A few take the opportunity to tell others of their struggle to accept God's plan. By doing so, these men encourage people everywhere in whatever battle they face. *Lion's Awakening* was inspired by the life of one of those athletes.

I've taken his real-life example and woven it into Landon's fictional account. Landon, Emma, and all the other characters—except Joe Paterno—are fictional. Bellefonte is an authentic place, a charming town about ten miles from State College. The other towns are also real, as are Pizza Mia, W. C. Clarke, Rite Aid, and Talleyrand Park. Of course, Penn State University, Beaver Stadium, and The Creamery are actual places visited annually by hundreds of thousands.

.

CHAPTER 1 ═══

Football tickets. Four of them. Six rows back, the first seat three spaces to the right of the fifty-yard line. Great tickets to any game. But these weren't to just *any* game. They were tickets to a sold-out, scalper's heaven, football extravaganza. They were the gateway to one of *the* clashes in all of college football this season. With them, a lucky fan would be able to capture every bit of the highlight reel in real time and living color. This battle pitted Penn State against its rival Ohio State in a match up that would likely determine who made the coveted trip to the Rose Bowl in January. These tickets were a gold mine.

Landon Steele could only glare at them.

"Bob, why do you do this?" Landon fumed and paced.

Every football season for the last four, Bob Hughes had sent tickets from the PSU front office to Landon's desk—while Landon was away from it. The first year they were two seats not quite at nosebleed height, but definitely in binocular range. The following year Bob had secured two that were closer to the ground and on the twenty-yard line. Last year's offering had been seats in nearly the same spot, but Bob had included four tickets. Each year's game had been between PSU and one of its Big Ten opponents. All of the selections had been stellar match ups. The campus had buzzed for days before each one.

Every fall Landon had returned the tickets, thanked Bob for his thoughtfulness, and made plans to be out of town on game day.

But those games paled in the light of this one. Only once in forever did a game of this magnitude occur right here in Beaver Stadium. For this eleventh game of the season, both teams were undefeated. Both were ranked in the top five. Both were considered serious contenders for the national championship. And in front of Landon lay tickets to four of the best seats in the house.

"Die-hard fans would swap their grandmothers for you." Landon leveled a gaze at the innocent offenders. The phone rang. He started and then lunged for the handset. "Landon Steele speaking."

"Where's your secretary?" Bob Hughes asked in his good-humored manner. "Did you send her off to buy some more accounting worksheets and pencils?"

"Hello, to you, too, Bob," Landon replied, stifling his frustration at his father's long-time friend. "You know that I take my lunch break every day from noon to one, and she takes hers from one to two when I come back. That's why

1

you have deliveries made here *before* one, but you call *after* one so that you don't have to go through Rosalee. I'm afraid your clock is a bit off though. It's 1:55. You're lucky she's not already back."

Apparently oblivious to Landon's assessment, Bob continued. "So you got my delivery, did you?"

"Right here in front of me."

"Can you believe those seats? I almost kept the tickets for Sara and Tony and their kids. Would have made me 'Grandpa of the Year.'"

"They still can. I'll send them back later today."

"You'll do no such thing, young man. It's been four seasons. You'll graciously accept those tickets, invite your mom, your dad, and some other over-the-top Lions supporter. Then you will sit near the fifty and yell like crazy as Penn State cracks open the Ohio State Buckeyes this Saturday. That's what you'll do."

"I can't."

"You can, Landon."

"Too many memories."

"You don't have memories any other times?"

"Sure I do. They'll be worse at the game."

"How do you know? You haven't set foot anywhere near a gridiron for four years."

Landon crumpled a nearby requisition sheet and threw it at the door. Why couldn't Bob understand?

"Saturday's forecast is sixty-five and sunny." Unseasonably warm for mid-November in Happy Valley. "Get outside and enjoy it. Bring your parents. Your dad will holler like a maniac, and your mom will cozy up beside him and scream in his ear."

Landon knew that Bob was right. He wondered how he could explain away those tickets if Mom and Dad ever found out about them. They'd be crushed to have missed such an opportunity. Nonetheless, Landon would return Bob's gift this afternoon as usual and visit his parents this weekend in Philipsburg as he did most home-game Saturdays. The thirty-five minute drive got him away from the football frenzy and nearer the ones who understood his situation best.

"Your dad and I had a nice chat this morning," Bob said, interrupting Landon's thoughts. "I'll see you around, Landon. No need to thank me." The click ended Bob's call and left Landon gaping at the receiver.

2

"Thank you? Thank you!" Landon exploded. "I want to wring your neck, Bob Hughes. How dare you? Give *me* the tickets but tell *my dad* about them. You meddling, officious, overbearing, pushy know-it-all. You don't have a clue."

The intercom buzzed. "What?" he barked.

"Sorry to interrupt you, Mr. Steele. Are you all right? I just returned and heard voices." His secretary's apologetic tone relaxed Landon's clenched fists.

"Yes, Rosalee." He forced himself to exhale. "I'm fine."

A pause ensued, followed by, "Oh, okay, sir—if you're sure."

"Just venting. Sorry."

"Can I do anything to help?"

Dear, thoughtful Rosalee. She was old enough to be Landon's mother, if not his grandmother, and she was practically an institution at the university. She could have moved up the ladder to just about anywhere, but she wouldn't.

Landon could hear her mantra even now. "No way am I leaving this office, not until I'm so stiff they have to pry me from this chair." She hadn't yet given any indication that anyone should get the crowbar.

"Please, give me about twenty minutes," Landon said. Twenty minutes would be more than enough time to scratch out some words of regret and thanks. "I'll have a letter ready for Bob Hughes. If you'd see that it's delivered, I'd be grateful."

"Of course, sir. Twenty minutes."

Landon flopped down into his black leather desk chair and rubbed his throbbing temples. A short time later he hunched forward, resting his elbows on the desk and his chin on his hands.

Out of the corner of his eye, he glimpsed the picture of his mom and dad, the only photo Landon kept on his desk. The snapshot had been taken last fall, on a Saturday when the three of them were raking a mountain of leaves from the maple and oak trees shading his childhood home. When Dad declared he needed a break, Landon had headed inside for a glass of water. Looking through the window, he studied his parents who stood a few feet away. Dad rested one hand on top of the rake handle and the other at Mom's waist. She stood at his side but was facing him and had enclosed him in a squeeze around his middle. Their faces hovered mere inches apart, and their eyes divulged secrets as they grinned at one another. Even after nearly thirty years of marriage, they were crazy about each other. Landon's heart flip-flopped and his face reddened at their intimacy. Grabbing his mom's camera, he hurried out to take their picture. The posed version lacked the "spark" that Landon had glimpsed moments before, but this photo would always be one of his favorites.

He reached for the frame. He had wonderful parents. He would not have survived the last few years without them. How could he deny them this rare opportunity? But how could he possibly endure reliving his past by revisiting Beaver Stadium?

━━━━━━

At 2:45 p.m. Bob Hughes's secretary buzzed his office.

"Sir, a letter marked urgent just came for you."

"Urgent?"

"Yes, sir."

"Who's it from?"

"It has your stamp on it. It looks like you sent it to someone here on campus and that person returned it to you."

Bob sighed. "Bring it in, please, Nancy."

Nancy entered his office moments later. Grasping the envelope, he could feel the ticket shape. Landon. "Thanks. I'll take care of it." Bob knew that he'd have no trouble finding someone to take the tickets. Sara's family might still be able to make arrangements even though it was already Thursday afternoon and the game was Saturday.

With a heavy heart, he lifted the envelope flap and reached for the contents. When his fingers met the paper, he gasped and riveted his gaze on what he held: one ticket with a small notepaper clipped to it. "We'll need only three. Thanks."

━━━━━━

Friday morning Landon parked in his assigned lot, shuffled a few blocks, and entered W. C. Clarke's at 7:30. A few regulars greeted him with, "Mornin', Landon," as they passed through, clutching their sustaining cups of daybreak java. The aroma of roasting coffee beans flooded the entire building and wafted up and down the street, playing the Pied Piper to everyone within its enticing lure. Perky freshmen, dignified professors, and on-duty policemen alike flocked to Clarke's for the best coffee in State College.

More foggy-headed than usual, Landon navigated the morning crowd, making his way to the counter to pour and pay for his cup of liquid fortification. A pile of dollar bills and some change cluttered the counter top, a testament to the "honor system" method of payment at W.C.'s. He put his money down, didn't bother making change, and headed toward the exit.

"Whoa, Landon. If I didn't know you better, I'd think you went on a binge last night. You look terrible, buddy," said Pete Thomas, a campus night watchman just coming off duty. He stationed himself between Landon and the door.

"Yeah, well, I didn't."

"Problems?"

"Just one," Landon mumbled, wishing Pete would blockade someone else and let him pass.

"If one problem makes you look like this, man, you're in big trouble."

"Tell me about it." Landon sidestepped, careful not to spill his coffee, and quickly shoved the door with his shoulder. Back outside, he heaved a sigh. "Call your dad, already. No matter what you decide, you and your dad have to talk. You need some sleep."

Sleep wasn't something Landon got a lot of, even without the issue of offending football tickets. Memories haunted, unfulfilled dreams beckoned. If he slept four hours at a time, he'd had a restful night. Catnaps sustained him: twenty minutes at lunch time in his car or office, a half-hour after supper most nights. Often at night a pain, not physical but emotional, stalked him from his bed, to the couch, to his favorite recliner. No matter where he went, he couldn't escape. Last night the digital clock on the DVD player read 2:43 when he'd dragged himself from the sofa and settled into the chair. Tucking the fleecy throw around his neck, Landon had shifted slightly to his right, heaved an exhausted sigh, and closed his eyes.

Forty minutes later shouts of "No! No! Noooo!" had catapulted him forward. What was that? Was someone in trouble? Stock still, Landon had listened, his heart thudding. One, two, three seconds elapsed. Only then had Landon sensed the wetness on his cheeks. Wiping furiously at his face, he'd slumped back. His heart rate diminishing, Landon recognized the truth. Once again, the anguished cries were his own, and as they had so many times, they thrust before him four-year-old images that were sharper than those any high-definition television could deliver.

———

Game day. The visitors' locker room in Iowa City, Iowa, was abuzz.

"Hey, Steele. What's it feel like suitin' up for PSU for the last away game ever?"

Landon paused from adjusting his shoulder pads. Less than a foot away, Bernard "Jordy" Jordan, the Lions' sophomore offensive tackle, shoved his left foot into his left shoe, hefted both onto the bench in front of him, and strained to tie the shoelaces.

Landon reached for his navy jersey with the white 58 on it and chuckled to himself as he watched the nearly-300-pound lineman bend his prodigious blue-clad belly over his bent knee. "Kind of sad, Jordy. Can't believe four years have gone so fast."

"Yeah, well, next year you'll be puttin' on the pads of some NFL team and makin' the big bucks. Who do you hope drafts you?"

"Any team that will let me play."

"Oh, c'mon, man. You gotta have a favorite. Where do you and the Butkus Award want to start out?"

"I haven't won the Butkus. There's …"

"You haven't won it *yet*," Jordy interrupted. "Just a few days and some paper work."

"I hope you're right, but Stevens from Notre Dame has almost as many tackles as I do. He's from a school with lots of tradition—including several Heismann Trophy winners."

"But we're not talkin' the Heismann. We're talkin' the Butkus, the award given to the best linebacker, and you just happen to be that guy. And you're from Penn State, which just happens to be Linebacker U."

"Like I said, I hope you're right. I need a strong game today."

"Those Hawkeyes better look out, 'cause we're here to help you claim that trophy."

━━━━━━

Landon shivered every time he recalled that day. The air temperature read forty-five, but a cold rain pelted down, spotting helmet shields and puddling in squishy slop along one hash mark. Running backs slid as they tried to take corners. Wide receivers dropped routine catches. The weather was miserable, and for many players, their performances matched the conditions.

Landon was one of the few whose game lived up to the hype surrounding it. By midway through the fourth quarter, he had racked up three tackles, broken up a couple passes, and nearly intercepted another. The score stood at 7-6 with Penn State leading.

With fewer than five minutes left, Iowa received a punt and began to move downfield, much to the dismay of the Penn State coaches and defensive squad. As captain, Landon huddled his unit together. "Come on, guys. No more Iowa first downs." He called the play, looking around the circle to make eye contact with each man. "Go Lions."

On first and ten, the Hawkeyes tried a reverse, but Landon wasn't fooled. He held his position. When the play eventually headed back in his direction, he dropped the ball carrier for a two-yard loss. On second and twelve, Bly, Iowa's quarterback, attempted a pass but was high and off the mark.

Third down would be another pass. Everyone expected that. What Landon hadn't expected was that Iowa's quarterback would fake to his left and trick Landon's fellow linebacker, Leo Jones, into leaping into the air for the would-be pass. When Leo launched himself, Bly drew back his arm and lofted a fifteen-yard spiral that was headed for an open receiver.

In the center of the field, Landon had seen the play unfolding in front of him almost as if it were in slow motion. He saw Bly's pump fake and recognized Leo's mistake. Just as Bly cocked his arm the second time, Landon raced toward the tight end. Three steps away from the Hawkeye, Landon watched the receiver leap, catch the spiraling pigskin, and reel it in, clutching it to himself. Still in stride, Landon propelled himself into the opponent's ribcage, blasting the football with his helmet and shooting the brown projectile into the air and across the mud.

Landing on top of the outstripped Hawkeye, Landon scrambled to his feet, half-running, half-crawling through the slick mud toward the elusive leather oval. With a leap that would have made a toad proud, he snatched the ball to his chest just before ingesting a mouthful of brown muck.

What Landon's slow-motion internal camera hadn't caught was the nearly half-ton mass of players that clambered toward the ball. His camera had also missed Iowa's mammoth left tackle, the guy with the monstrous thigh that somehow lodged itself under Landon's calf. When one player landed on Landon's ankle and the bulk of another hit his knee, the lineman's thigh became the fulcrum over which Landon's left tibia and fibula could not bend. The splintering reality struck with a sickening crunch and excruciating pain.

In that one play, Landon secured a victory for Penn State. He tied up the necessary votes for the Butkus Award. He guaranteed himself a position as a first-round draft pick.

And he lost everything he'd ever hoped for.

What Landon had been unable to see, cameramen all over the stadium had captured—his living nightmare. In three ticks of the clock, Landon's football dream had vaporized.

Four years later, the internal replays still haunted him. And they always ended with his own gut-wrenching words: "No! No! Nooooo!"

CHAPTER 2

With his still-steaming but half-empty travel mug in his hand, Landon forced himself to jog the last block to his office building to prove that he still could. Instead of lifting his spirits, the jog triggered thoughts of one of the morose ironies of his injury. Within a little over a year, he had recovered nearly 100 percent of the use of his left leg. All the glasses of milk, coupled with years of weight training and a lack of unhealthful habits, had forged strong, resilient bones which responded to treatment far better than the doctors had hoped. He could run nearly as quickly as before and even manage the stops, turns, and spins so essential to a linebacker. Landon's problem wasn't one of physical healing. His hurtle was reestablishing his football reputation.

After his recovery, he had sent a highlight video to every NFL team, a montage of his greatest college plays and the post-surgery evidence that he could still make those moves. Only one team scout had responded. The conversation had been short.

"Sorry, son, but if you haven't taken the hits for over a year, I can't take the risk."

No one was willing to draft a linebacker who had crushed his fibula and suffered two compound fractures to his tibia. No matter what his accomplishments at PSU, Landon Steele was just another name on a vast roster of college standouts who might have made it in the pros.

If only his injury had occurred after he'd signed a contract, then the team doctors would have labored night and day using state-of-the art equipment to resurrect Landon to his former greatness. The cold, hard facts were, however, that Landon had been left with an unfulfilled dream, a shattered leg, a wrecked life—and no professional interest or money to help him regain any of them.

Reaching the third floor, he struggled to shake off the gloom. He paused in front of Rosalee's desk to wish her a good morning, review his schedule, and get any news. Turning from her toward his own door, he heard the phone ring. Rosalee reached for it.

"Landon Steele's office. How may I help you?"

Landon inserted his key into the lock at the same time Rosalee waved in his direction.

"Your mom," she mouthed before responding ale just now coming in." Landon pointed one finger in the air, "Give him a moment to set down his things, and he'll be wit

Entering his office, Landon heard Rosalee's half of the Harold and I will be there on Saturday for sure. People say v college football, but we wouldn't miss it."

With a lump in his throat, Landon cradled the receiver and press "Hi, Mom. What can I do for you?"

"Landon, do I call you only when I need something? I hope not. That s so—so—mercenary of me." Without giving him a moment to answer, she add "You sound a little down this morning."

"Rough night. I'll be all right as soon as my morning caffeine kicks in. What's up?"

"Sure you're okay?"

"I'm okay, Mom. Why'd you call?"

"Uh—well—I'm ashamed to admit it. I called because I need a favor." At Landon's chuckle she said, "And don't laugh at your mother."

Landon stifled himself to a grin. "You're funny when you're paranoid."

"I'm not paranoid, but I don't want you to feel used. I'm still trying to get used to having an adult son. This is uncharted territory for me."

"Me, too. But I've been out of the house almost four years. How long will you need?"

"I don't know. Maybe until I die, but at least until you get married."

"Don't rush the first thing, and don't hold your breath on the second. Now, what's the favor?"

"Are you coming up tomorrow?"

After Landon had wondered all night about how to broach the subject of this weekend, his mom had opened the door. "Actually, no. Thought I'd come tonight." Inspiration struck. "Cook one of my favorites?"

"You bet! What sounds good?"

"You know what I like. Surprise me."

"I'll do that, and I may surprise your dad by not telling him you're coming. You'll be here at what time?"

"Probably not before seven. I'll stop by my apartment after work and get what I need."

"Okay. See you then. Bye, dear. Drive carefully. I love—"

"Mom, what about your favor?" Landon hoped she hadn't hung up.

My goodness, I forgot." Her laughter at the other end of the line mingled with his. "I'm not paranoid, but I might be losing my mind. I think there's a difference. Oh, well, at least I'm happy."

Landon let her ramble; the longer she talked, the better he felt.

"I'm making some bruschetta for a luncheon on Monday, and I really would love about a pound of fresh imported mozzarella, the kind you can get at ..."

"At W. C. Clarke's." Landon finished for her. "I just came from there."

"You were buying cheese this morning?"

Landon cringed at the thought of caffeine and cheddar. "Today's roasting day. Only dead people or lunatics who don't drink coffee skip W.C.'s on roasting day."

"Coffee in a cheese shop. I don't understand it, but I know their mozzarella is heavenly. It makes such a difference. Could you also pick up some good olive oil—not too large a bottle. I don't use it very fast."

Landon had been scribbling as she spoke. "Fresh mozzarella—about a pound—and not too large a bottle of good olive oil—whatever 'good' is."

"Just tell the people there. They'll know what I need."

"I hope so. I won't be any help."

"Maybe not, but you're the best delivery man ever. Thanks so much. We'll see you around seven. Love you, Son."

"Love you, too, Mom. Bye."

At 6:14, Friday evening, Landon entered his apartment, one minute earlier than he'd hoped. The errand he'd run for his mom meant that he would really have to hustle. Setting his black brief case on the floor just inside the door, he removed his dress shoes, wiggled his toes, and jogged to the kitchen. He needed water. Seconds later he chugged a full bottle. "Ahhhh." Tossing the plastic into the recycling bin, he strode toward the bedroom, where he emptied the contents of his pockets onto the bed. He changed from his gray slacks, white shirt, and PSU tie to a pair of khakis and a black polo.

His duffel bag awaited him, front and center on a shelf in his closet. Flinging it to the bed, Landon absently began throwing in his usuals: shorts and a T-shirt to sleep in, well-worn jeans and sweatshirt for Saturday, the necessities for underneath, along with his shaving kit and shower essentials. He was returning to the closet for slacks, dress shirt and tie for church on Sunday when he remembered; he needed something to wear to the football game—tomorrow's football game.

Ignoring his tight schedule, Landon grasped the sides of his short hair and flopped face down onto the bed. The change from his pocket leaped from the comforter like hot oil in a frying pan. "What have I agreed to? How will I ever survive?" He buried his face in the thick blue comforter.

Moments later he raised his head, his mind recalling a verse that he had often claimed during his college years. "I can do *all things* through Christ who strengthens me." Its message had grown faint in the years since his accident. Pressing his face to the bed cover once again, Landon clenched its softness in his fists and released a muffled yell. When he finally looked up, a glance at the clock confirmed his suspicion. He was going to be late.

Grabbing the first blue and white clothes he could reach, he chucked them into his bag. Then he snagged his duffel, the hanging clothes, and his wallet before dropping a pair of sneakers in front of him and jamming his feet into them. At the door, he stopped and retrieved the shoes he'd just removed. Once outside, he locked the door and dashed to his car.

━━━━━━━

With two minutes to spare, Landon rounded the corner onto Cherry Lane and turned into the first drive on the left. Amazingly, he had managed to make up the minutes he'd lost at his apartment. If his mom commented on his being right on time, he would mention the lack of heavy traffic. Not his average rate of speed.

Taking only the grocery items with him, he let himself in at the front door and was immediately greeted by enticing aromas.

"I'm here. Whatever you made, Mom, it smells great."

Simultaneously, his dad emerged from the hallway, and his mom poked her head around the doorway from the kitchen.

"Stuffed shells, tossed salad, homemade bread sticks. What do you think?"

"I think I should come for supper more often." Landon bent to give her a hug. "Your cheese and olive oil, ma'am."

"Oh, thank you, sir. My luncheon ladies will be ecstatic. Dinner's all set."

Landon turned and hugged his father. "Hi, Dad. Did you know I was coming?"

Mom answered for Dad. "When I started baking a pie, he got suspicious. I had to tell him."

"I seldom get pie any more except when you come home." Landon's dad winked and clapped him on the shoulder. "Let's eat. I've smelled this sauce all afternoon. I'm ready to put a little of it onto a piece of cardboard and dig in."

Mom guffawed and patted Dad's slight paunch. "You poor thing, you're positively wasting away."

During salad, Landon's jitters emerged as butterflies flitting in his throat. By the time Mom had served the pasta, they raced like greyhounds through his chest. At the meal's end, nervous elephants thundered in the pit of his stomach.

"Pie now or later?" Mom asked.

"What do you think, Dad?"

"I think coffee now and pie later."

"I think you're half right. I say coffee now; pie *and* coffee later."

His mom smiled at the two of them and said, "I'll put the coffee on and load the dishwasher. See you shortly."

Landon stood and started to gather up the plates, but she slapped at his hand. "I'll do this. Go."

Not for the first time in his life, Landon wondered whether his mom was clairvoyant. Did she sense his anxiety? Had Dad said something about the tickets? Whatever the case, the time was now.

Landon waited until his dad settled on the couch and then sat next to him. "I need to ask you something."

Dad crossed his right ankle over his left knee. "What is it?"

"Bob Hughes told you about the tickets for tomorrow's game, didn't he?"

"Just yesterday. Seemed convinced you'd send them back to him."

"Did he say anything else?"

"Nothing except to ask me to convince you to use them." His father's brows drew together. "You're going to, aren't you?"

Landon's back stiffened. "Two of them, anyway. I don't want you and Mom to miss out."

"You returned your ticket?"

Wondering why he had kept the third ticket, Landon sidestepped. "I haven't been back. The memories." He gulped loudly. "Too painful. Not sure I can."

"Can? Or want to?"

"Want to? You think I *want to* avoid football?" Landon slapped his hands on his thighs and stared at his dad. "I had my life's dreams right here," he said, raising a palm toward his dad. "And then in one play, everything disappeared." His hand plummeted to the couch. "No Butkus Award, no being drafted, no playing in the NFL. Nothing but weeks of injuries followed by months of rehabilitation, all so that the most exciting thing I do with my life is jog down the sidewalk."

"Many men with football injuries can't even do that."

"Don't quote me the stats, Dad. I know. 'I'm one of the lucky ones.'"

"Not 'lucky,' Landon. Blessed. You don't realize how blessed."

"I don't feel blessed."

"Being blessed isn't about feelings. It's about truth."

Landon gripped the sofa cushion and clenched his teeth.

His dad continued, "They carried you off that field badly injured but with most of your body intact and your mind totally unharmed. Eventually, you recovered completely."

These football discussions never changed. Why couldn't his dad grasp the disappointment that haunted Landon every day?

"You earned your accounting degree and landed a fine job. The only thing you lost was a professional football career, a tremendous opportunity, for sure, but certainly not a necessity. You *are* blessed, Landon, even though you choose not to believe it."

Landon sighed and rubbed the back of his neck. "Football is my first love. Why would God ..."

Dad raised his hand, halting Landon's words. "Say that again."

"What?"

"What is football to you?"

"It's my first love."

"Still?"

"Always."

"Interesting you should say it that way." Dad leaned to his right and collected his reading glasses and a thin soft-backed book from the top of the Bible that sat on the end table.

Landon recognized the book as the guide his dad's Bible study group was working through.

Dad leafed a few pages into the book and then scanned one page closely. Settling his glasses on his nose, he began to read. "'Perhaps no place in scripture more vividly contrasts doing things for God and being in love with God than does Revelation chapter 2, verses 1-4.'"

At the reference, Landon lowered his head and braced himself for what he knew was coming.

"'To the angel of the church in Ephesus write: ... I know your deeds and your toil and perseverance, and that you cannot tolerate evil men, and you put to the test those who call themselves apostles, ... and are not, and you have perseverance and have endured for My name's sake, and have not grown weary. But I have this against you, that you have left your first love.'"

When his dad stopped reading, Landon looked up but said nothing. He hoped his father would quit there. Dad continued.

"'Christians in Ephesus were doing all the right things on the outside: working diligently, enduring hardships, avoiding evil men and their influences, even protecting the church from false teachers. But God wanted less action and more love. He wanted their hearts most of all. He knew that other things—even good things—had pushed Him out.'"

Dad laid the book back on the stand. With a gaze that Landon recognized as one of both sympathy and rebuke, he said, "Maybe you stay away from football because your love for it is stronger than your love for God, and you're angry because He isn't willing to take second place." Setting his glasses on top of the book again, Landon's dad rose. "I'll go out to the kitchen and help Mom bring in the pie and coffee."

The condemning words scorched Landon's mind and heart. He lowered his head into his upturned palms and muttered, "Dad's right." Tears stung his eyes as he looked up and whispered, "It shouldn't be that way."

Two empty dessert plates and an untouched piece of apple pie sat on the coffee table while the cuckoo clock sounded its eleventh chime. Landon's mom said, "I'm going to bed. Is it settled? Shall I pull out my blue and white for tomorrow?"

"What do you think, Son?" Dad asked.

"I'll try."

His mom's soft brown eyes became liquid. She reached over to squeeze Landon's hand. "We'll do all we can to help." A moment later she smiled. "We haven't been to a game in so long, I might be too excited to sleep." She rose and gathered the plates and coffee mugs. "Don't stay up all night solving the problems of the world. I'll see you two in the morning. Love you both."

When she had gone, Dad spoke. "You look as if you could use some rest. Will you be able to sleep?"

"Maybe. I never know. Deciding to face this thing might help."

His father leaned forward. "Remember what you've admitted tonight. But don't resign yourself to the idea that football can have *no* place in your life. It's okay to love football as long as you love God more."

With that, Dad rose. Landon joined him and engulfed his dad in a bear-like hug. "Thanks."

They drew apart. "You're more than welcome." Dad massaged his arms and shoulders as though restoring circulation to them. "Just so you know, you still have the clutch of a linebacker. I'll see you in the morning."

———

Saturday's weather was all that Bob had predicted—sunny and nearly fifty degrees by mid-morning—balmy for November in the Nittany Valley. As expected, what would normally be a thirty-five minute road trip followed by a few minutes to park, turned into a stop-and-go traffic marathon and a parking ordeal that lasted nearly three hours. Electing to forego the tailgating festivities, Landon and his parents arrived at the peak of the pre-game invasion. Directed by policemen, campus security, and multitudes of people hired specifically to park cars, Landon finally reached his appointed spot. "Man, that's one part of game day I'd forgotten about. Players road on the bus, got off near the tunnel, and ran through when we were ready. What a rat race."

Grinning, his mom stepped from the back seat of the car. "Welcome to the pack."

Fifteen minutes later, the three jostled along in the masses. Crossing the threshold into the stadium, Landon glanced at the crisp white lines on the field, saw the chain gang with their down markers at the ready, heard the warm-up notes from the Blue Band. And felt his heart stop. He gasped, forcing himself to breathe.

"Hey, buddy, keep moving," someone yelled, shoving Landon from behind.

Landon stood, rooted where he was. He couldn't inch one step farther. He had to get out. Turning, he lowered his head, ready to tackle anyone who stood in his path.

His dad's large hands closed on his shoulders like vise grips. "Landon. Landon, look at me."

"I can't take it." He jerked from his dad's grasp, rushed by him—and collided head-on with his mom.

Taking quick steps backwards, she struggled to regain control. Milliseconds later a hand jerked out and clutched her fleece hoodie at the back of her neck. Too late to rescue her entirely, the grasp did, however, lessen her collision with unrelenting concrete.

"Mom, are you hurt? I'm so sorry." Landon knelt beside her.

"Yeah, lady, are you okay?"

Landon looked up and saw a tall, scrawny kid with hair so fiery red that folks at the University of Tennessee could have collared him as a Volunteer and used him as the poster child for their trademark orange. Sprouting from that lanky frame was the arm connected to the hand that had just released his mom's shirt.

Poster boy bent down and asked again, "Are you hurt?"

Betty's eyes darted from one to the other before she said to Landon, "Could you help me up?"

Dad pressed Landon aside. "Are you okay?"

"Not quite sure, but I think so." Looking quickly behind her she called, "Thanks so much."

The teen's face mirrored the brightness of his hair. "You're welcome. Sorry you hit the ground."

"You did what you could."

Ashamed at his own recklessness, Landon added, "Thanks again."

"No problem. Enjoy the game," he said, springing toward two younger boys whose equally fluorescent hair tagged them as his brothers.

Dad guided the three of them to the edge of the traffic flow. "Can you enjoy the game, Betty?"

"Of course I can. I've taken harder falls. What happened, Landon? Suddenly I couldn't get out of your way fast enough."

Landon fingered the change in his pocket before answering. "The field, the band, the fans—I panicked." He pressed the base of his palms to his temples. "I'm such an idiot."

Dad slapped his shoulder. "Ease up on yourself." He stared intently at Landon. "Remember what football gave you—what it means to you."

When someone bumped her again, Mom said, "We can't stand here much longer. Are we going to our seats or back to the car?"

Landon forced a small grin. He handed the tickets to his dad. "You lead the way. Mom can stay back here with me. If I decide to make a run for it, at least she won't be behind me."

Diving back into the crush of people, the three progressed slowly but without further misadventure. Row six. Looking to his right, Landon noticed a group of what he took to be college-aged men sitting just beyond the three seats that were the Steeles'. None of the men wore shirts. Each had some combination of a blue and white PSU logo painted across his chest.

Nodding toward the crew up ahead, Landon reached for his dad's elbow. "Let me go first."

His dad sat next to Landon, and Mom took the seat on Dad's left.

Kickoff was scheduled at 1:00, twenty minutes from the time they settled in. Landon watched the cheerleading squad and then turned his attention to the preparations for the singing of the national anthem. After that he scrutinized the yellow-sashed security crew as they made their presence felt throughout the stands. Only seconds before the starting lineups were announced did he allow himself to focus on the white-clad men huddled at one sideline. The home team, the Nittany Lions.

Coach Joe Paterno, well past retirement age, but still young at heart, stood several inches shorter than many of the players encircling him. Their strength and size could have intimidated him. Instead, it seemed to invigorate him. Landon watched as the octogenarian general rallied his troops.

He still loves this game.

His favorite Coach Paterno moments replayed in Landon's head. Their stunning realism eclipsed the playing of the National Anthem and masked the tossing of the coin. Not until the Buckeye kicker lofted the ball toward a Penn State receiver did Landon shake himself from the memories and realize the game had begun. A football game that he was watching from inside Beaver Stadium.

CHAPTER 3

Landon clenched his jawbones tightly. He clutched the bleacher beneath him. With each pop of the pads or clash of opposing helmets, he flinched and squeezed harder.

Both teams suffered the jitters at first, each one going three-and-out on its first possession. On its second try, however, Penn State mounted an effort that moved the ball downfield, close to field-goal range. With third down and one yard to go, the Lions' running back got the ball, took one step forward and instantly collided with the Ohio State safety, an All-American whose tackle slapped the ball-carrier to the ground with a resounding thud.

A hush smothered the stadium as the young man lay motionless, and several seconds slipped by. Landon's heart raced. Memories as strong as a choke hold squeezed the breath from him.

Then, as suddenly as he had hit the ground, the running back jumped to his feet, shook his head and arms, and jogged to the sidelines.

When Landon could breathe again, he turned to his dad. "I think he just got the wind knocked out of him."

"I think you did, too."

"Yeah, I guess so." A half-smile crossed Landon's face.

Throughout the course of the first thirty minutes, Landon's heart rate fluctuated between fast and turbo, and by the end of the second quarter, his hands seemed molded to the seat he still grasped. The lead had bounced back and forth, both teams showing why they were highly and nearly evenly ranked. At halftime, the scoreboard read Ohio State 17, Penn State, 15.

As soon as the clock registered zero, Dad left for the men's room, hoping to be back before play resumed. Landon stood where he was. He wanted nothing more than a good stretch. And that would have remained true if a woman in front of him hadn't bought a hot dog. Recognizing its tantalizing smell, Landon felt famished.

Sliding to his left, he tapped his mom's shoulder. "Mom, I'm getting a hot dog. You want one?"

His mom turned toward him. "I think I'll pass. I ate enough at breakfast to hold me." She stopped abruptly. "Where are my manners? Landon, I'd like you to meet my new friend, Emma." She motioned to the young woman seated on the

18

other side of her. "We've been getting to know each other during the television timeouts. Emma, this is my son, Landon."

The short brunette looked around Landon's mom and extended a hand. "Nice to meet you, Landon—" Her eyes dilated and her jaw dropped. "You're Landon Steele—*the* Landon Steele."

Her amazement, coupled with his befuddlement, beckoned the blood from every other portion of Landon's body to his neck and face. "The only one I know of," he blurted. "Should I know you?"

Emma gasped then covered her gaping mouth. "I'm so sorry." Now her face began to glow. "We've never met. You shouldn't know me from anyone."

"But you know me?"

"I'm a Penn State grad. A sophomore here during your senior year. *Everyone* on campus knew who you were, especially after *Sports Illustrated* published the article about you and included your picture."

When Landon furrowed his brow, she giggled. "Your face hung in the rooms of so many female co-eds, it's a wonder you weren't attacked by their boyfriends on a daily basis. Good thing they knew how hard you could tackle."

Landon's mom, who had remained silent throughout their exchange, piped up. "Did your room have Landon's picture?"

Landon grimaced at his mom's frank inquiry, but as Emma's discomfort became apparent, he leaned forward to hear her answer.

"Actually, my roommate and I each had one."

Landon's mom elbowed Emma. "No wonder we hit it off so well. You have good taste."

"Oh, Mom." Landon groaned. "I'm going back to my seat now and wait for the hot dog guy. Should I get Dad one?"

"Definitely. Ketchup and mustard for him."

"Would you get one for me, too?" Emma asked as she dug into her pocket and pulled out some cash.

"Sure." Landon raised one hand in the air to get the vendor's attention and then took her money in the other. Why hadn't he thought to ask her if she wanted anything? In a short time, a hawker approached to his right. Hot dogs and money began the back and forth trip as the blue and white crew played the part of go between.

"Emma, switch places with me so that you can get your hot dog and your change without having to reach around me," Mom said.

Landon cringed. She was so obvious.

Both the hot dogs and the change, along with a couple of sodas, made the line from peddler to patron without mishap. When Dad returned, he took the seat where Emma had been and then enjoyed his unexpected treat, finishing just as the PSU kicker catapulted the football toward the opposing end zone.

While they ate their hot dogs, Landon stole glances at Emma. She was short—five feet, three or four inches, he guessed, and thin. He liked the dimples that formed when she smiled. And she smiled a lot. He liked that, too. Her dark brown eyes that had stared so openly at him, now darted around as she stretched to watch the second-half kickoff. The wind blew tendrils of her shoulder length brown hair.

Emma wore dark blue jeans, a white, long-sleeved shirt, and a white Penn State sweatshirt. She was pretty, not in a glamorous way, but definitely pretty. She and his mom chatted during timeouts, but during the game, she was as riveted to the action as Landon was.

When the Penn State quarterback connected with the wide receiver for a twenty-five-yard gain, and the stands erupted, Emma jumped to her feet as quickly as he did.

"Go, Penn State," she yelled, turning toward him. Her eyes gleamed. "First and goal on the eight."

Landon grinned at her, but when she turned back to the game, he studied this enigma beside him: pretty enough to turn a guy's head, plucky enough to save his picture from a magazine, and savvy enough to follow the game. Quite a combination.

The second half was a back-and-forth heart stopper. The close score and Emma's presence drew Landon's mind away from himself.

In the third quarter, Penn State took its first lead of the game. Emma clutched hands with Mom, and the two of them jumped and cheered like schoolgirls. When the final quarter came around, the Lions' field goal kicker added three points, giving PSU an eight-point advantage.

As the ball floated through the uprights, Emma grabbed Landon's arm and squealed in his ear.

Never had he been at a football game in the company of a young woman. Back when he was playing, most of the females he knew were interested in the game only because it got them nearer him and his notoriety. He'd determined that, for the most part, young women and football should remain apart. Watching Emma, he wasn't so sure.

Even though down by eight, the Buckeyes didn't quit. Ohio State mounted an impressive drive that chewed up much of the fourth quarter. Landon, a captain to his core, coached the defense. "Stay in position," he yelled when the outside linebacker missed his assignment. Several times he roared, "Make that tackle." With the ball resting on the nineteen-yard line, and OSU needing fifteen yards for a first down, it appeared that the Lions had halted the assault.

Third down. Landon watched the quarterback as he dropped back to pass, and a memory as clear as a newly washed window flashed in his brain. The pump fake, the cornerback jumping in that direction, the split second when the receiver was open.

"Get back there!" Landon hollered, leaping up. "Get back!"

Too late, the PSU cornerback recognized his mistake. By that time, the receiver was dancing into the end zone, being pummeled by exultant teammates.

As Landon growled, Emma asked, "Will they go for two?"

"I would. They want the tie if they can get it."

The Ohio State coach agreed. After only a few ticks of the clock, the score was deadlocked.

Less than three minutes remained. After the kickoff, Penn State started at its twenty-yard line. Three downs later, the punter returned the ball to the Buckeyes.

The clock read 1:53 when Ohio State's offense took the field again. If Penn State could stop them from scoring and get the ball back, the Lions would have a chance to score before the game ended in a tie and went into overtime. After the first run, Ohio State called its first timeout to conserve precious seconds. Another running play resulted in only a couple yards and the Buckeyes' second timeout. On third and long, the Buckeye quarterback's pass landed incomplete.

The Ohio State punter took the field, stepped off his kicking distance, and readied himself for the snap. When it sailed higher than expected, a gasp engulfed the stadium. The punter leaped into the air, tipping the ball with one hand and catching it as it fell into his arms. Then, avoiding tackles, he somehow found an open man and tossed the ball laterally to a receiver who thundered his way down the field and into the end zone. An Ohio State gaffe had morphed into a six-point lead.

A collective groan erupted from Beaver Stadium. Time was running out.

Ohio's missed point-after attempt restored a glimmer of hope to the Lion faithful, but Penn State would have just over a minute and only one timeout to work with. The Lions needed a miracle—and a touchdown.

On the kickoff, the Penn State receiver muffed the catch, recovering his fumble, but pinning his team inside its own twenty-yard line. On the next play, however, the blue and white faithful came to life when the quarterback's first-down pass was a thing of beauty that hit the wide receiver on the numbers and advanced the team to the Ohio State side of the field, with a new set of downs. From the forty-yard line, the quarterback passed again, resulting in an eight-yard gain. Penn State was moving ever closer. When second down netted no yardage, and an unsuccessful run on third down forced the home team to use its final timeout, groans permeated the atmosphere.

Fourth down and two to go. If Penn State could gain two yards, its hopes were still alive; if not, Ohio State would get the ball back and run out the clock. Before the ball snapped, Landon felt small fingers desperately clenching his left wrist. When they had settled there, he didn't know. Nor did he understand the urge to cover them with his hand. Emma turned toward him, her forehead creased with anxiety.

The center's hike, the linemen's push, the runner's lunge came right on cue, like the choreography in a Broadway musical. But for Penn State, the dance ended inches short of the yard marker. A moan filled the stadium, and shocked gazes marked the Lion faithful. Penn State had lost.

Ohio State players high-fived and chest bumped each other, while the Buckeye fans whooped and hollered. The Steeles and Emma sank back into their seats. Landon stared blindly at his feet for several seconds. Then he turned to his left.

Tears streamed down Emma's cheeks. Seeing his glance, she swiped at her wet face. "I know I'm being silly. It's just a game." She pulled a rumpled tissue from her pocket and wiped her eyes hastily. "Sometimes it doesn't seem like one, though."

Her words—all of them—were so true that he had to smile. He nodded in agreement. "I know what you mean."

"I'll be all right. I just hate to lose. Especially to Ohio State."

"I'm with you there." He nudged her shoulder. Then he spoke to his mom. "Are you two ready to fight the mob?"

Dad motioned for Landon and the others to follow. "Let's start moving," he said. "The lines will get worse before they get better."

When everyone was out of the row, Marshall extended a hand toward Emma. "Hello, young lady. My wife and son have been introduced, but they seem to have forgotten about me. I'm Marshall Steele."

"Hi, Mr. Steele," Emma said, taking his hand in hers. "I'm Emma Porter. You have a nice family." She glanced at Betty and Landon and then grinned, adding, "But I'm sure you already know that."

"I do, but I'm happy that you agree. So," he continued, "what brings a young lady to a packed PSU game alone? You're a brave soul to come by yourself into this horde."

Landon had wondered about that himself. He edged closer to Emma so that he could hear more easily. "It's quite a long story." She looked around at the crush of people. "But I guess we have time. Like I told Betty and Landon, I was a student here—two years behind your son. I earned my business degree and had planned to come back to study for my master's. But during the spring that I graduated, my mom was diagnosed with lung cancer. By August she was sick enough that I felt I needed to be at home."

Landon's mom grasped Emma's hand. "Oh, honey, I'm so sorry."

"It was really hard, but I know I did the right thing in not returning. I had begun to wonder about earning my MBA. It didn't seem to be what the Lord wanted. When I decided to stay in Pittsburgh, my hometown, I enrolled in the Culinary Arts Institute there, something my mom had always thought I should do." Tears formed in Emma's eyes. "In eighteen months, I earned my associates degree in pastries and candies, especially chocolates. I loved it, and the campus was only minutes from my house. Even on full class days, I spent time with Mom, and I was always there to help at night. After finishing at the Culinary Institute, I decided to combine my business degree and my skill with chocolates. I'm opening my own shop."

Her eyes sparkled, and excitement emanated from her. Landon grinned.

"Growing up, I thought I'd always live in Pittsburgh, but when I attended PSU, I fell in love with all the little towns around here, especially Bellefonte. I had my heart set on opening Heavenly Chocolates right there. In July the Lord began granting my desire. I hope to debut the first week in December so that I can take advantage of the Victorian Christmas celebration and the other holiday festivities."

Landon's mom asked, "And your mom?"

"She died last spring."

The two women hugged. "Emma, that's so sad."

A strange emotion clutched Landon's heart. What would it be like to be without his mom? He admired Emma's ability to bounce back.

"It is. I miss her, but being busy with this new business has really helped. I know she would have loved to see me as a chocolatier. She loved chocolate as much as I do." Emma breathed deeply before glancing at Landon's dad. "All of that, and I haven't even reached the part about today."

He chuckled. "Looks like we still have time."

"Hailey, my roommate while I was here, and I have remained best friends. Her aunt and uncle live in Bellefonte. That's how I came to know the town. I visited them a few times with her."

A bottleneck in the crowd brought everyone to a halt.

"When I decided to set up shop here," Emma continued, "they volunteered to let me stay with them until I get on my feet and find a place of my own. Uncle Mort graduated from Penn State back in the '70s and has done lots of work for the university over the years. He has connections here on campus."

When Landon saw a group of rowdies pushing and shoving toward Emma, he shielded her and glared at them.

"Thanks. I didn't even see them coming."

"No problem. What were you saying?"

"When I told Mort that I was going to be here this weekend and would love to come to the game, he called in a favor or two—or six—and found this wonderful ticket." Engulfing them in a sweet smile, she added, "I got so much more than a great seat."

Landon gulped. Then he smiled. "So, for your business, do you have a location, a license, a city permit—everything?"

"Yes, the equipment was purchased and the first year's lease paid with money Mom left me." Again the teary eyes. "My business plan is set. The marketing strategy is in place. I still need to secure an attorney and an accountant in this area, but Uncle Mort knows someone."

His mom and dad wore Cheshire cat grins. Landon gawked openly.

"Did I say something funny?"

Landon cleared his throat. "No, but I'm an accountant at Penn State."

"An accountant?" Her face registered disbelief.

"I went from tackling people to wrestling numbers." Even as the words came out of his mouth, Landon marveled that he'd been able to joke about it—and so quickly.

Emma nodded and smiled. "Good comeback! But I bet I'm not the first to ask you that. Your adoring fans probably assail you every time you come to a game."

Out of the corner of his eye, Landon watched his parents. Apprehension clouded their faces. He tugged at his shirt collar before answering. "No, they don't. This is my first game back."

"Your first game this season? Why haven't—"

"My first game in four years." His face was Alabama crimson.

"Four years!"

Landon could almost see the cogs turning in her brain.

"But that means you haven't been to a game since—"

"Since my injury."

"Oh. I'm sorry." Confusion and embarrassment crossed her features. "It must have been more extensive than I realized."

"My leg healed quickly." They moved a step or two before he continued. "The rest of me hasn't." He sighed, clearing his thoughts. "Today I came. And I survived. A psychiatrist would probably say that I'm on my way to a cure."

"And what do you say?"

"It's one small step."

———

"You know that big breakfast I had several hours ago?" Landon's mom asked once they had exited Beaver Stadium. "I think it has worn off."

Dad didn't even raise an eyebrow. "I was wondering how long you would last. Do you want to go somewhere and find a sandwich?"

"Not exactly."

"What exactly?"

"I'd like to go somewhere and find some ice cream."

"The Creamery!" Emma chimed from behind Landon's mom.

"Exactly."

"Me, too. Let's go." Without hesitating, Emma stepped around Betty and scanned the still-large crowd. Abruptly she took off again, zigging and zagging, repeating "Excuse me" while she maneuvered her petite frame through tight spaces, which somehow opened up for the rest of them.

So much for her needing someone bigger to make a path.

When they reached the end of the Creamery line, she said to Landon, "I hope your mom's not famished. We could be ..." Her voice became unintelligible as a group of Ohio State supporters roared by.

After the ruckus faded, Landon bent his head toward her, catching another whiff of her perfume. "What were you saying?"

"I said I hope your mom can last a while. We could have quite a wait."

"Do you know what you want?"

"Always a dilemma for me. I flip-flop between several."

"Which ones?"

"Keeny Beany, Bavarian Raspberry Crunch, Mallo Cup, and Chocolate Cherry Cordial." She rattled off her answer even before she began to study the menu board. "Oh, there's one that sounds interesting, too. Goo Goo Cluster."

Landon scanned the sign for the ones she named. Moments later, he chuckled. "They're all chocolate."

"They're all chocolate *with a twist*," she corrected.

"You're a chocoholic."

"No, I'm a chocolatier who's always looking for good ideas. A place like this is research for me. If a combination tastes good as ice cream, it can probably be, or has already been, made into a candy. I just have to find a formula that works for me."

"Research, huh?" Landon rolled his eyes and grinned. "I've heard some pretty creative excuses for eating ice cream. That's the best ever."

Patting her trim tummy, she quipped, "I don't mind sacrificing my body for the sake of science."

Landon laughed and leaned closer. "Your sacrifice hasn't been too great."

Her eyes glimmered as she caught his meaning. "Thank you." Without hesitation, she added, "I'm glad I cut out your picture."

CHAPTER 4 ══════════

Just before eight on Monday morning, Landon stood in front of Rosalee's desk as usual. What was unusual was the small, brightly colored box sitting there. "Did I forget your birthday? Thought it was in March."

"It is," she affirmed. "Today's not my anniversary or Secretary's Day or anything else that I know of."

"What's with the box, then?"

"After you read the card, you can tell me."

"What?"

"Read the card, and then you can tell me."

"It's for me?"

"It has your name and this building on the envelope."

"Hmm." He lifted the box. Moving it closer, he breathed deeply. "Ah, chocolate."

"I didn't know you were a chocolate lover."

"I'm turning over a new leaf. Thanks, Rosalee."

Once inside his office, he set down his briefcase and the box. He removed his coat and hung it on the rack. Ignoring his Monday morning mail, he turned to the box on his desk and the card attached to it.

Landon,

> *Thanks for such a great Saturday. I couldn't even mope around after the loss. When I got home that evening, I was in a creative mood. Here's what I came up with. Hope you enjoy it.*
> *Emma*
> *P.S. About that accountant—?*

More curious than ever, Landon set the card aside and removed the brightly colored cellophane. When he lifted the lid and peeled back the paper, the essence of chocolate tempted his nose while edible artwork delighted his eyes.

Six chocolates nestled in red tissue—two each of three different creations. One was a miniature dark chocolate teacup, topped by a dollop of white chocolate to represent whipped cream. After picking it up, he read the label it had been sitting on: Raspberry Hot Chocolate. Landon placed the cup in his mouth and bit down. Chocolate melted on his tongue while raspberry oozed around it. A cup of the real thing couldn't be as good as this.

He nearly reached for the second teacup, but chose, rather, to sample an egg-shaped milk chocolate covered with delicate swirls. Its label read, an Eggcellent Caramel. It truly was. A soft ambrosia that tickled every taste bud. This piece was as delicious as the first, maybe even better.

The third choice, Heart and Joy, was shaped like two concentric hearts. According to the tag, it was a combination of hazelnut, coffee, and milk chocolate. Licking his lips after the last bite, Landon added one more item to his list on Emma. *She makes the best chocolates I've ever tasted.*

After sampling all three, he set the box down. Too much sugar coupled with the caffeine from his cup of W. C.'s would have him jumping on his desk rather than writing at it. He started to put the lid on the package but paused mid-way.

"Rosalee," he said, opening his door, "try one of these chocolates." Reaching her desk, he held out the box.

"Ooh, fancy. They're almost too pretty to eat."

"Almost. Have one anyway." He explained what each was, and she selected the caramel.

"Oh, my. This is scrumptious. And how is it that you are receiving chocolates?"

"I met a chocolatier on Saturday,"

"You did, did you? Where was this?"

"At the football game."

"You met a chocolatier at …" She nearly choked on her last bite of caramel. "You were at the game?"

Tingles crept into his cheeks. "I finally accepted Bob's offer."

"And the chocolatier?"

"Her name's Emma Porter. She's setting up shop in Bellefonte." He handed Rosalee the business card that had been just under the cellophane. "Sat next to Mom. The two of them were best friends before halftime."

"And *you're* getting the chocolates because …?"

"Mom introduced us."

"I see."

Landon thought she was seeing more than just a few chocolates. "She needs a good accountant."

"What a sweet arrangement."

He guffawed at her pun. "I'm going back to my office now."

"Thanks for sharing."

———

Having leaned over a table for several minutes, Emma stood up, bent back to relieve the stress in her spine, and stretched her arms. "Time for a cup of tea." She headed toward the kitchen of her small shop and to her old friend, a teakettle that had been her mother's.

Wandering around while she waited for the whistle, she looked at the clock. Five thirty. She'd been at the shop since ten that morning, framing artwork and designing arrangements for the display. She should think about going back to Mort and Sylvia's. They wouldn't have waited supper for her since she had asked them not to, but she was getting tired and hungry. Maybe the tea would perk her up so that she could work a bit longer.

While pouring boiling water over the mandarin orange tea bag, Emma heard her phone come to life with Hailey's ring tone. She jumped, nearly spilling the scalding liquid over the side. Releasing the teakettle, she scrambled to find her cell.

"Hi, Hailey. I'm so glad—"

"No time for small talk. I think that your somewhat garbled message said, 'I met Landon Steele.' Did I hear right? Are you talking about the man of our co-ed dreams?" Hailey hadn't even paused for a breath.

Emma laughed. "Yes."

"Yes, what?"

"Yes, that's what I said."

"And?"

"He's nice."

"He's *nice*? That's it?"

"He's really nice."

An exasperated sigh met Emma's ears. "Don't make me crawl through this phone. Give me details!"

Still giggling, Emma flopped into a chair. "We met at the Ohio State game last Saturday. I was sitting next to his mom. At halftime she introduced us. Oh, how embarrassing."

"His mom embarrassed you?"

"I embarrassed myself. As soon as she said, 'This is my son Landon,' I blabbed, 'You're Landon Steele. *The* Landon Steele.' Before long, I had divulged that we both kept his *SI* picture."

"What did he say?"

"His first words were, 'Should I know you?' So then I had to explain—to someone that I really don't know—how I know him. Embarrassing."

"But he talked to you, right?"

"He did. Then his mom had me switch places with her, and Landon and I sat next to each other for the rest of the game."

"Aaaaaaaaah!" Hailey's scream pierced Emma's ear. "This is too incredible." Another yell. "So, what's he like? Still his same magnificent self? Still those killer blue eyes?"

"Oh, Hailey," Emma said on a sigh, "he's dreamy. Better than in the picture."

"Not possible."

"Oh, but he is."

"What's he doing now? Where is—" A sudden clunk interrupted Hailey's litany. "Emma? Emma? You still there?"

Emma gasped. "Sorry, I dropped the phone. Right now he's—Landon's—standing at the door. Bye!"

"What? Wait!"

Scurrying across the room, Emma ended the call and tossed the phone onto the display case. *Sorry, Hailey.* Then her toe caught the chair leg, and she nearly sent herself sprawling. Hopping on one foot, she rubbed the injury but kept going, her eyes riveted to the glass door to be sure the photogenic image was more than a mirage.

━━━━━━

Landon winced. *That had to hurt.* When she started to hop, he wanted to laugh but squelched the urge just in time. Still clutching one foot, she opened the door. "Hi!"

"Did you hurt yourself?"

"My foot a little. My pride a lot."

"I'm sorry—about both."

"Really?" She rested her hands on her hips and stared at him. "I saw the grin."

This time he couldn't stop his smile. "All right, I confess. It really was funny."

She was grinning now. "You're probably right. Come on in," she said, standing aside to let him pass.

"Smells good in here." He looked around. "Almost as good as the box I got this morning. The samples were delicious. Rosalee, my secretary, loved hers, too."

She tucked a strand of hair back into place before she looked up. Even her eyes reminded him of chocolate.

A teasing smile curled her lips. "Were you surprised?"

"Very. How'd you find me?"

"Uncle Mort, who still has—"

"Connections," he finished for her.

"I no sooner sent it than I feared you might think I was stalking you."

"Are you?" He couldn't resist asking, just to see if she would blush. She did.

"Well, since your mom introduced us ..." Grinning, she asked, "Are you worried?"

"I think I can protect myself. You don't have any linemen-type brothers, do you?"

She shook her head.

"Boyfriends?"

Emma's eyes widened. "No, none of those either," she whispered, before looking away.

He smiled to himself before glancing around the shop. "Looks like you're almost ready to open."

"Almost. My grand opening is set for December 6. I have a couple deliveries that will arrive a few days before that—perishable items. The air conditioning isn't fully operational, but with cooler weather, it shouldn't be an issue. Up for a tour?"

"Sure."

"I'll give you my vision while I lead the way."

"Even better."

She slipped past him.

They entered the small kitchen. "It's not big, but chocolates don't require a lot of bulky equipment. A range top, microwave, and chocolate warmer will be plenty. The space wasters are the molds." She opened several drawers and doors. "Since this area was designed with their storage in mind, I hope I'm prepared."

"Why so many different types?"

"Different molds work better with different chocolates. And new ones come out every day. Once the shop's up and running, I'll give you a lesson in Chocolates 101, if you'd like."

He lifted his eyebrows and widened his eyes. "With free taste tests?"

She grinned. "Absolutely. Chefs live by taste tests."

"Sign me up."

For the next half hour, Emma peeled back the layers of her new venture: the supplies, the special tools, and the display case, which was equipped with a temperature control to keep the chocolate creations as perfect as possible. At each juncture she explained her plans.

"My big project for today, besides display case design, is to finish matting and framing these." She gestured to several prints, each depicting a candy or grouping of candies. Accompanying each piece of artwork was a Bible verse.

Landon read aloud, "Taste and see that the Lord is good." He moved to the next. "How sweet are Your words unto my taste! Yes, sweeter than honey to my mouth!"

After reading the third, "My soul melts with heaviness: strengthen me according to Your word," Landon paused. "I like these." He picked up the one nearest him and examined it closely. "Art and scripture linked to your product. Very clever."

"It's my way of acknowledging God's leading in my life." She hung her head and sighed. "Let me rephrase that. These are reminders for me to trust God's leading. Sometimes I worry."

"About what?"

"What if people don't come? Have I planned adequately? Do I have enough cash to stay afloat until I establish myself? Will I survive the first year even though the statistics against it are staggering?"

"All very good questions." He read the panic in her eyes. "Starting a business is tough."

She leaned on the display case and turned toward him. "I know. A good product is just the beginning. If only I could make candy and not worry about the rest."

"Don't worry. But do plan."

"Sometimes I think I'm crazy for trying."

"You've gotten some help?"

"Through the Small Business Administration. My advisor, Lenny Paine, started and operated a bakery in Pittsburgh. He taught me so much about marketing perishables, especially in maintaining inventory." A gleam lit her eyes. "He also assured me that a successful business requires much more than a clever slogan."

Landon set one foot on the seat of a chair. Propping an elbow on his bent knee and his chin on his hand, he asked, "You already knew that, right?"

She smiled. "Yes, but one of my favorite instructors at the Culinary Institute was fond of repeating, 'Good food is its own best advertisement.' Lenny took issue with that statement."

"I would, too." Landon wanted to offer some platitude about being sure that everything would work out fine, but he'd seen one business after another start up, only to go bankrupt within a year. He opted for a safer topic.

"Have you eaten?"

"Not yet."

"How about if you show me a place in Bellefonte where the good food speaks for itself, and I'll buy you dinner."

A dimpled grin lit her face. "Give me a minute to lock up."

━━━━━━

Emma drove her red Ford Focus out of the parking lot and headed for a family restaurant down the street. She had given Landon the simple instructions, and he was to meet her there. A familiar ring tone broke into Emma's jumbled thoughts.

Emma snatched her phone. "Hello, Hailey."

"I couldn't wait any longer."

"I'm driving. I can't talk now."

"Call me when you get home."

"I'm not going home." Emma couldn't keep the excitement from her voice.

"Where are you going?"

"Landon's taking me to dinner—well, he's buying dinner—we're going to dinner together—well, not exactly together—driving separately, but—I'll call you later."

"Listen to yourself. You can't even talk straight. But you'd better be able to by the time you call. I need details."

"Bye, Hailey. Don't call me. I'll talk to you later."

"Yeah, yeah, yeah." Her friend tried to sound put out, but Emma knew she was only kidding. "Details, remember. And lots of them."

━━━━━━

Landon was waiting when Emma opened her car door. He extended his hand, noticing how small and soft her hand felt in his.

"Thanks," she said.

When she stood, he asked, "How tall are you?"

"You're really wondering how short I am, aren't you?"

He laughed and nodded.

"Five feet, three inches. And you?"

"Don't you remember?" he teased. "*Sports Illustrated* included all my personal stats."

She slapped his arm. "You're taking advantage of my co-ed crush."

"Not ashamed to admit it." He bent low, invading her space as he reached to open the restaurant door. "So how tall am I?" he whispered.

"Twelve inches taller than I am." She ducked inside ahead of him.

Grinning and shaking his head, Landon followed her.

━━━━━━

It was after nine o'clock when Landon entered his apartment. He and Emma had spent two hours at the restaurant, leaving only when she insisted that they shouldn't tie up a table any longer. Then they had talked for another half hour in the parking lot.

A few minutes into their conversation outside the restaurant, she had opened her car door. Taking this action as a not-too-subtle hint that she wanted to leave, Landon mumbled, "You're ready to go?"

"Just trying to level the playing field."

When she stepped up onto the doorframe, then pulled the door to her, leaning her hands on it, he understood. "An instant eight-inch growth spurt." He stepped closer to the door. "Maybe I'll have to buy you some short stilts."

"Only if you want me to break my neck."

He settled his hands on either side of hers. "You can laugh at yourself. I like that."

"I like it better when I don't have to."

"You have a great laugh." He couldn't explain what that laugh did to his heart. Was she aware? "If not stilts," he said, trying to clear his thoughts, "how about a small stool?"

Again that lilting laugh. "Am I supposed to keep it with me all the time?"

34

"Only when I'm around."

"How would I know you were coming?" She was teasing him. He was an easy mark. "Maybe I could keep it in my car." Her eyes twinkled more brightly than ever. "Then wherever I go, I'll have it. And besides," she said, shrugging her shoulders, "even when you're not around, it will help me whenever I'm 'vertically challenged.'"

Her amusing banter drew Landon in, and he leaned over the car door, his forehead nearly touching hers. After taking a deep breath, he said, "You smell like chocolate—even your hair."

She pulled away. "An occupational hazard."

"I like it." He touched her arm. "Chocolate is much better than the smell of a locker room—my former occupational hazard."

"Call me crazy, but I bet you wore even that well."

"If you believe that, you are crazy." A group of customers exited the restaurant and headed in their direction, talking loudly as they came. "We've been discovered." He looked at his watch. "I should be going."

"I should too. Mort and Sylvia will think I've taken up residence in my shop."

"Your shop," Landon said, slapping the doorframe. "We haven't talked about accounting. That's one reason I came."

Her eyes flashed. "There were others?"

He'd said more than he meant to. "One or two, maybe."

"You could come back."

Her eyes melted any hesitation he felt. "How about Friday?"

She frowned. "I can't this weekend. I'm going home to see my dad and brother."

Seeing Emma shiver, Landon remembered that they were standing outside in near-freezing weather. He considered covering her hands with his.

"This is the last time I'll be able to visit them for a while. I hope to leave by 1:00 Friday afternoon so that I'm there in time to make supper."

"Thought you didn't have a brother."

"I have a brother." As she was speaking, her foot slid, and she tilted sideways. Landon grasped her arms until she righted herself. "Thanks."

"No problem. Now about this brother."

"You asked if I had a lineman-type brother. At five feet, nine inches tall, and rail thin, he hardly qualifies. Height doesn't exactly run in our family."

"Really?" He winked at her. "Would Thursday work?"

"Thursday would be great."

"Around 7:00?"

"Thursday around 7:00."

"At the store or somewhere else?"

She crinkled her brows. "Whatever is best for getting the paperwork in order."

"At the store. Bring your business plan and any contingencies relating to it. I'll check some things at the shop. Then we'll need to spread everything out and get down to work."

"Not much space for spreading out at the store. After we finish there, we can go back to Mort and Sylvia's house. They won't mind."

"I could bring a pizza."

"Yummy! The works?"

He shook his head. Then he gave her his best lost-puppy look. "Half, the works; half, double cheese."

She nodded. A smile lit her face but faded quickly, replaced by a gaze that flashed an electric current straight to his heart. The jolt must have made a complete circuit, because he observed the change in her eyes, saw her pronounced swallow, and watched as she wet her lips.

Too much, too soon. The words radiated like hazard lights through Landon's brain. He cleared his throat. Then he helped her down from her perch.

"Thanks for dinner." Her voice was soft and breathy. "I'll see you Thursday." Once settled behind the wheel, she added, "Good night, Landon."

He watched as she started the car and then waved as she pulled away.

During the fifteen-minute drive home, Landon relived the moments outside the restaurant. He hadn't dated much in high school or college. Football and his studies had been his life. Hours in the weight room and at the library had limited his social time. Not that he couldn't have dated—there had been countless opportunities and endless volunteers for his attention. But he had kept his focus.

He'd never kissed a girl on a first date, had never found it hard not to. But tonight he'd struggled with himself. The "electric storm" between the two of them had blindsided him.

From pizza to passion in a heartbeat. Emma Porter had claimed his attention and was already doing strange things to his heart.

CHAPTER 5 ═══════

By Wednesday afternoon, Landon was kicking himself. Why hadn't he asked for Emma's phone number Monday night? He had no way to reach her except at her shop, and he really needed to see her business plan before Thursday so that he could review it. All day Tuesday he had given serious thought to going back there, but since he'd teased her about stalking him, he hesitated to show up at Heavenly Chocolates again.

At 4:45 he was totaling some of the last accounts for the day and trying to think of a feasible excuse to drive to Bellefonte after work, when his phone rang.

"Landon, it's Bob. Glad you went to the game." Bob never wasted much time on greetings. "Sorry we couldn't manage a win. How did things go?"

"They went okay. Thanks for the tickets."

"No problem." He cleared his throat. "I need a favor."

"What?"

"Promise me you won't say no without thinking about it."

"What is it?"

"For the last home game, I need someone to run the thirty-second clock."

"You've got a guy for that."

"*Had* a guy, Landon. He suffered a heart attack. His doctor says he won't be up and about by the last game. Even if he is, the doc won't clear him to be at the stadium. Says that stress could have triggered the attack."

"There are people all over campus who would trample their mothers for this opportunity."

Bob's hearty chuckle filled the phone line. "No doubt about that. But I'd like you to try it."

"I can't."

The clock keepers had to be riveted to the game. *Intense* didn't begin to describe the atmosphere around them. Everyone lived and breathed football. Simply imagining the saturation of insider jargon and up-close contacts sent a wave of loss and bitterness down Landon's spine. He would be absorbed in the action yet immeasurably separated from it.

"You can, Landon. It's the same as going to the game. You just have to do it."

"No, it's not. On Saturday I nearly bolted from the stadium as soon as I got there." Landon cringed at the memory. "Without moral support and lots of distractions, I wouldn't have made it to kickoff."

Bob's cough reached Landon before his voice did. "Yes, I heard about one of those 'distractions.' A little snippet of a gal, isn't she? Mort Sawyer and I go way back. He called me early Friday morning, begging me to scrounge one precious ticket. Did you sit next to her?"

"Eventually, yes."

Landon heard a thud as though Bob had thumped his hand down onto his desk. "Then you owe me a favor. I helped you overcome your phobia of football games, *and* in a roundabout way, I introduced you to a lovely lady—Mort and Sylvia say she's cuter than a button." A meaningful pause ensued. "Well, what do you say?"

"No."

"She as cute as they say?"

Landon flushed the color of a Coke can. "She is. And she knows football. But I'm still not running the clock for you."

"It's just one game."

"One too many."

A pause filled the space. Then Bob spoke again. "Maybe someday it won't be."

Setting the phone down after saying goodbye, Landon released the breath he hadn't realized he'd been holding. He felt guilty letting Bob down, but the thought of being immersed in football sent memories like left jabs to his heart.

Bob was a caring man and a good friend—better than he knew—for he had unwittingly provided the answer to Landon's dilemma about locating Emma. After all, how many Mortimer *Sawyers* could there be in Bellefonte?

———

Standing in her bathroom and wrapped in a terry cloth robe, Emma heard the ringing phone. Mort and Sylvia's landline. She reached for her hair dryer and cranked it into high speed, singing as she dried and styled her short thick mass. She had nearly finished when she noticed a thin hand beckoning at the door.

"Aahh!" All at once she screamed, jumped and dropped the hairbrush. "Sylvia, is that you?"

"Yes, dear. I'm sorry I frightened you."

Emma set down the dryer and cinched the terry belt. "Come on in."

The sliver enlarged until a flustered Sylvia timidly poked her head into the bathroom. "I'm so sorry, Emma, but there's a phone call for you. I think it's your brother. I thought you'd want to take it."

"My brother?" *Why would Bud be calling?* "Thanks, Sylvia." She took the phone, and Sylvia retreated.

"Hello, Bud. What's wrong? Why didn't you call my cell?"

A short pause. "It's not Bud—I hope nothing's wrong—I don't know your cell phone number."

"Landon?" Emma's heart stopped beating for the second time in less than a minute. "Sylvia thought you were my brother."

"I was wondering who Bud was." His voice sounded relieved. Then it became teasing. "Sorry to disappoint you and Sylvia."

"Surprised. Maybe even shocked. But not disappointed."

"You speak for Sylvia, too?"

Emma couldn't stop her giggle even though she knew she sounded like a star-struck teenager. Landon was quick and funny.

She left the bathroom, crossed to her bed, and settled onto it, leaning her head against the headboard. "Sylvia is an incurable romantic who has been trying to play matchmaker for Hailey ever since our freshman year. When I tell her that you're my accountant—well—let's just say that the wheels of her brain will be spinning in all directions."

"I haven't done any accounting yet."

"True."

"So, if I'm not your accountant, who am I?"

A wonderful, slightly vulnerable, kind, witty, incredible man packed into one gorgeous frame. "Um—well—uh." *What kind of addle-brained answer is that?*

"Hard to explain, huh?"

"My mind has turned to pudding." *Pudding? What are you saying?* "How would *you* explain you?"

"I'm the guy who forgot to ask for your phone number on Monday night. The guy who seriously considered driving through Bellefonte searching for a red Focus in one of the driveways."

Suddenly the pudding ooshed from her brain and made an incoherent blob of her tongue.

She hesitated so long that Landon asked, "Emma, are you there?"

Emma cleared her throat, and suddenly the pudding slid away, too. "I'm here. You would have driven around looking for my car?"

"Call it an adventure."

"What if I'd gone out for the evening?"

"Guess we'll never know. Just before decision time, Bob Hughes called me. You and I have mutual connections. Bob has been both my dad's friend and Mort's colleague for years. As soon as he mentioned Mort Sawyer, I had a new strategy."

"You looked in the phone book."

"Much easier than driving around."

Again she giggled.

"What's funny?"

"Nothing, really."

"You're laughing."

"A girl can giggle for other reasons."

"What other reasons?"

"I'd rather not say."

"You could tell me, but then you'd have to kill me?"

Her quiet laugh morphed to a snort, and she fell sideways, her face buried in a pillow, where she continued her outburst to the backdrop of male laughter and jibes.

"Did you just snort? Don't deny it. I heard a definite snort." When she didn't answer, he asked, "Emma? Emma? Where are you?"

Emma pulled herself upward, swiped her disheveled hair from her face, and forced herself to breathe deeply. Landon had called her name at least four more times before she composed herself enough to reply. "I was going to adamantly decline to answer, but then you made me snort, and now—"

"I *made* you snort?"

She couldn't smother her snicker. "I haven't heard that corny movie line for so long that it struck me as hilarious."

"I'd give you my entire repertoire of movie one-liners, but I'm heading out. Just one question. I need to read your business plan before tomorrow night. Could I swing by and pick it up?"

Emma smiled into the phone. The words he spoke were business, but his voice carried a tone of pleasure. "Sure. I'm headed to mid-week service, but I should be back by 8:30. Would that be okay?"

"Great. See you at 8:30."

"Need directions?"

"No, I'll find you."

Emma liked the sound of those last three words. "How about my cell phone number—just in case?"

"I won't be able to talk with Sylvia."

Emma laughed before reciting the digits.

The next evening, Landon ordered their pizza to be ready at 6:55. He wheeled into Pizza Mia, a Bellefonte pizzeria, paid the bill, grabbed the steaming box, and headed out. Within three minutes he had parked and was carrying the pizza toward Emma's front door. She met him there before he knocked and held the door wide.

"Hi. Set everything there." She motioned to one of only two small wrought iron tables in the store and then leaned toward the box as he set it down. "I'm starving."

"Pizza first, accounting later?"

"Definitely." She lifted the lid and let the aroma waft up. "Looks wonderful."

"Pizza Mia's comes highly recommended by Rosalee, her kids, and grandkids."

"Napkins are here somewhere, but for plates, we're out of luck."

"No problem. I grabbed a handful of napkins at the pizza place. We can use these." He pulled them from his coat pocket before setting two Dasanis beside the pizza box. "Hope water's okay."

"Water's great."

About two minutes later, everything was set, and Landon helped Emma with her chair. "I'll pray," he said as he sat.

Emma bowed her head, and then raised it again when he tapped her arm. "My family always hold hands when we pray for a meal." He extended his hand toward her. "You mind?"

She gulped and placed her hand in his.

Emma had no idea what Landon prayed. He could have mentioned rockets to the moon or snowballs in July for all she knew. She was, however, powerfully aware of his hand—strong and warm, with long, lean fingers. She tried to focus on his words to God, but her mind inevitably flew back to the touch of that hand.

Then an unbidden thought crossed her mind, an occurrence that had occasionally troubled her over the last couple of days. It raced through her brain and pierced her heart. Thankfully, it also returned her mind to the present and to the two words of Landon's prayer that actually did register with her: *Emma* and *Amen.*

What had he said about her? She wished she knew. Her pang of conscience, combined with her troubling thoughts, left her befuddled. When she looked up, Landon was watching her. It really was not possible, but those blue eyes seemed bluer every time he looked at her.

"Are you in there?" He tickled her palm with his fingers.

She sighed and gave him a half-smile, reluctantly letting go of his hand. Averting her eyes, she lifted a gooey, topping-packed slice from the box. "Let's eat this while it's still warm."

His demeanor told her that he knew she was sidestepping something, but he didn't press.

A half hour later they sat with the nearly empty box between them. "That was great," Emma said. "I guess we should get to work. What's first?"

"I need to walk through the store checking some items against your business plan." He stood and stretched before pulling a small tablet and pen from his shirt pocket. Within a few seconds he was jotting things as he surveyed the space.

Following him with her eyes, Emma gathered the trash and wiped the table. How many women entrepreneurs wished for an accountant like Landon?

━━━━━━━━━━

When they reached Mort and Sylvia's, Emma introduced Landon to both the Sawyers. From Sylvia he received a welcoming smile. "So you're the one I thought was Emma's brother." She looked quickly toward Emma, and Landon remembered Emma's earlier description: incurable romantic. Sylvia's eyes positively gleamed. She was plotting, no doubt.

Mort stepped forward and shook his hand. "One of the best linebackers Penn State ever had. Nice to meet you. Sorry about your injury."

Landon's heart raced. He hadn't expected the recognition. "Thank you, sir. Nice to meet you, too."

Sylvia showed him to the dining room.

"Emma has free reign of our home. If you need anything, just ask her."

"Thank you."

Landon spread papers out in front of him, while Emma left the room with the Sawyers. When she returned, she was carrying a file folder which she set across the table from him and began leafing through.

Landon watched her as she searched. Emma was motion personified. At the game she had sat only temporarily, incessantly leaping to her feet and jumping up and down. She walked fast and talked faster, especially when she was excited. Even in her quieter moments, like right now, her lips moved silently, and her right foot tapped impatiently. Before long, she looked up from the folder.

"What do you need?" he asked.

"I have a spreadsheet I'm using to log all my time at the shop. More for my own records than for anything else. I want to record your time on it, too." She suddenly stopped riffling through the stack. "Here it is."

Landon reached forward and shut the folder, closing her hand in it. "I'm doing this for a friend."

Bright gleams shot from her eyes. "No, Landon. You're not." She jerked her hand and the page from the folder. "Tonight you are here as my accountant. I'm going to pay you."

Landon sat back in his chair and returned his hand to his own stack of papers. He watched as she set her jaw and stretched her sixty-three inches to its fullest. "It's not necessary."

"To me, it is," she said, placing the paper in front of him. "If you won't let me pay, I'll look for another accountant."

In a game of football, Landon could have taken her down with one half-hearted swipe, yet in this room, her fiery stare and fighter's stance left him totally defenseless. He sighed, looked at his watch, and wrote 7:53 in the column labeled *Start Time*. He added his name to the row and then looked up at her.

"Ready?"

"Yes." Her shoulders relaxed. "Do you need me here, or will I be in your way?"

"I need you." He didn't elaborate. Instead he slid out the chair next to him. "Have a seat."

She stood where she was. The foot-tapping resumed. She shuffled more papers.

"Emma, are you okay?"

"Yes—no—I thought I was—I don't know." She lifted a hand to her hair and twirled one dark strand around her index finger. "I'm nervous about all of this." She gestured to the pages in front of him.

"Why?"

Tears lurked in her eyes. "This business is my dream come true. What will I do if it fails?"

Landon rose slightly, reaching forward to gently grasp her arm. "Come and sit." With mild pressure he eased her around the end of the table before releasing her.

Her gaze toward the carpet, Emma shuffled to the chair. Landon quickly wrote 7:56 in the margin, crossing out the earlier number. Then he slid the page beneath the paper that it had been on top of.

"Overall, your business plan looks very good," he said once she was settled.

Her gaze jerked upward.

"You have most things laid out well." He pulled up the document and placed it on the table between them. "It's clear and concise."

"Overall?" She stressed the word as though it was an insult. "Most?" She sat straighter in her chair. "You would have written a better one?" Her tone was defensive.

How had the conversation taken this turn so quickly? "I didn't say that."

"Mr. Paine and I spent weeks on that plan." She planted her hands on the chair arms and scooted forward in her seat, angling toward him.

"And it's a good one, but I—"

"You would have done it differently."

Landon grasped the arms of his own chair and angled himself toward her just as she had done. His thigh rested in front of her knees, essentially trapping her in the seat. She had asked his advice. He would give it. "In one or two points, I would have."

Refusing to flinch, he stared at her and waited. The cuckoo clock, striking eight, testified to their standoff.

On the last chime, Emma blinked. "What would you change?"

Landon held her gaze a moment longer before answering. "Cash flow could be a problem. I think you underestimated the amount you need."

"But Mr. Paine—"

"Is retired. He ran his business at a different time."

Emma's face blanched as if he'd informed her that a tornado had destroyed her shop. Landon wished he were finished. There was more she needed to hear.

"Another problem is your income estimates. They rely too heavily on foot traffic." He turned the page as he spoke.

"You know something about the people of this area that the demographics don't show?"

Landon set the paper in front of Emma. Then he shoved his chair back and stood. "Talk with your Small Business advisor. Maybe he can recommend an accountant."

"You're not going help me?"

"I don't take clients who don't trust my advice."

Emma stared at him. One second she appeared stunned; the next, she snatched her cell phone and began punching the keypad.

Landon stood beside her in disbelief.

"Hello, Mr. Paine. This is Emma Porter."

Mr. Paine, the Small Business Administration guy.

"I need you to talk to someone. Here he is."

Before Landon could refuse, she thrust the phone into his hand. An elderly man's voice called, "Emma? Emma?"

When Landon tried to return the phone, she crossed her arms. The voice persisted. Landon plunged ahead.

"Hello, Mr. Paine. I'm Landon Steele, an accountant who's looking over Emma's business plan."

Emma eagerly listened to Landon's side of the conversation.

"Right in front of me." He paused and then replied, "I can tell."

Landon's curt remarks made Emma wish that Mr. Paine were on a speaker phone.

"The cash flow figures trouble me."

A lengthy pause ensued. Landon wrote several numbers on a blank sheet at his right while Lenny led the conversation. Finally Landon spoke again. "Relying on foot traffic, especially until customers become aware of her business, also causes concern."

A series of yes and no answers followed. Then the conversation took an unexpected twist.

"I grew up near here." Landon followed his statement with pauses interrupted by, "My parents still live in the area." "I'm in State College at Penn State." "About fifteen minutes," and, "Not quite four years."

He closed with a hodgepodge of quick responses. Then he extended the phone to her.

"Emma, listen to this young man." Lenny's tone commanded attention. "He has good instincts, and he's a local boy who understands that area."

"We had it all worked out."

"Young lady." Emma recognized that tone—the one that made her feel like his daughter rather than his client. "Ours was a basic plan, not a hard and fast rule."

"But Mr. Paine, all the time we spent—"

"Will be wasted if your business fails. Don't be too proud to take sound advice."

Emma felt as though she'd entered a time warp and was back in junior high. Her plans seldom fell into place then. She'd put so much time and energy into this dream. Was she on the verge of seeing it fail, too?

"Let him make his case. If you still aren't convinced, call me back tomorrow. We'll go over everything again."

Emma hesitated while his words sank in. "Thanks, Mr. Paine."

"I know you're disappointed."

That's an understatement for sure.

"Keep your chin up, girl. Being an entrepreneur isn't for the faint of heart."

"I'll try."

"Let me know what you decide."

━━━━━━━

After he returned the phone to Emma, Landon needed to get away. Not too far, but far enough to be out of sight. He went in search of a glass of water. He hung around looking out the kitchen window; then he decided things wouldn't get any easier the longer he stalled.

Carrying his glass with him, he rounded the corner and saw Emma standing beside the chair she had been sitting in, her back turned toward him.

She was mumbling to herself, shaking her head occasionally, and waving her arms.

Poor Mr. Paine.

Then he saw the phone on the table. At least she wasn't venting at her Small Business advisor. He thought about putting his glass down and leaving, but his coat hung on the back of a chair near her.

He shifted his weight. He took another drink of water. In mid-gulp he watched Emma slump back into her seat. Tears spilled over instantly. Why hadn't he left five seconds sooner?

His mom wasn't one who cried easily, and Landon had no sisters. He'd never learned to cope with weeping females. He stared at the ceiling and then hung his head. In four steps he closed the distance between them and stopped beside her.

Emma continued to cry. She really needed a tissue. There were none in sight.

At last, Landon had a purpose. He looked around the dining room. On a small buffet sat some china plates. Next to the plates lay a stack of neatly folded cloth napkins. Not exactly what he had hoped for, but they would work.

When he placed the napkin in Emma's hand, she looked up.

"I thought you'd gone." Her voice rasped.

"Not yet."

"Hanging around to gloat?"

The second those hateful words left Emma's mouth, she regretted them. Remorse knifed her once again when Landon stepped around her, retrieved his jacket, and started for the door.

"Wait."

He turned back but stood where he was.

"Please stay—at least long enough to let me apologize." She used the napkin for her eyes and nose. "I'm sorry. You've been nothing but kind, and I've been—"

"Hard-headed? Thin-skinned?" He leaned against the doorframe.

He wasn't making this easy. "Plus a few more."

"You know I'm trying to help."

She did know. The affirmation brought another round of tears to her eyes and Landon to her side.

"Buck up, Em. Things will be okay." He sat down next to her and waited.

With a shuddering breath, she said, "I don't deserve your help, but I'm glad you stayed."

Landon looked at his watch. "Are you up for this tonight?"

Emma's eyes grew wide. "You're still willing to help me?"

"Are you willing to listen?"

Again the guilt. She looked straight at him for the first time since the phone call. "I'll do my best."

"I can live with that."

"Will you accept my apology?"

"Will you accept my advice?"

Emma heaved a huge sigh. Landon raised his eyebrows.

"This business has become a part of me." Her hands covered her heart. "Your criticisms seemed like a personal attack—and when I'm attacked, I fight."

———

"I don't think you can obtain the necessary number of sales that way." Twenty minutes had elapsed since Emma's apology and Landon's agreeing to stay. She had excused herself and then returned looking much more refreshed. They were tackling the business plan once again. "Let's do the math."

"But I've already …" She looked frustrated.

He hurried on. "Hear me out. If your profit margin is 11 percent, and you want a profit of $36,000 per year, you would need sales of nearly $327,300."

He showed her the calculations. Emma studied the figures and then nodded.

"If the store is open 260 days a year —five days each week—you require over $1260 of sales each day to reach your goal. If the average customer spends $10, over 126 people would have to come in *and buy* in order to meet your total. At eight hours a day, that's just over eight sales of at least $10 every hour."

"But customers could spend a lot more than $10 each. Handmade chocolates aren't cheap."

"True, and they shouldn't be." His affirmation seemed to ease her nerves a bit. "But are you willing to gamble your whole investment on walk-in customers' daily cravings for chocolate?"

Landon watched her defenses mount.

"No, I'm not. I want to cater parties and social functions—events where I can sell multiple chocolates to lots of people. I have that in my business plan."

"That's what I'm saying." He pointed to her business plan, which he had opened to the section on marketing strategy. "You mention catering, but it's not specific. You don't give names, dates, places. The lack of particulars concerns me."

"But I am looking into those things. Mort has given me some names, and I've made contact with the events coordinator for the annual Victorian Christmas celebration here in town. But it's so hard to know how to give cost estimates to potential customers until I've actually opened my doors. Without cost data, they are reluctant to commit. It's a vicious cycle." She rubbed her temples.

"Maybe I should go. You've got a hectic day tomorrow and a busy weekend." He closed the document.

The eyes that met his now were the smooth chocolatey ones he longed to see.

"I didn't want the evening to end like this."

"Don't worry about it. Go and take something for that headache while I gather things up."

She walked him to the door a few minutes later. Before she could reach for the knob, he said, "I have an idea I want to run by you before I go."

Her sidelong glance and drawn out "Okay" betrayed her skepticism.

"It's nothing hard—or that serious." He smiled at her.

Her grin was quick and lit up her face, but the earnestness in her warm brown eyes distracted him so much that he nearly forgot what he wanted to say. "While you're in Pittsburgh, I could talk with my dad and mom. Dad's a banker. Mom's involved with several civic clubs. They may know of events or of people who host events. Philipsburg is a bit far from Bellefonte, but my parents' network may include contacts nearer to you. They would do whatever they can to help. What do you think?"

In a heartbeat, she planted a kiss on his cheek. "I'm so glad that Mort found me that ticket. Thank you, Landon."

As he walked to his car, Landon chuckled to himself and raised his hand to the spot where her lips had been. He hoped she'd still be thanking him later when she glanced at the timesheet she had insisted he use. While she was getting some Tylenol, he had slipped it out from under the top page and drawn a line through the information he had written earlier. On the next line, he'd re-entered the date and added: *helping a friend, 0:45; offering accounting advice, 0:15.* At the end of the line he had written, *Landon,* placing a small *58* to sit on the base of the *L.* Before her return, he'd tucked the sheet back under the stack.

CHAPTER 6

Friday night Landon made a trip to see his mom and dad in order to explain Emma's situation.

"*You're* here to get *our* help for *her*. Is that right?" Behind his dad's rhetorical question was a glimmer of jesting. He cast a knowing glance at Mom.

"What does your friend need us to do?" Mom already had the paper and pen in her hands. By the time Landon left Saturday morning, she was making phone calls and promising to keep him posted.

Landon's Saturday afternoon was consumed by research, mostly on the Internet. An idea had been brewing in his brain—and brewing was exactly the right word. His idea was coffee.

Being a caffeine lover himself, he could thoroughly understand the draw of the addictive beverage. He could relate to people who stood in line waiting for the perfect cup of liquid pick-me-up. He also knew that coffee drinkers loved to couple their caffeine with a sweet partner. Chocolates seemed like an obvious choice. Bringing customers in for coffee would, he suspected, have a positive effect on candy sales as well.

His other thought was that coffee would have a much lower overhead and, therefore, a much higher rate of return. Saturday's research seemed to prove him right. Clicking on dozens of web sites, reading several reviews by both industry insiders and customers, Landon discovered two basic options. The first was the standard pour-through type of brewer. It boasted of larger quantities at a time with a lower cost per cup. The second option was the single-serving machine, which offered a faster cup of coffee but at a higher cost per serving. Each machine had its pros and cons. The more Landon read and pondered, the more he became convinced that the single-serve machine was the better choice for Emma.

To coffee drinkers, freshness was a must. After twenty minutes, fresh coffee was no longer fresh. She would be too busy to make coffee three times each hour. She needed something that would be fast and easy, requiring little oversight or cleanup. The single serve machines were designed to have coffee goodness at the customer's fingertips in less than one minute. Additionally, the varieties of single-serve portions were so numerous that a person could spend more time in decision making than he would in actually getting the java once he had made his choice.

Landon's next quandary was over the type of single-serve brewer. Some used plastic-cup servings, while others were made for flat, disc-like pods. The cup style was trendier, it seemed, but, according to reviewers, the pod was slightly less expensive and equally efficient. The best pod brewer was, however, much more costly than a highly rated cup-method machine.

After several hours of digging for information, Landon's brain felt like a pinball machine with hundreds of ideas bouncing around inside it—and he hadn't yet broached the idea to Emma. Getting the idea past her would be the next hurdle.

Needing to clear his head, he slid his feet into some running shoes and headed outside. It was much cooler this weekend than last, with the high in the low forties. Leaving his driveway, he jogged ahead. The twilight run invigorated his muscles, but it did little to ease the disquiet in his brain. He kept seeing Emma's tense face and hearing her words, "What will I do if it fails?"

He recalled his response to her on Thursday. "Don't worry, Emma. Pray hard and work hard. The Lord will help you." When the words left his mouth, Landon hadn't thought himself a hypocrite, but in retrospect, he knew he was. He coasted to a halt near the empty bench at the stop for the city bus. Evidently no one needed a ride.

"Lord, I haven't really prayed about Emma or anything else in a long time. Until last weekend, I never realized how far I am from you." He plopped onto the seat and stretched his arms along the back of it. "I want to help Emma. I think I can, if only she'll let me. But she is stubborn."

"Ouch!" He examined the side of his left hand. A sliver of wood from the bench protruded from his skin.

He dropped the offender to the ground, but not before a Bible verse jogged his memory. "Why do you look at the speck that is in your brother's eye, but do not notice the log that is in your own eye?"

I'm not the one who doesn't want to listen to the advice of someone whose opinion I asked for.

Was he arguing with himself? Maybe. Was he telling the whole truth—even to himself? Definitely not.

Studying the concrete at his feet, Landon recalled the days after his football catastrophe. He'd asked several people for help in adjusting to his situation: former teammates who hadn't been drafted, coaches who had advised other injured players, and his pastor, who often counseled troubled people. Only occasionally, however, had he taken their advice. He hadn't meant to hurt them or disregard their help; he simply felt that they didn't know his problem clearly.

Why should I expect Emma to listen to me?

Landon looked skyward. "Show me how to help her."

After he'd left the Sawyer's home Thursday night, he recalled adding 58 to his signature, a practice he'd adopted during his freshman year at PSU. That number had helped him remember how fortunate he was to be a part of the Nittany Lion squad. The "number in a name" had become his trademark, a trait that many had noticed and asked about. Because of this practice, Landon had had numerous opportunities to share Christ with others.

When his football career ended, so had the inclusion of his number. He rationalized the omission by saying that he wasn't number 58 anymore. Someone else had that privilege. Deep inside, though, he knew the real reason—he didn't want to talk about the God who had robbed him of a football career. He had honored God, but God had let him down. Not since his injury had he felt the closeness he had once shared with the Lord.

On Thursday night at the Sawyer's, the 58 seemed to glide from his pen as spontaneously as his testimony had once rolled from his lips. He couldn't say that he was ready to meet God where he had left Him, but maybe he was getting closer.

Landon eased himself from the bench and set off toward his apartment. Ten minutes later he was back at his computer desk devising a plan—a formula that would help Emma sell chocolates without making her feel pushed or obligated.

He had just finished jotting down some ideas when his phone rang.

"Landon, I have some names and telephone numbers that I want you to give to Emma."

"Hi, Mom. That was fast." He cradled the phone between his neck and shoulder while he grabbed a pen and some paper from his computer desk. "Did you spend the whole day on the phone?"

"Not quite, but I do feel talked out. My tenacity paid off, though. The prospects look good. I told each of these people to expect a call from Emma next week. You did say that she'll be back by Monday, didn't you?"

"Tomorrow night, I ho—I think," he corrected.

She laughed. "Your dad's right. This isn't your normal where young women are concerned. But I think it's nice—and I know she's sweet. Just be careful."

Her motherly advice delivered, Mom dictated the names and phone numbers of the five people who had voiced an interest in Heavenly Chocolates.

━━━━━━━

By Sunday morning, Landon was antsy. He had tried to reach Emma while he grabbed a sandwich for supper on Saturday. When she didn't answer, he left a message. Around 8:00, she called back, but he was in the middle of a game of racquetball with his friend Mike and didn't listen to her message until he was driving home.

"Hi, Landon. Sorry I missed you. Dad's okay. Bud's good. We're at Aunt Chloe's house—Mom's sister. Probably won't be back to Dad's till late. I'm hoping to return to Bellefonte tomorrow night. I'll call …"

The phone had stopped recording just then. When was she going to call? She hadn't yet. He hoped she would before he left for church. If she hadn't reached him by then, they wouldn't be able to talk until after the service, and he didn't want to wait that long.

He was as anxious as a field goal kicker in over-time. Part of him felt like a love-struck teenager who couldn't wait to hear her voice again; the other part seemed more like an over-zealous first grader eager to spill his big news before he exploded with excitement.

At 9:30 on Sunday, Landon hurried out the door, later than he usually left for church. When his left shoe hit the asphalt, his foot shot out in front of him. He threw his arms into the air and tried to thrust his weight forward to maintain his equilibrium. But then his right foot betrayed him, too, and he felt himself hurtling down the driveway, in a display of helter-skelter gesticulations more animated than those of an orchestra maestro.

When his performance ended, Landon lay sprawled across the hood of his car, his hands clutching at the sides of the vehicle and his feet still searching for any pavement that didn't seem like part of a conveyor belt run amuck.

Ice! It was everywhere—a shimmering glassy cloak that warped straight tree limbs into U-shaped anomalies and added crystalline appendages to mailboxes and birdfeeders.

The metal to which Landon now clung was concealed in the glistening sheath. Slowly he attempted to plant his feet and rise. But the slight decline of his driveway made his condition precarious, for the icy rain had slithered underneath the front edge of his Camry. Wherever he set his foot, it met a treacherous plane, slicker than any newly waxed floor.

Slowly, Landon inched to his right, stretching his leg toward the tire. He hoped that the wheel had shielded some pavement from the onslaught and that he could gain a foothold. At last his right foot held firm. He shifted his weight in that direction, depending on this anchor leg to support him while he righted himself.

As he released the car with his left hand, his phone rang. "No. Not now." He plunged his hand into his pocket, lost his balance, and rapped his elbow on the hood.

"Ouch!" he growled, regaining whatever footing he could.

Finally he maneuvered the phone to his ear. "Hello."

"Landon, it's me, Emma."

"Hi, I'm glad you called."

"You sound winded. What are you doing?"

"Hugging my car."

"What?"

"Ice storm. I didn't even glance out the window before I barreled outside, and I nearly landed on my back. The next thing I knew, I was clutching ice-covered silver metal."

"Are you all right?"

"Technically, yes."

"I'll let you go so that—"

"No, don't." His voice was more desperate than he intended it to be. "I've been waiting for your call."

He heard her sigh. "That's nice." Then she giggled. "I must admit that I would like to have seen what you just described."

"Some friend you are."

"The best! And to prove it, I'm hanging up. I'll call back in five minutes—after you've had time to untangle yourself."

"Better make it ten. My apartment's uphill."

━━━━━━

"How'd you do it?" Emma asked without preamble after Landon's hello.

"Do what?"

"How'd you get back inside?"

"Maybe I didn't. Maybe I'm still desperately clinging to a Toyota while you're callously making fun of me."

A quick chuckle floated through the phone. "I'm sorry."

"Oh, sure, you are." He laughed, too. "Maybe no one ever told you, but an apology is much more convincing if you're not laughing when you say it."

She giggled some more, and then for the next ten minutes, she regaled him with the saga of her visit: a Friday night dinner that was anything but a culinary triumph, due—she emphatically assured him—to a faulty oven thermostat; the practical joke she played on Bud; and Aunt Chloe's tale of the time she and Emma's mom got lost in Pittsburgh when they were kids.

Landon listened, marveling at how she drew so much pleasure from even the smallest things.

Not until she said, "How was your weekend?" did he remember how impatient he had been to talk to her.

"I'm glad you asked. I spent most of it delving into marketing ideas for a certain entrepreneur that I know." He recounted both his trip to his parents' house and his mom's news about potential customers.

She gushed and giggled, thanking him profusely.

"I have other news, but I need to talk to you in person."

"Sounds intriguing."

"Overstatement, for sure. More like *interesting*." He hoped she would agree. "When are you coming home?"

"I'm not."

His hand jerked so suddenly that he spilled some of the coffee he'd just poured. "You're not coming home? Of course you are. You have to. Your business ..."

"No, I don't have to. I already did."

Landon exhaled while his heart restarted. "That's not funny. You nearly gave me a coronary—and I spilled coffee on myself."

"It must be a little bit funny, because I'm laughing." She was.

"Payback is sweet."

A sharp intake of breath, then more laughter. "So you're the vindictive type, are you?"

"We'll see." He grinned as he crossed the room, opened the door, and dislodged a piece of an icicle hanging from the knocker. Carrying it to the freezer, he tucked it safely inside before he refocused his attention on her words. She apparently wasn't too worried about his reprisal.

"The ice storm that we got here early this morning was supposed to arrive as snow in Pittsburgh around eleven o'clock last night. I know this because Aunt Chloe's unfulfilled desire in life was to be a meteorologist. Nothing about the weather escapes her. When we arrived at her house last night, she was in a dither about my 'getting out of the city before the snow flies.' I took her advice and managed to stay ahead of the storm."

But not completely away from the icicles. His eyes gleamed when he realized the irony.

"What time did you get in?"

"Shortly after midnight. But it took over an hour to unload the car and find a place for all the things I brought back with me. Then I was too wound up to sleep. The last time I looked at the clock, it was nearly 3:30. I'm slightly bleary-eyed."

"Go back to bed. Everything's closed because of ice."

"I might, now that I've had breakfast. I was famished when I woke up."

"Your aunt didn't feed you?"

"Aunt Chloe's desire was to be a meteorologist—not a chef. I love her to pieces, but the woman simply cannot cook. Even the charred leftovers from Friday were better than Aunt Chloe's offering. I didn't eat much."

"Poor starved creature." He exaggerated the words. "Why didn't you stop along the way?"

"With a storm looming behind me? No way. My right Nike hit the pedal, and I got here as fast as I could."

"So when are we getting together? I have news, remember?"

"Tomorrow after you finish work?" she suggested. "I could cook for you—Sylvia's oven works fine."

Not the answer he had hoped for. "Hmmm—that could work."

"Do you have plans?"

"Not for tomorrow night. But since you're back early, I was thinking later today."

"After an ice storm?"

"Ice has to melt sometime." Landon concocted as he talked. "Go take your nap. I'll pray for a heat wave and then drop by the Sawyer's this afternoon. How's three o'clock?"

"Terrible."

He winced at the immediate rejection.

"Mort and Sylvia always nap on Sunday afternoon, and they do not like to be disturbed. Those two are normally such a mild-mannered pair, but not if you wake them from a nap. I don't want to chance it."

Landon's ego had recovered somewhat.

"I'm not driving even to the shop in this kind of weather. Besides, it's not very conducive there to sitting down and hashing out ideas."

"I could come pick you up. We could work here." A long hesitation prompted him to add, "All my paperwork is here. If you really want to cook, I'll let you borrow my oven."

"Does it work?"

"The last time I used it, it did."

"And that was …?"

"I'd have to think about that. My cooking is done on top of the stove."

"Maybe we both should eat a big lunch and forget about supper."

"Or maybe we can stop on the way back here and get something."

"Okay. It's a deal—on one condition."

"Name it."

"You'll come only if the ice has melted, and you'll call before you leave."

"That's two conditions."

"Leave it to an accountant to quibble over numbers. Do we have a deal?"

"I'll see you at 3:00—after I call twenty minutes earlier."

Emma slapped at the persistent alarm clock. She shrugged her head from under the down comforter. Focusing on the dial, she read the fuzzy numbers, 1:30. She had slept over three hours since returning to bed after her talk with Landon. She knew she should get up, but the room felt chilly. A glance out the window revealed a gray day and what appeared to be steady rain.

Suddenly she was back home basking in the warmth of her own bed and her mother's love. "Just ten more minutes, Mom." Tears stung her eyes, as she rehearsed the often-repeated plea to her mother. Dreary days did this to her. She pulled the cover over her head and sobbed, missing her mom's voice, her encouragement, even her rebuke—"Emma Joy, get out of that bed—now!"

Emma didn't get up. Her sobs eventually subsided to whimpers, which soon gave way to more sleep. Her next coherent thought was that her phone was ringing. Her phone! Mort and Sylvia's nap!

She bounded from the bed, nearly tripping herself when her feet became entangled in the quickly discarded comforter.

"Hello."

"Temperature: 45 degrees. Roads: rain covered but ice free." Landon's mellow voice freed her from her fog. "I'll be there in twenty minutes."

Twenty minutes. Panic. She glanced at the clock. It now read 2:40. Where had the hour gone? Why did Landon have to be so punctual?

"Drive carefully—and slowly." She hoped he would interpret her words as concern for his safety and not for the stall tactic they were.

Before she had said goodbye, Emma was already laying out clothes to wear. She grabbed her favorite jeans, tossing them and a sweater onto the bed. The sweater was warm, and it fit perfectly. She might be in a sleep-induced haze, but she knew she wanted to look good.

The next twenty minutes passed in a blur. Emma was tiptoeing to the window in the Sawyer's living room when she saw Landon's car turn into the driveway. She grabbed her leather jacket and purse and stepped out onto the porch.

While Landon parked, a memory from Saturday night ran through Emma's mind.

"Have you met any nice young men in that little town of yours?" Aunt Chloe's favorite question came while she, Bud, and Emma were washing dishes. Even though she should have expected it, the query caught Emma off guard, and she hesitated.

Handing Emma the plate he had dried, Bud cast her a knowing glance.

"Well—yes—I have."

Aunt Chloe pulled her soapy hands from the sink and turned toward Emma. "Really, dear? How exciting! Tell me about him."

"His name is Landon Steele. He was a big-name football player while I was at Penn State."

Bud's eyes shone as if he could remember seeing Landon in action.

"He seemed sure to be drafted into the NFL. Several teams were interested. Then late in the season, he suffered a severe injury to his leg."

Aunt Chloe's smile dissipated.

"By the time it healed completely, no team wanted him."

"That's too bad."

"It sure was," Bud interrupted. "The guy was great—had a nose for the ball and the speed to track down any player who had it."

"You remember him, Bud?" Aunt Chloe's surprise showed on her face.

"Course I do. Anybody who follows the Lions knows who Landon Steele is."

"But you never met him while you were in college, Emma?"

"I *saw* him a few times." She caught the grin on her brother's face. "Actually, I *saw* him quite often because I had his picture."

"What?"

Bud chuckled as Emma told about the interview, the magazine photo, and the dorm rooms which Landon's face had adorned.

"So when his mom introduced us—we sat next to each other at a football game—I recognized him right away."

"Was he surprised?"

"*Stunned* is the better word."

"But he didn't seem to mind?"

"No, not after I explained. He even laughed about it."

"I told you. The guy is great." Bud punctuated his sentence by swatting Emma with the dishtowel.

━━━━━━━

The silver car door opened slightly, a black rod emerged from inside, and within seconds a large umbrella expanded above the door.

Emma watched, admiring both the smoothness with which Landon handled the bulky umbrella and his thoughtfulness in remembering it. His polished manner testified to the businessman he had become rather than the football player he once was. His physique, however, still bore the outline of an athlete.

At his waist, slim fitting jeans met the leather of his bomber jacket, setting off his narrow midsection and accentuating the broad shoulders above. His sand-colored hair contrasted with the dimness of the day, and his eyes reminded her of summer skies dispelling the gloom of November. His lithe gait gave no hint of his ever sustaining a serious leg injury. Landon was more than easy on the eyes. She blushed when she realized she was gawking.

"Hi." He reached the porch and gave her hand a quick squeeze. "I made it."

"I'm glad." She returned the pressure on his hand before releasing it.

"Watch your step," he said, taking her elbow. "The stairs are a bit slick."

Holding the umbrella between them, Landon guided her to the passenger's side door. After opening it, he shielded her from the rain while she got in. Then he shut the door and hurried around to the driver's side.

Emma sat in amazement. Only eight days earlier, her store had consumed her every waking moment. For the last week, however, thoughts of Landon had crowded in as she worked. And once or twice, this former linebacker had encroached on her dreams.

CHAPTER 7 ══════

"**S**o what's this mysterious something that you have to tell me?" Emma asked, when he had backed out of her driveway.

"I'll let you know when we get to my place."

She crossed her arms and pouted. "That's not fair."

He laughed and then changed the subject. "Tell me about your brother. Is his name really Bud?"

"No, it's Chester—after my dad."

"You don't hear that name much anymore."

"Probably for good reason." She wrinkled her nose in displeasure. "Dad goes by Chet, and it fits him. But when Bud was born, Dad didn't want two Chets in the house. So we all called my brother Chester—until he started first grade. Somehow, when the two of us went back and forth to school each day, I began calling him Bud. Dad didn't like the idea, but he got used to it, eventually."

"Are you close?"

"We are, even though he's six years younger than I am. When we were growing up, he entertained me with all of his antics, and I took care of him. For about two years, while he was in middle school, he became the annoying younger sibling. At least that's how I thought of him." She paused momentarily, and Landon glanced over to see her staring out the passenger window. Seconds later, she continued. "We became close again after I left home. I don't see him often, but we talk a couple times each week."

"That explains why Sylvia thought I was your brother."

She smiled. "Probably."

"Tell me about your dad."

Emma looked at her lap and clutched her fingers together as though her hands were suddenly cold. "What do you want to know?" Her voice had gone from whimsical to wary in the time it took him to ask the question.

Stopping at one of the few traffic lights in town, Landon turned toward her. When she returned his gaze, it seemed that pain had colored her chestnut eyes a muddy brown. He waited, not sure of what else to do.

She finally spoke. Her voice was bland, and her gaze seemed locked on the hands that rested in her lap. "Dad is a mechanic at a forge in Pittsburgh. He repairs and does maintenance on the equipment there—everything from the furnaces for production to the microwaves in the lunch room."

Not once had Emma looked up as she spoke, and Landon wondered why. Her words seemed innocuous. Once again silence permeated the car.

"Dad can fix almost anything—except himself."

Understanding dawned, and Landon asked, "You mean because of your mom's death?"

"A lot more than that." Finally she looked up. "I have very few memories of my dad being happy." When Landon cast her a puzzled expression, she explained, "He says that life gave him a 'raw deal.'"

"How so?"

"His recitation starts with the death of his parents when he was eighteen. A horrific car accident. Grandpa died at the scene. Grandma, a few days later. After their deaths, Dad's younger brother Paul and sister Annie needed care, but no one in the extended family stepped up to help. The financial responsibility fell on him. Even though he'd already been accepted at Dusquene University, he joined the army. He never went to college, never had any time to live just for himself."

"Hard break, especially for a kid."

"It is," she conceded, "but he overlooks a lot of positives." Her demeanor revealed both sadness and frustration. "In the army, Dad earned enough to allow his brother and sister to stay in their family's home. When he agreed to pay her a small salary, a spinster aunt came to live with Paul and Annie. Aunt Maddie gave them a whole lot more than Dad paid for, and his siblings became the family Maddie never had."

Landon glanced at Emma whenever he could and still drive safely. Her face showed a gamut of constantly changing emotions.

"Dad's service training taught him skills that landed him a good job when he got out at twenty-four. His position pays well and has excellent benefits. He's never been without work."

"Not many can say that."

"You're right, but Dad takes his employment for granted—as something that he earned and is entitled to." She brushed a strand of hair from her face. "Shortly after his discharge from the army, the city began expanding toward the neighborhood in which Dad had grown up. Real estate prices skyrocketed. He made a hefty profit when he sold the house—and that's when he met Mom."

Her voice stopped, and Landon looked over at her. A tear slid down her face. She gulped.

"They were married for over twenty-five years. Bud and I wish he could see how blessed he was." Emma's voice cracked. "She was the best. Her father was the real estate agent who helped him sell his home and buy another. She worked in the office."

"Love at first sight?" Landon asked, though not with the enthusiasm he had expected.

She sighed deeply. "The way Mom explained it to me, Dad was smitten. She was cautious."

"She didn't share his feelings?" *Unrequited love, a story as old as time.*

"Just the opposite. She cared a great deal—quite quickly. And her parents thought Chet Porter was a perfect choice for their daughter—nice home, good job, willingness to shoulder responsibility."

"But ..."

"Call it a sixth sense or intuition or whatever else, but Mom had reservations. She could never put her finger on what made her nervous—until after they were married."

Landon turned in at the entrance to an apartment complex. They had reached his home without picking up anything for supper, but he hadn't wanted to interrupt her.

When she realized they were stopping, she asked, "Are we here already? I'm sorry. I shouldn't have—"

"You should have." He removed his seat belt and leaned toward her. "I'd like to hear the rest. What did your mom find out once they married?"

She turned doleful eyes toward him. "My dad's an alcoholic. He started drinking during high school. By the time he met my mom, he was hooked." So much grief welled up in her eyes that it spilled out. "Maybe the saddest part of all is that Dad can hide his addiction—most of the time. That's why Mom never found out until later. That's why, even today, few people know that he needs help."

"How do you hide alcoholism?"

"You drink every night after work, but no more than you can handle. On the weekend, you binge. Then you have Sunday to recover."

"He's done this your whole life?"

"Yes. Until Mom died, she did her best to see that he kept himself under control. After she passed, he got worse. Now he doesn't always wait until the weekend to go on a bender. His work is suffering, and people are finally becoming aware. Bud deals with more problems than I ever had to."

Landon reached out and pulled her to himself. "I'm sorry, Em."

She momentarily relaxed in his arms, then moved away saying, "You're the only person I've ever told besides Hailey." She grabbed his right forearm. "Please, keep my secret."

Her secret. She bore no blame for her father's addiction, but she felt guilty nonetheless. That thought crushed Landon. "How can I help?"

"Pray for Bud—for his safety."

"Your dad gets violent?"

"Not usually, but he's drinking more than ever." Emma reached into her purse and pulled out a tissue. "Bud has never really had a childhood. When he was still in grade school, he began watching out for Dad. Later our mom got sick, and Bud helped with her care." Emma drew a ragged breath. "When I moved back, I was able to relieve him of some of the burden of Dad. But since Mom's death, Bud's life is harder than ever—he's never played sports in school or joined any club."

Never played any sport. The idea jolted Landon. *What would that be like?*

"He's almost eighteen, but he doesn't have his driver's license. To get one, he needs an adult in the car with him for fifty hours, and Dad's not fit for that. He's had his permit twice, but has had to let it run out." She raised her hands and then let them fall helplessly. "I feel so guilty I'm not there to help him. I nearly gave up this opportunity, but Bud wouldn't let me. In spite of all he copes with, my brother has such a kind heart—like our mom did—and he wants this dream of mine to come true."

Landon had never met Bud, but he empathized with Emma's brother already. Her vision had captured him, too. "Is that part of the reason you feel so much pressure to have the shop succeed?"

"I can't let Bud down."

Landon enclosed her hand in his and bowed his head. He couldn't remember the last time he'd prayed aloud with someone. Still, he felt compelled to do so. "Lord, please help Mr. Porter to let go of his addiction. And please help Bud—protect him, bring someone to encourage him. Help him get his license. In Christ's name, Amen."

"Thank you, Landon." She exhaled a long cleansing breath. "Let's go inside. I'm excited to see what you've been up to."

Just like that, the bold, bubbly Emma was back.

Landon gave her the short version of the layout of his apartment—the kitchen, the bathroom, and the living room; then he motioned her to the folding table he had set up in the living room. She glanced around.

"This place looks like you, masculine but polished." She smiled in his direction. "Modern furniture with a black, silver and red color scheme. Very trendy. I like it."

He smiled at the compliment. "I'm glad. I do, too." He glanced at the clock. "It's only 3:30, a little early for supper—which we didn't get anyway—but would you like something to drink?"

"Yes, please."

"Do you drink coffee?"

"Ugghh! No—never. I can't understand how anything that smells so good can taste so horrible."

Landon's confidence plummeted. *She hates coffee. Why didn't you ask her about it before you spent hours in research? But it's not entirely hopeless.* Her discouraging words had held one ray of hope. *She likes the smell of coffee. She doesn't have to drink it; she just has to sell it.* The self-to-self pep talk bolstered his courage—a little.

Landon poured Emma some juice, and within five minutes, the two sat side by side at the rectangular table—a purchase that he had made just after he landed his job. Space was essential for completing tax forms, and the extra work area allowed him to keep the kitchen free of clutter.

Once Emma was ready, he set three folders in front of her. Each one contained pages that he had copied from the Internet and grouped according to the type of coffee maker and its necessary supplies.

Placing his elbows on the table, he looked at her and said, "Since Thursday night I have been trying to come up with a way to help you draw more foot traffic through your store. I wanted something with a fairly high rate of return and low maintenance. Saturday morning I had a brainstorm. Until we walked in the door, I thought it was *the* solution—now I'm not so sure."

"What changed since then?"

He reached across in front of her and opened two of the folders. "Here's my idea."

She looked from his face to the files. Her jaw dropped. She gulped and stared. Then her chin sank to her chest.

Landon writhed and grimaced. He shifted in his chair. His eyes widened in disappointment.

Emma's shoulders shook violently, and choked sounds escaped her lips.

"Emma? Emma, please—" He smoothed his hand along her arm while lifting her chin and turning her face toward him. "Em, please don't—"

Sparkling eyes searched his face. "Please don't—what?"

"You're laughing." He jerked away, resting his fists on his thighs. "I'm sitting here dying because I think you're in tears, and you're laughing so hard that your body is shaking." He feigned disgust.

Emma placed her hand on his shoulder. "You're so cute when you're flustered." She moved closer and whispered, "But don't worry, I won't tell your tough-guy buddies about your sensitive side."

With his right hand he snatched her palm from his shoulder, while simultaneously stretching his left arm around her and catching her left wrist in a snug hold. In the time it took Emma to breathe deeply, he had engulfed her in a commanding grip. "What sensitive side?" His eyes gleamed with daring—and something else.

She gasped at his question but neither replied nor pulled away.

His arms full of Emma, Landon could think of only one word, *soft*—a concept that his father had commented on years earlier. "Son, women are soft. Their hearts are soft, to love us; their emotions are soft, to comfort us; their bodies are soft, to please us. The Lord uses the same things to form both men and women, but somehow, the woman is a softer version than we are, and it goes much deeper than anatomy."

Even Emma's shoulder, which Landon now pressed into his chest, seemed to yield to him delicately. Her hand and wrist molded easily under his fingertips. His dad's words, though true, failed to express even half of the softness Landon currently understood.

She turned her head—just a few inches from his—toward him. "You *are* sensitive And very strong."

Her words revived him from his trance enough that he sighed, "And you're soft—so soft."

"As in *weak*?"

"As in *soft*."

———

Weighty seconds passed as Emma registered the meaning of Landon's words and understood the situation the two of them were in. Reluctantly, she withdrew her hand from his as she whispered, "Thank you."

He released her wrist and straightened in his chair. "Back to coffee."

She smiled briefly. "Much safer, I think."

For the next several minutes, Emma mostly listened as Landon explained what he had discovered. Though not a fan of coffee herself, she had to admit that she was in the minority in that regard. She could also appreciate the idea of chocolates and coffee together. A mocha candy was already on her list of those she would offer at her grand opening.

She noticed that Landon was avoiding suggestions as to what she *should* do. He simply presented the facts. Finally she asked, "So, what do you think is the best option?"

He paused. "That's your call, not mine."

Recalling her reaction Thursday night, she understood his reticence. "Yes, it's my decision, but I really would like your opinion. I don't drink coffee, so this is all new to me."

"The brewing and selling side is new to me, too. I'm usually on the buying and drinking end."

"What would you recommend, though—if you had to?"

He arched his eyebrows. "Do I have to?"

"Technically, no." She laid her hand on his forearm. "But I really would like your opinion."

Before making direct eye contact, he glanced at her hand on his arm. "If I were in your position, I would go with a brewer that makes individual servings. That method will be easier for you to keep up with, and you won't need to be checking on it and making a fresh pot of coffee."

"I think you're right. Not being a connoisseur myself"—she rolled her eyes—"I need something that takes all of the guesswork out of making the perfect cup. I'm notorious for getting wrapped up in my work and becoming oblivious to what's going on around me. It will take all my powers of concentration to stay ahead of the peripherals—I don't need anything else to complicate my day."

"Which individual serving machine do you like?"

"I honestly don't know. I'm somewhat confused by the lingo." She pulled up the specs for one model. "If I'm reading this page correctly, it seems that this system can't be connected directly to a water supply. That sounds like a lot of hassle, refilling the pot every time it runs out. I also wonder about how often I'll have to empty the used pods."

"Once again, we agree. Taking into consideration those things and one more—the reputation of the company—I'd go with this one." He reached toward the other file and picked up a fact sheet on a machine from a well-known maker of commercial brewers.

"I like this one, too, but what does it cost? I don't see a price on any of them."

Emma watched as Landon fidgeted with a button on his polo shirt. Then he cleared his throat. "I wanted your decision to be based on more than price, so I left them off."

"But you do know how much each one is, right?"

"Yes, and if the adage 'You get what you pay for' is true, then you would be getting a lot of machine right here." He tapped the picture on the page he held. "This one's not cheap—just into the four-figure range if you buy retail. You wouldn't be, but the wholesale price is hard to come by without a business license number."

Emma felt her jaw drop. "That machine costs over a thousand dollars!"

"It retails for that, but—"

"A thousand dollars!" She grabbed the sheet from his hand and gaped at the offending picture. "All it does is brew coffee—not make your breakfast or mop the floor. Even with a substantial wholesale discount, I can't afford it. Start up costs have nearly wiped out everything except my emergency fund." She plopped the paper onto the table and turned directly toward Landon. "And this—machine—would be just the beginning." She delineated each of the next items on her fingers. "I'd have to pay to have it plumbed. I'd need coffee pods and cups, along with sweeteners and creamers, and who knows what else. I wouldn't even know where to begin in deciding which flavors to choose or how much to purchase." She switched to the other hand before continuing her list. "I have so little time left before the opening, I can't take time to shop for the best price on it or the extras. And another thing—"

Emma's tirade ceased when Landon grabbed her upper arms and covered her lips with his.

━━━━━━━━

Emma's gasp and her backwards jerk hit Landon like a Jordy Jordan tackle from the blind side. He forced himself away and held her at arm's length.

"I'm sorry I startled you." When she didn't respond, Landon added, "I surprised myself, too. But you were talking so fast. Thought you might hyperventilate. I did the first thing I thought of."

Emma took two ragged breaths. "Very effective as a conversation stopper." She stared at him. "But hyperventilation is still a definite possibility."

"Yeah—for two of us." Landon shook his head at what he had done.

Her searching gaze met his. He wrestled with the idea of kissing her again, no apologies attached. Then her smoldering look faded, and she grinned. "I guess I *was* going on a bit."

He arched both eyebrows. "A bit?" Releasing her arms he picked up a legal pad lying in front of him. "Do you want to hear my proposal?"

Emma's eyes nearly bugged out of their sockets.

Landon blurted, "About the coffee brewer—my proposal for coffee."

"You have a proposal for coffee?"

He hung his head and mumbled, "Talk about putting your foot in your mouth." Before he could embarrass himself further, he noticed Emma's face directly in front of him, her head lower than his, her chocolate eyes searching his blue ones.

"Let's start again, okay? You untangle your tongue, and I'll try to keep mine in check. I'd like to hear that proposal."

Landon forced himself to focus on coffee. He lifted his head and said, "What if I would buy the brewer—consider it an interest-free loan to you—and you would make monthly payments to me until you paid it off?"

"An interest-free loan?" Skepticism clouded her features. "It's a good thing you're not a banker. Your colleagues would have you institutionalized for even thinking such a thing."

"Actually, I ran this idea by my dad, and he agrees that it could work."

"Landon, you're talking about several hundred dollars here, not a buck ninety-eight. I can't let you do that. I have no guarantee how soon I would be able to pay you back or even that I could. What if this endeavor goes belly up?"

Landon flipped a page on the legal pad and handed the tablet to her. "Like specialty chocolates, gourmet coffee isn't cheap for the customer. But here's where the two are different." He pointed to the numbers. "When you consider the cost of ingredients, gourmet coffee is inexpensive to produce." Showing her the page with the samples of coffee pods, he added, "Each of these costs about twenty-five percent of the retail price for the cup of coffee it makes. Take it from a guy who buys a lot of coffee." When Emma smiled, he added the capstone to his argument. "Even with the extras, like creamers and sweeteners, and taking cups and lids into account, the markup is easily one hundred percent—spend a dollar and bring in two. That's music to an accountant's ears."

━━━━━━

Coffee! He wants to buy a brewer for my shop so that I can sell coffee alongside my specialty chocolates. Dear Lord, am I crazy for even considering it?

Emma fretted and chafed in her seat as Landon explained the advantages. The weighty decision burdened her mind. When his voice died away, she knew he was expecting an answer. But what could she say?

"Be still and know that I am God." One of Emma's favorite verses raced unbidden through her mind. *Father, I know that You're God—and I trust You—but is this Your leading, or am I being influenced by someone special who really seems to care?*

"What do you think?" Landon's gaze searched her face.

Suddenly Emma was hearing God's words from a childhood Sunday School lesson. "'Have I not commanded you? Be strong and courageous! Do not tremble or be dismayed, for the LORD your God is with you wherever you go.'"

I trust You, Lord. I want to be strong and courageous.

Emma reached for the legal pad. She handed it and a pen to Landon. "I'll need everything in writing: what the loan will cover, the monthly payment arrangements, everything." She sent him a steely glare to convey her resolve. "Then I'll need your promise that you'll help me to shop for all the things that create a cup of gourmet coffee."

CHAPTER 8 ━━━

O n the first Monday of December, Landon rose earlier than his usual 6:30. He completed his newly initiated morning routine: shower, wardrobe, Bible, and breakfast. But instead of pocketing his change, gathering his briefcase and pointing his Camry in the direction of PSU, he made a last-minute stop at his refrigerator, retrieved a card from the counter, and adjusted his tie one final time. Outside, he hit the unlock button and unloaded his arms, carefully placing everything in the front passenger seat.

Twenty minutes later he parked in the lot next to Bellefonte's Talleyrand Park, collected two items from the seat beside him, and hurried toward the center of town. The cold kept most people inside, but a few hardy souls jogged bravely through and around the park, their breathing creating cloudy puffs ahead of them. Only the ducks in the stream that ran along the edge of Talleyrand seemed oblivious to the chill. Landon saw one plunge his head completely underwater, pointing his tail skyward. A few seconds later the stalwart fowl emerged, shaking his head vigorously, while munching on some tasty morsel he had evidently discovered during his frigid foray beneath the surface. Landon shivered.

By 7:15 he stood outside Heavenly Chocolates, the crisply painted letters shining brightly against the gleaming glass door. He stopped on the sidewalk to the right of the portal, partially shielded by both the window blind and the sandwich board which proclaimed, "Grand Opening." He glanced inside.

Chocolates filled the showcase, each one in its separate position, clearly and elegantly labeled. The two small tables, covered with red cloths and sporting vases with a single white rose, welcomed people to sit. In one corner on a quaint yet sturdy wrought iron stand rested the chrome and black coffee maker that Landon boasted about and Emma addressed as "that monstrosity."

Two days after getting Emma's approval for the brewer, Landon had delivered the contract she insisted upon. By the end of that week, he had located a local wholesaler who sold the coffee maker she had chosen. Then, armed with Emma's business license, he ventured off, returning with the prodigious brewer and armloads of cups and other paraphernalia, exercising great care to "keep all receipts." Emma's hard line on retaining documentation could have made her a great accountant.

Once the machine was safely unpacked, she had insisted on reading the directions for its setup, use, and care. When her exacting demands were met, she granted him dibs on the premier cup.

His choice of pods—an amaretto cream—delivered a combination so delicious that, after his first sip, Landon had declared, "Oh, Em, if only you were a coffee connoisseur. This is the best."

Her response was a sidelong glance coupled with a shake of her head. "Are you in love?" she quipped.

As he took another cautious sip of the steaming brew, he glanced over the cup and caught her gaze. "I might be."

She didn't respond aloud, but her flush and the gleam in her eyes spoke volumes.

Remembering that look as he peered inside her shop, Landon smiled. He was beginning to think he was in love, but certainly not with a coffee machine or any divine creation it could produce.

Inside, Emma stepped from the kitchen into his line of sight. She had pulled a white apron over her head and was adjusting it and tying the strings behind her as she walked. Her hair bobbed with each step. "Ah, Emma," he whispered, "do you know what you do to my heart?"

He glanced in the window at his own reflection. He'd worn a blue shirt with darker blue pinstripes, one that Emma had seen him in on Sunday the week before.

"I like you in blue," she had said, "even though it hardly seems fair."

"Fair?"

"How is any girl supposed to resist those blue eyes when a blue shirt makes them even bluer?" She'd batted her lashes at him.

"I think I'll wear blue more often." He had.

Now he ran the fingers of his free hand through his short hair, adjusted his tie, and knocked on the glass in front of him.

―――――――――

Hearing a knock on the door, Emma jumped. "We don't open till 8:00." Then she recognized Landon, his blue eyes shining as he smiled. Her heart fluttered. He was so good looking, and he was standing at *her* door. Exhaling deeply, she scurried to let him in.

"What a nice surprise." She stepped aside for him to enter. "I'm so nervous, I can't think straight, and I ..."

Landon pulled his right arm from behind his back and handed her the bouquet he held. "Happy First Day of Business," he said before bending to kiss her cheek.

"Oh, Landon! Roses!" Red roses. Did he know the traditional meaning of that color? "They match my decor." Tears bubbled over as she hugged him tightly. "Thank you—for everything. You've done so much—and now these. They're beautiful." Emma placed her free hand on Landon's biceps and raised herself to return his peck on the cheek. His arm muscle tightened perceptibly, sending a thrill through her hand and heart.

"You're welcome—for everything—but I didn't do much." He glanced around. "The place looks great and smells *heavenly.*" He elbowed Emma. "All it needs now is a paying customer." She watched as he sidestepped her and headed for the coffee maker, quickly selected his choice, and set the machine in motion. Then he moved to the display. "I'd like three caramels, please—two for me and one for my secretary. You can put them all in the same bag."

Emma stood as if she were molded in chocolate. Not until Landon strode toward the cash register, did she regain her mobility. Flustered, she took one long waft of the roses in her arms, set them on the nearest table, and scurried past Landon. Before selecting his choices, she donned plastic gloves. Then she carefully placed three of her creations in a small bag, folding and taping the top of the sack securely. Stripping the gloves from her fingers, she began punching the cost of his purchase into the register.

Her hands halted in midair. "What am I thinking? After all you've done, this is on the house." She reached to void the entries, but Landon captured her fingers and squeezed.

"Remember what you told me?"

She looked into his clear blue eyes and wondered how he expected her to remember her name.

"'If you won't let me pay, then our time here is finished,'" he recited as he handed the bag back toward her.

Emma regretted those words. "But, Landon, I want to do this for you."

"And I want to be your first paying customer."

She hesitated.

"I wore blue," he said, staring at her.

Emma melted beneath his cobalt gaze. Why had she ever told him about the effect that his wearing blue had on her? "You don't play fair." Reluctantly, she took the ten-dollar bill from him and returned his change.

Landon accepted the money with one hand and grasped Emma's with the other. "I like to win." He lifted her hand and kissed the back of it.

Was he trying to win her heart? She hoped so.

Emma smiled as Landon kept her hand in his and brought her from behind the counter to his side. Together they crossed the room to retrieve his coffee from the brewer.

"Would you like any creamer, flavored syrup, or sweetener in that, sir?" Emma asked in her best professional voice. "We have several to choose from."

Landon grinned. "No, thank you. This flavor is perfect as it is."

"And you're sweet enough already." Not subtle, but oh, so true.

As Emma placed a lid on the cup, he reached inside his jacket and pulled out an envelope. "Have a great first day," he said, handing it to her.

"Another present?" she asked, examining the card before looking up. "You didn't need to do this." She tapped his arm with the envelope. "But it means a lot. And so do the roses." Reaching for his hand, she gave it a gentle squeeze. "Thanks again."

"You're welcome—and just for the record—" His fingers returned the pressure. "I didn't choose red because they match your colors."

After closing the door behind Landon, Emma leaned against it and wondered if there was anything more wonderful than a terrific guy who understood the language of roses and brought you red ones.

By 10:30 Landon had encountered two vendor accounts whose balances from November were still outstanding and one potential vendor who missed his scheduled meeting. Unless the guy had a great reason for not keeping his appointment, Landon knew that PSU would not be selling the man's wares any time soon.

Then at noon Rosalee called on the intercom. "Mr. Steele, I hate to do this to you, but I've come down with one of my migraines. Can you handle things for the rest of the day?"

Rosalee's migraines, although rare, were severe. "Rosalee, go home. Don't worry about things here. I hope you feel better by tomorrow."

With all the setbacks of the morning, Landon decided to take his lunch earlier than usual. He walked a few blocks and bought a deli sandwich, then returned to his office and propped up his feet, hoping that the afternoon would be brighter.

And it was, but not with a warm and sunny glow. Instead, the hours blazed with a sort of crash and burn intensity. Reviewing end-of-November accounts, Landon discovered a posting error on a spreadsheet. Even though it involved only a number transposition and accounted for a small sum, the time it took to locate the problem and to correct it was anything but inconsequential.

While he was correcting the problem, the phone rang. Landon forgot about Rosalee's absence and let it ring a few times before reaching for it.

"Why are you answering the phone?" Stewart Greer, his department head, inquired bluntly. "You don't have time for that. You haven't finished November's reports yet. I need them—now!"

"Rosalee is sick. I found an error. I'm correcting it. I'll have the reports to you as soon as possible."

"As long as that means this afternoon." Stewart was not a patient man. "And one more thing. Dave Carter is out on emergency leave. His dad died suddenly." Landon's heart sank. *Poor Dave.* "You and two others will have to divide up his work load until I find a temporary replacement."

As much as Landon wanted to help, he knew that the extra load meant working long hours—probably most of the week.

Not once during the day did he find time to call Emma. Until the bereavement phone call came, he had held onto the hope of driving to Bellefonte that evening. The added responsibilities precluded that notion. By the time he had completed what he felt must be done before he left that night, the clock read 8:30, and he was exhausted—and famished.

He considered hitting a fast-food drive through, but his good sense prevailed, and he opted for his favorite little family restaurant tucked away only a few blocks from his apartment. The wait staff didn't promise to have a person in and out in the time it took to sing an advertising jingle, but they were prompt and courteous, and the food, excellent.

After ordering, Landon prayed for his meal and then settled in with a Coke and someone's discarded *Centre Daily Times*. It wasn't hot off the press, but it was the closest he had come to current events all day.

Landon was scanning the stories on page 1 when his friend Mike settled himself on the other side of the booth.

"Hey, buddy. Didn't expect to find you here. You look whipped."

"Long, hard day," Landon said.

"I didn't think you office guys had hard days—sitting in those fancy leather chairs, having your secretaries run all your errands."

"Yeah, you PennDOT boys have it so tough."

The two friends had been carrying on this good-natured debate since the day Landon was hired at Penn State. By then Mike had worked for the Department of Transportation for nearly three years.

"Are you really just getting off work?"

"Yep."

"So, what are you having?"

"Hot meatloaf sandwich with mashed potatoes and gravy."

"Good choice! If I hadn't eaten an hour ago, I'd be tempted to steal some."

"Don't even think about it." Landon reached for the fork in front of him and pointed the tines at his friend. "My noon sandwich wore off about five."

Mike ordered a chocolate shake. "Are we still on for racquetball on Thursday?"

Landon glanced at his watch before answering. "I hope so. I'll have to let you know later this week. Dave's father died yesterday. He'll be out for a few days."

"Had he been sick?'

"Not that I knew. Had a heart attack and was gone."

"What a blow that must be."

"Yeah."

The server brought Landon's coleslaw and Mike's shake. Landon glanced around her to check the clock across the room.

"Are they slow tonight, or are you really hungry? You're clock watching."

"Neither."

"Late for something?"

"No," Landon hedged. "Just later than usual. I want to see what time it is."

"You're a terrible liar. What's up?"

Landon never could keep things from Mike. The guy sniffed out news as a bird dog flushed quail. "Emma's shop opened today. I saw her this morning. I wanted to go to back after work to see how the first day went."

"You saw her before work—and you wanted to go back tonight?"

"To see how business was. I'm her accountant."

Mike nearly created a geyser with his chocolate shake. After gulping back the potential stream, he asked, "And how many of your other clients do you see twice a day—just to check on them?"

Uncomfortable heat crawled up Landon's neck, but he hated to look away and give Mike the satisfaction of making his point.

"Don't tell me you're sweet on the candy lady. You've only known her a couple weeks!" When Landon didn't respond to his friend's outburst, Mike slumped against the back of the booth. "You are, aren't you?"

"I might be."

Mike shook his head. "This isn't like you. Wanting to see her twice within twelve hours." He straightened up and then plunked his elbows squarely on the table, measuring Landon's response. "You've mentioned her a few times. More than a few, I guess. I had no idea."

"Emma is—like no one else."

"Three heads? Seven feet tall?"

Landon rolled his eyes. "Kind, funny, godly."

"And what's she look like?"

Landon finished off his slaw just as the server brought his meal and refilled his Coke. After he had cut the first bite of his sandwich, enjoying the excuse to keep Mike wondering, he said, "She's pretty." He plunged the generous serving into his mouth, licking his lips as he savored the combination of flavors.

Mike opened his mouth. Then he stifled whatever he had been about to say and sat with a puzzled grin on his face and waited until Landon had swallowed.

"What?" Landon asked.

"I don't get it. All you say is, 'She's pretty,' but she has you jumping through hoops in only a few weeks' time."

Landon tilted his head slightly and exhaled sharply before turning his attention back to his meal.

"Is she expecting you tonight?"

His mouth full, Landon only shook his head.

"You called her?"

When his mouth was empty, Landon said, "Not yet."

"But you're going to as soon as I leave."

"I'm not calling her from a restaurant. I hate that."

"You could have called her on your way here."

"I was too down. Didn't want to ruin her excitement."

"But you can tell your troubles to me?"

"You showed up at my table and invited yourself to stay." Landon wiggled his eyebrows before returning his attention to his plate.

Mike muttered something to himself. "Just don't let yourself get too far too fast. You know how women are."

"*You* know how women are. I seldom date."

"All the more reason you should be cautious."

"I can take care of myself—she's a foot shorter than I am."

"With women, height has nothing to do with it, believe me." Mike slurped the last of his shake up the straw and finished it off with a loud sucking noise. "Gotta run. Be careful, buddy—and I'm not talking about your driving."

———————

The car clock read 9:40 when Landon pulled into his drive. His apartment was dim, lit only by the security light outside. In the bleakness all he could discern was the blink of the answering machine.

"Six messages? I'm popular today. It's not even March," he said, crossing the room and flipping on the reading light next to the phone.

He pushed the button.

"Landon, it's me, Emma. It's 10:30. I'm busy. Thanks so much for the flowers. Bye."

A few seconds elapsed.

"Hi, Landon. It's me again. Sylvia is relieving me for a few minutes so I can breathe. It's still busy. I read the card. I laughed. Then I cried. Bye."

Landon recalled the party-hat-wearing bulldog and chuckled to himself. The inside greeting was equally silly. His written message hadn't been. He hoped her tears were happy ones. Once more he heard her voice.

"All right, I admit it. That monstrosity is worth the space it takes up. I'm not quite ready to say it's the best, but you are for thinking of it. See ya soon."

The best. If only she hadn't added "for thinking of it."

The machine erupted again. "I know I'm crazy for calling your house when I know you're not there, but I didn't want to interrupt your busy day with all this silliness. One more hour before closing. I love my new job!"

Landon had never had so much fun checking his machine. Then, on the fifth message, the voice of Stewart Greer brought him back to reality. "Landon, this is Stew. Dave called. His mom is taking his dad's death very hard. Dave's concerned for her physical and mental health. He'll be gone at least until a week from Wednesday. Give me a day or two, and I'll find someone to fill in for him."

More troubles for Dave. First his dad, now his mom. At least he had vacation time on top of his bereavement leave. Maybe the entire week wouldn't be so hectic for the rest of them in the office if Stewart was planning to bring in someone else.

One more message to go. "Please be Emma," Landon wished aloud during the brief pause.

"It's me—again. When I got home at 6:00, I really hoped to have a long talk with you this evening, but as soon as I sat down, the adrenaline rush faded. So I had dinner and finished up everything I needed to do. I'm going to bed early. I'll talk to you tomorrow. I have something important to ask you." There was a brief pause before she added, "Thanks for helping to make this day all that I hoped it would be. You're my hero."

He caught her words and grasped their bittersweet meaning: he wouldn't be seeing her face tonight, but he would drift off to sleep with her words on his mind and in his heart.

━━━━━━━

When Landon rang the doorbell at the Sawyer's shortly before eight on Tuesday evening, Emma met him at the door. She was wearing a winter coat—not her usual stylish leather one—but a fluffy affair, probably down-filled. Its white puffiness made her upper torso appear to be garbed in a giant marshmallow. On her head she'd perched the modern version of the aviator's cap, a blue and white knit hat with flaps that covered her ears and strings that hung past her shoulders. Atop the imitation airman's hat, sat a white pompom that looked like a mini version of the marshmallow that enclosed her.

Landon's eyes widened, and a grin tilted his lips upward. "Are you going somewhere?"

"*We're* going somewhere. I need to get out. Let's walk to Talleyrand. The Christmas lights are up, and the park is beautiful at night."

"Okay, I could use the exercise. I didn't make it to the gym after work."

"Another late night?" Emma started across the porch but then stopped. "Will you be warm enough? You probably weren't expecting this wintry jaunt."

"I wasn't." Smiling, he tugged one of her hat strings, setting the cap at an odd angle. "But I have a sweatshirt with me—the one I was going to wear at the gym. Let me grab it."

At the car, he retrieved the shirt from his gym bag. Removing his jacket, he handed it to Emma, loosened his tie and drew it over his head. Then he pulled the sweatshirt over his oxford. Glancing at her, he said, "You're staring."

Instantly she looked away. "I'm sorry. That was rude."

He tipped her chin up. "I didn't think so."

"But you noticed." Emma shifted her weight.

"Noticing the stares of a pretty woman is what guys do."

His statement of the obvious made her smile. "That I believe," she added sarcastically.

"Like women don't notice men!" He reached for his coat.

"We do." She chuckled but didn't relinquish the jacket. When his hand rested on hers, she added, "I spent weeks looking at your picture. Sometimes I still can't believe it's really you. I guess I stare to make sure."

Seconds elapsed before Landon spoke. "I'm amazed at your honesty."

––––––––––

Emma gave him the coat and waited as he put it on. Then, tucking her hand into the crook of his elbow, she propelled him down the driveway with her. They had walked several yards before she spoke again. "I'm amazed at your humility. All those people crowding around you, wanting an interview, your autograph, a date—and you aren't full of yourself."

"That was four years ago."

"Do people really not know who you are?"

"You mean who I *was*."

"I mean who you are—one of the best linebackers PSU ever produced, the holder of most of the linebacking records."

Landon stopped abruptly, jerking Emma to a halt as well. "Let's not talk about football." He pointed toward the bridge that spanned the stream. "Come on, I want to see if the ducks are still up."

Emma remained silent as she and Landon reached the park, started across the bridge, and looked for their feathered friends. When they didn't find any of the hardy fowls still afloat, she said, "I guess they've already gone to bed."

"Yeah, I guess so. They're early risers. I saw some yesterday when I came to the shop."

Without responding, Emma turned her back toward the water. She rested her elbows on the railing of the bridge and then gazed around the park. "Isn't it beautiful? I love Christmas—the decorations, the carols, the whole holiday atmosphere." She scanned the scene once again and then sighed. "I know that Christmas is all about Christ, but some things make it even more special."

"Like presents." When he turned to face her, one elbow on the railing and his feet stretched out in front of him, his face held a look of anticipation like that of a nine-year-old boy standing in front of a stack of gifts with his name on them.

How Emma would have loved to know him as a child, to see those eyes sparkle as he opened presents. "At Christmas, God gave us the best present ever. I guess I can see where the tradition may have begun."

"So you're not a Scrooge, 'Bah, humbug!' and all that?"

"Definitely not."

"Have you started your list? Rosalee reminds me every workday in December just how long I have left."

"Are you a last-minute shopper?"

"Isn't every red-blooded American male?" When she giggled, he asked, "What's on your Christmas list this year? Anything I could find early?"

Emma's heart flip-flopped. Had Landon just opened this door? "Well—actually—there is one thing I would like from you—and I wouldn't even mind if it was late."

Landon leaned toward her, stopping only when he was close enough that she could feel his breath on her cheek. "I'm listening," was all he said, in a voice somewhat huskier than normal.

Emma cleared her throat and plunged ahead, talking quickly. "I want you to be my date at the Capital One Bowl in Orlando, Florida, on New Year's Day, when Penn State takes on Alabama. Mort has four tickets. He asked Sylvia, Hailey, and me to go, but Sylvia wants to give her ticket to you. Mort said you and he could room together. Hailey and I will share another room. All you have to do is come. Mort has thought of everything. It will be so much …"

"No, it won't." Landon backed away slightly.

She turned toward him and placed a gloved hand on his arm. "Of course it will. The Nittany Lions and the Crimson Tide."

"I won't be there. I can't go to a Bowl Game." Landon turned and paced a few steps.

"But, Landon, this is the Capital One Bowl, the one you would have played in if …"

Spinning back toward her, he said, "I know it's the Bowl I would have played in during my senior year." The intensity of his voice had risen. "Don't you think I wonder about the Capital One every year? I hurt my leg, Emma, not my head."

She clutched her stomach as if he'd just punched her in the midsection, then shoved herself up from the railing and quipped, "I know where you were hurt. I was there when it happened."

"So was I."

His blue eyes turned grayish, and Emma realized how much *steel* there was in Landon. "And for every day as the bones healed, for every grueling twist or turn that had always been so easy, for every rejection letter or phone call. I lived through it all—day and night for four years. Football is past."

"But you went to the Ohio State game."

"The only one."

"It was a start—a way back."

"There is no *way back* for me, Emma. Why can't you get it? You're a college grad."

No way back? Emma couldn't believe her ears. Without a word, she turned and retraced her steps. She needed to think. Had she missed some crucial element of Landon's story? Was she being unreasonable? A walk among the festive lights might help her find some answers.

Quickly descending the steps, she stepped into the muddy grass. Her foot slipped, and she landed hard with one leg in front of her and the other behind her. Her jeans sopped up the muddy wetness of the lawn. She was pulling herself and her soggy pants up as though she were closing a pair of scissors, when she felt Landon's hand steadying her.

"Emma, wait."

"I need to think. Alone." She withdrew her arm. "I'm confused and cold and wet." She continued up the sidewalk.

Before she reached the edge of the park, Landon was in front of her, his hands grasping both her arms.

"Emma, you have to listen to me."

"No, I don't." He'd accused *her* of being dense, but how hard a concept was *alone?*

He released her but remained in her path. "Hear me out." He looked around and spotted a nearby bench. "Let's sit over here."

"You've made up your mind and given your answer—and insulted me in the process."

Landon raked his fingers through his hair, exhaling as he did so. "I'm sorry. Really. Please sit with me."

She pointed to the soggy mess she wore. "I'd rather stand." She crossed her arms and waited.

Fearful that he didn't have much time before Emma changed her mind and bolted home, Landon started talking.

"I love Christmas, too." Her expression remained fixed. "Because of you, I've looked forward to this one more than any other since I was a kid." He leaned toward her. She set her outstretched leg behind her and shifted her weight away from him.

"I'll buy you a great gift. We'll spend Christmas wherever you want—here or in Pittsburgh or at my parents' or anywhere else you can think of. If you want to go on a trip, we'll go. If you'd rather stay at Mort and Sylvia's and sleep until noon, I'll come later."

He could see the intensity in her eyes. "I'll drive you to the airport when you fly out for the game. I'll pick you up when you get back—whatever time, day or night. I'll help out at the shop while you're gone."

"Why are you still at Penn State?"

Landon's head jerked back. "What's that got to do Christmas?"

"Just answer the question."

Landon failed to see the connection, but he didn't say so. She was skittish enough as it was. "Because I grew up around here. My parents are nearby."

"That's not what I asked. I asked you why—if football has such a devastating effect on you—you chose to stay in the one place that holds more football memories for you than anywhere else."

He drew himself up and squared his shoulders. "The university made me a job offer. Maybe they felt sorry for me. Maybe Bob pulled some strings, I don't know."

"You were an Academic All-American. You could have found a job anywhere."

She was right. The job had made the decision easier, but it wasn't the reason.

Landon shifted his weight from one foot to the other. "At graduation I still had months of training and conditioning before I was ready to be a linebacker again. If I stayed at Penn State, I would have the support of my parents and access to those with connections to football, people who could help me get back into the game once I recovered."

She stared at him, not seeming to grasp his meaning.

He clutched her shoulders and bent over until his face nearly touched hers. "I was going to play football again, Emma." His blue eyes searched her brown ones. "I never wanted to stay in the accounting department at PSU."

Emma didn't shake herself free, but she didn't back down, either.

"But you have stayed, Landon. Even though you never returned to football, you've kept yourself right in the middle of the Nittany Lions, close enough to feel the excitement. Now when Mort makes this magnificent offer, you turn him—and me—down flat. No discussion, no explanation, just a resounding no."

"Try to understand."

"You're making it difficult. You say you'll do anything for me while I'm away, and you'll gladly take me anywhere I want for Christmas, but you won't do the one thing and take me the one place I've asked you to."

Landon couldn't believe her callousness. "You make me sound selfish, like I'm being obstinate for the fun of it."

Her demeanor silently spoke the words, "Well, duh."

"You think *I'm* being selfish! What about you? You know what I've been through. You know how I feel about football, but you ignore all of that and ask me to go to a Bowl Game with you—the hardest one of all for me to forget."

Emma shifted her weight toward him, clasped the sides of his coat, and gazed up at him. "I watched you at the Ohio State game. You were so into every part of it. I could have understood what was going on without seeing the field. Your face was a mirror."

Befuddled, Landon raised his hands in the air. "Okay, so I love football. What's your point?"

"Here's my point." She released his jacket but brought one index finger to his chest, prodding him as she emphasized her words. "Three weeks later, after Mort creates this wonderful surprise, and I dream about our going to the Capital One Bowl together, you suddenly decide that one more football game will put you over the edge."

"You're dreaming about going?" He clutched her hand to halt the emphasizing finger. "Sounds pretty selfish to me."

Landon waited for Emma to cry or argue or maybe kick him in the shins.

"If wanting to see that excitement on your face again, to feel your love for the game—if that's selfish ..." Her voice cracked, and she paused. "Then I'm the most selfish person in the world." She pulled her hand from his grasp, turned, and started up the street.

CHAPTER 9

After she left, Landon stood, dazed. Was he to blame for Emma's not understanding his dilemma? Why hadn't he told her about the recurrent nightmare? After a few nights' reprieve, it was back, as agonizingly vivid as ever. He hadn't told her about his panic attack inside the stadium, either. He hadn't wanted to admit his weaknesses.

The thought that troubled him most was a new one. Had he really reacted during the Ohio State game as Emma said? If she was right, the paradox of his life had grown gargantuan. How could he love something so much yet struggle to be anywhere near it?

He sank onto the nearby bench and rested his chin on top of his fists. By the time he collected his thoughts and glanced up the street, he could see Emma ready to turn a corner onto the Sawyer's lane. Once she turned, she would be out of his view. Could he catch her before she reached home? Should he try to even though he knew she didn't want him around?

If he hurried, he could at least watch to see that she arrived safely. Staying well behind her but keeping her in sight, he followed Emma up the sidewalk. He would not have needed to exercise such stealth. She never looked back. With steps that were clipped and purposeful, she reached the Sawyer's house. Landon watched her climb the stairs to the porch, unlock the door, and let herself in.

Resisting the urge to go inside and confront her once more, he unlocked his car door and slumped onto the seat. He started the Camry and revved the engine, hoping that Emma would hear and fling the door open, dashing out to meet him. Instead, only silence and darkness remained.

Emma strode into the Sawyer's home, giving the door a shove behind her. Each step away from Landon had increased her frustration. "How long is he going to let this—phobia—or obsession—or whatever it is control his life?" She sputtered on as she bent to remove her muddy shoes.

"You're back sooner than I expected." Sylvia bustled into the room. "How was your …? Where is Landon?" she asked, looking around.

"I don't know, and at the moment, I don't care."

Sylvia gaped at Emma. "Surely you don't mean that."

"I do mean that. He's so full of himself."

The older woman's eyes grew even wider. "Are we talking about the same Landon—the one who gave *you* ideas for your shop and helped *you* get ready to open and brought *you* flowers yesterday?"

"Yes," Emma sputtered. "The very same one. He turned me—and you—down, Sylvia. He's not going to the Capital One Bowl. I barely had time to get the invitation out before he barked 'I won't be there.'"

"Did he say why?"

Sylvia's tranquility fueled Emma's exasperation. "Oh, he reminded me of the football phobia he's had since his accident and offered some drivel about taking me anywhere else I wanted to go and doing anything else I wanted to do."

"And you said?"

"I asked him why in the world he's still at Penn State if football has such a devastating effect on him—and then I reminded him that we met," Emma's volume had risen with each word she uttered, "at a football game."

"And how did you leave things between the two of you?"

"*I* left *him* at the park." Emma tried to ignore the stunned look she saw on Sylvia's face. "I'm going to bed. Maybe after I shower I'll be able to forget about him for tonight and just go to sleep." She hung her jacket and hat on the coat rack. "If not, I'll pretend that my extra pillow is Landon and take my anger out on it."

———

Early Wednesday morning Landon dialed Emma's number. When he heard her say, "This is Emma. Leave a message, and I'll get back to you," he waited for the beep.

"It's Landon." His carefully planned words suddenly dropped from his brain like the signal in a bad phone connection. "I want to talk to you," was all he managed to re-gather. "Please call me."

His phone remained silent all day and throughout the evening. Over the next few days, Landon called her several times. He got no response.

Saturday night after supper at his parents' house, Landon repacked his duffel bag. On his way out to his car, his mom stopped him. "You know we would love to have you stay the night and go to church with us tomorrow."

"I know, but I'm going back tonight."

"Bring Emma the next time you come."

"Mom, don't push." He could hear the sharpness in his tone. "I can't make her talk to me."

And that was the agonizing truth. The thought brought Landon no comfort.

The only thing in his playbook at the moment was to catch up to her at her church the next morning, a congregation that met just outside Bellefonte. He'd never been there, but he knew of the place, and he and Emma had talked about his attending with her some Sunday. Tomorrow was the day; Emma was clueless. Was she bold enough to snub him outright? Definitely. Would she? He hoped not.

Entering the church parking lot on Sunday, Landon saw her as she neared the front door. She hadn't seen him. He turned down the first row he came to. Halfway up the line he found her Focus—the Nittany Lion bobble head on the dash was unmistakable. The space next to hers was empty, but only until Landon reached it.

By the time he parked, found the room for the college and careers class, and located a seat, Emma sat clustered among a group of young women. The only vacant places were on the other side of the room. He chose one a row behind her. The instant he sat, he questioned himself—again—as to the wisdom of this plan. Emma was near enough to conjure up daydreams but too far away for him to do anything to help them materialize.

As soon as class ended, he wove and dodged through the group. He had nearly reached her when he heard, "You're Landon Steele."

Landon groaned inwardly. Of all the times for his celebrity to catch up with him. He turned and found himself face to face with a young man who appeared about his age.

"Yes, I am."

"I thought so." The exuberant guy stuck out his hand. "My name's Ryan. My younger brother Joe's being recruited to play for the Lions this fall—at linebacker. He's watched every bit of your footage that he could get his hands on. We all have. You're his hero."

Landon had heard this comment a few times over the years. Each time put him more on edge than the last one. *If they only knew.* "I'm just one guy in a long line of PSU linebackers."

"Yeah, the one with most of the records."

Trying to steer the conversation to more comfortable ground, Landon asked, "Your family from here?"

"Not far. We're from Julian. Joe's a senior at Bald Eagle High."

Landon knew of the nearby school district. "It's good to see a local boy make the team."

Ryan reached to his shirt pocket and pulled out a pen. He handed it and his church bulletin toward Landon. "We're visiting here today. Joe stayed back home so that he could go to our church with the love of his life. He'll flip when I tell him I met you. Could you sign this for me? He'll never believe me otherwise."

"Uh—sure." Landon scribbled down his name and jersey number and added, "Congratulations, Joe."

"Thanks, Landon." Ryan hesitated. "Great to know that a guy really can be both a football player and a Christian. The folks are worried."

"Mine were, too." Landon knew that both Mom and Dad had spent hours in prayer for him during his career. "It won't be easy."

Ryan gulped and nodded. "Lots of temptations, huh?"

"Everywhere."

"Mom and Dad say … Oh, man, I forgot. They're waiting for me. Gotta run." Ryan shook Landon's hand once more. "Thanks again." He bolted a few steps down a long hall and then spun back. "Our last name's Kelly. Watch for Joe."

Joe Kelly. Easy enough name to remember. But Landon wouldn't be watching.

The service had started by the time he sneaked into the back pew. He scanned the crowd, thankful, as he often was, for his height advantage. Emma was midway back in the center section. Once he located her, he had a plan. She had been able to elude him before the service, but he was determined that she wouldn't afterwards. As the congregation rose for the closing hymn, he slipped out to the parking lot. Unless Emma was planning to walk home, she would have to go back to her car.

━━━━━━

Emma fidgeted as discreetly as she could, squirming and turning to see as many people as possible in every direction. What was Landon doing here? When she left the classroom a few minutes ago and saw him, she had nearly choked on her breath mint. Had he stayed? She didn't see him, and he was fairly easy to spot. Maybe he finally got the hint that she wasn't ready to talk. Maybe, but she doubted it. She didn't know him well, but enough to realize that Landon was a planner, a thinker—not a get-an-idea-and-run-with-it kind of person like Emma was. He'd had time to ponder. What was his plan?

She'd fussed and fumed during the last few days, in one minute, reaching for the phone and touching the keys for his number and, in the next, clamping the device shut and tossing it out of her reach. Sometimes she blamed him for his phobia. At others, she cried over his pain. If only he weren't so likable and kind and fabulous. And stubborn.

Emma wanted to help him, but she didn't know how. And she wasn't sure he wanted help—not really.

Maybe I'm being harsh. He's been through a lot. She knew how hard a major loss could be. Her mom's death had stunned her for weeks.

Weeks, Emma, not years. He has to get over the death of his football career, not surrender the game altogether.

The thoughts that raced through her mind during the pastor's sermon were the same kinds she had been chasing during the last four days. Still she hadn't caught up to any clear decision.

At the end of the service Joelle Nelson bounced up to Emma.

"Miss Porter, Mom wants to know if you need directions to our house."

"I do. I'm somewhat directionally challenged, so I hope I don't get lost."

"I could ride with you."

"That would be great."

"I'll go clear it with my mom."

The high school senior disappeared into the crowd still milling around. She was the oldest child of Jim and Sue Nelson. Sue had stopped Emma at prayer meeting earlier that week and invited her to have lunch with them on Sunday and spend the afternoon. Emma was excited to get to know the family and to see their new home.

Emma and Joelle crossed the parking lot together a few minutes later. Joelle was describing her little brother's escapades during the recent ice storm.

"Mom told him that he could go outside since morning service had been cancelled. Johnny pulled his sled from Dad's workshop, slipping and sliding it all the way to the back door of the house. Then he let Baxter, our golden retriever, outside and tied him to the sled. Baxter wasn't too happy about Johnny's plan. By the time Johnny dragged the dog to the driveway so that Baxter could give him a sled ride, both of them had fallen more than once. Mom captured the whole scene with the camcorder."

Emma envisioned the energetic five-year-old, wrestling a large dog and a sled. She laughed and then remembered Landon's tale about that same morning.

"My friend Landon …" Emma's voice trailed off as they reached her car. Landon's head had emerged between his car and hers as he climbed from the Camry.

"Landon, what are you doing here?" Emma sputtered.

Joelle stopped in her tracks. She stared up at Emma with a "Wow!" look on her teenaged face.

Emma wished the asphalt would suddenly gape and allow her to vanish beneath its surface. When her brain was once again working, she handed her keys to Joelle. "Unlock the car and climb in. Start it up if you're cold. I'll be just a minute."

Emma stepped between the vehicles and met Landon.

"You haven't returned my calls," he said before she spoke. His tone was sad but not sarcastic.

"I'm thinking, Landon."

He backed up slightly and leaned against his car. "You can't think and talk to me at the same time?"

His searching gaze unnerved her. "That's just it. I don't seem to be able to. Either I'm so caught up in you that my mind turns to mush, or I'm so frustrated by you that I want to scream." She sighed loudly.

"Which is it now?"

"What?"

"Caught up or frustrated?"

"Stunned." Not only by his unexpected presence, but also by how much the few days of not seeing him made his nearness so much more powerful. Joelle's reaction had screamed what Emma was feeling.

"That wasn't one of the choices." She could see a glimmer in his eye.

Emma couldn't completely mask her smile. "I added another."

"Oh." He nodded twice. "We have to talk, Em."

"We will, Landon. Give me a couple more days." She had no idea how the extra time was going to help, but she didn't have an answer now. "I'll call you."

He tilted his head slightly and looked at her askance.

"I'll call. I promise."

"By Tuesday."

"By the middle of the week."

"A couple is two." His eyes somehow linked her with him as he spoke. "Two days from Sunday is Tuesday, not Wednesday."

Emma felt trapped by her own words. "I'll call by Tuesday."

"You promised, remember?"

"I promised." She finally allowed herself to look long and hard at him. The pain—and something else—she saw there made her stomach do somersaults. Pulling herself away from his magnetism, Emma started toward the driver's side.

"I miss you, Em." Landon's hand cupped her elbow.

"I miss you, too." She gulped hard before fleeing to the shelter of her car.

"That's your *friend* Landon?" Joelle gushed as soon as Emma had shut the door. "He's sweet."

Emma wanted to shush the girl and then set her straight, but when she saw Joelle's eyes about to bug out of their sockets, she only chuckled. "He is, isn't he?"

"Uhhh—yeah." Joelle's confirmation dared anyone to think otherwise. "Are you two seeing each other?"

"Yes—no—not right now. It's complicated." *To say the least.*

"Is he a Christian?"

"Yes."

"Does he enjoy being with you?"

"I think so."

"Do you enjoy being with him?"

"Yes."

"Do you daydream about him? I sure would." The teen's eyes gleamed with excitement.

Emma chuckled, even as she felt the red creep into her cheeks.

Joelle giggled. "No need to answer."

Emma shrugged, and the two shared another laugh.

"Whatever the complications are, I'd work them out."

Landon watched Emma pull from her parking spot and continue on her way. Maybe he should have been discouraged that she never looked back or that he didn't know anything more than he had before. He wasn't, however. Instead, the heaviness he'd felt for days was replaced by the idea that he had to wait no longer than two days before he heard Emma's voice again. He would force himself to wait.

When Emma turned onto the street, Landon noticed a man leaving the church. The crowd had thinned, so he covered the distance to the parking lot by himself. Something about his gait seemed familiar to Landon. Trying not to look too obvious, Landon studied him as he approached.

"Coach Spalding?" Landon could hear the incredulity in his own voice.

The elderly man stopped, stared hard for a few seconds, and then stepped forward. "Landon, how are you, son?"

"I'm okay. You?"

"Better'n I deserve." He stepped forward and clapped Landon on the back. "What brings you here? You're not a regular."

"No, I'm not. Are you?"

Aldus Spalding cackled loudly—the same chortle that prompted many players to call him "Laughing Spalding," a nickname that the coach didn't seem to mind. "Guess this is about the last place you ever expected to see me."

"To be honest, sir, yes, it is."

"A lot has changed since you graduated."

Landon knew that Coach Spalding had retired.

"You got somewhere you need to be?"

"No. My plans just drove out of the parking lot."

Aldus looked in the direction of Landon's head nod. "You've got me puzzled, but if you don't mind pork barbecue for lunch, I'd love to have you explain what you meant. My house is a few blocks down the street. Whadda ya say?"

"Only if you'll explain some things to me, too."

"It would do this old heart good."

━━━━━━

"If you opened a restaurant and had that sandwich on the menu," Landon said, pushing his chair back from the table, "I'd be tempted to buy one every day." He patted his abs. "Good eats."

"My daddy would be proud to hear that. It's his recipe. Been in the family for years."

"Did he own a restaurant?"

"Nah. He was a migrant worker. Moved all over the Deep South picking fruits and vegetables of every kind. Loved barbecue. Tinkered with the recipe for years till he hit on his favorite. Had my mama write it down. Daddy never learned to read or write."

"But you went to college."

"Sure did—just so I could play football. Played basketball, too. Back in those days, you didn't have to be nearly seven feet tall."

Landon grinned. "How far back were those days?"

"I'll be sixty-five next June. Those days were way back."

Aldus stood, lifting both his and Landon's plates. A few seconds passed; then he moved to the sink. Landon had heard rumors: a knife fight, a car accident. He never had found out the cause of coach's limp.

Returning to refill Landon's coffee mug, Aldus asked, "So, we've talked about your job, your family, and my daddy's pulled pork. Anything really important in your life? You haven't told me about your plans driving out of the parking lot."

Landon tipped his chair back on two legs. For some reason he felt compelled to explain. "Emma Porter."

"Emma Porter ...Emma Porter. Can't say that I know ..." Aldus slapped his knee. "Yes I do! She's that new girl, little bit of a thing. Started coming a few weeks ago. Haven't been introduced to her yet, but I know who she is. Big brown eyes. Cuter than a beagle pup."

Landon, who had begun nodding his head at each point of Aldus's description, blinked twice at the last remark.

His reaction didn't escape Aldus. "You ever see a beagle pup, son?"

Laughing, Landon looked at the floor and shook his head. "Can't say that I have," he answered a moment later.

"Nothing's any cuter. Big brown eyes—sad one minute, smiling the next. Ears so soft you could cuddle a baby in them, and a heart so full of love, that pup'll do, or at least try, whatever you ask."

Aldus's eyes had taken on a sad, far-away look, as though he were somewhere in his past. His eyes glimmered with unshed tears.

"You had a beagle pup?"

"More than one. Hope to have another before I die." The older man shook his head as if to clear the memory. "Now what about Miss Emma?"

Landon seldom spoke as much or as freely as he did during the next twenty minutes. Without really understanding why he should tell his former coach so much, he felt comfortable doing so. He left out little—even relating the nightmare, his crash into his mom, the embarrassing first conversation with Emma, their growing so close in only a few weeks, and the "blow by blow" of Tuesday's fiasco.

He ended his saga with, "She hasn't seen me or even spoken to me until today. She did this morning only because I showed up where I knew she would be. I was ready to tackle her if necessary."

Aldus reached across the table and slapped Landon's arm. "Now that's the Steele I know." His cackle filled the small kitchen.

"What do I do now?" Landon asked when the noise had lessened.

"About Miss Emma? Wait. Pray. Focus on you, not her."

If Spalding realized Landon's puzzlement, he ignored it. Instead, the older man rose slowly from the table. "I need to stretch. Walk with me."

Ten, maybe twelve, steps took them through the bright kitchen to a dimly lit living area complete with a small fireplace. Coach struck a match to the banked fire. Both men stood and watched as the flames quickly engulfed the few logs. Aldus approached the mantle covered with framed photographs and newspaper pictures.

"Have a look." He motioned to the memorabilia. "I need to get some medicine from the bathroom cabinet and then go back to the kitchen for the rest. I'll be a couple minutes."

Landon started on the left with an old black and white photo, a family of five: dad, mom, two daughters, and a son. The boy, about ten or twelve, was Aldus, for sure. There was also a picture of the coach in his Ole Miss uniform and one of him at graduation. None of these surprised Landon. The next one did.

It was a picture of a beautiful young woman in a wedding dress. Aldus Spalding, sporting a handsome dark suit, stood next to her and held her hand. Landon had heard that the coach was a confirmed bachelor.

The next two frames contained photos of the Spalding family. In the first, the coach held a little girl in one arm and draped his other arm around his young wife. The second picture included another daughter in the happy-looking group.

The photos gave way to newspaper articles with pictures. Most of them centered on Penn State linebackers. One showed the entire Nittany Lion team and coaching staff as the National Champions.

The last item was a color photo. Two grown women stood on either side of Aldus. Landon noticed the identical smiles on all three. Certainly, these two were the coach's adult daughters. Studying the photo closely, Landon couldn't miss the fact that they weren't holding hands, locking arms, or touching each other in any other way. Gone was the closeness of the earlier photos.

"Now you've seen my life."

When Aldus spoke, Landon turned.

"Not much to show for nearly sixty-five years, is it?"

"You were married. You have children."

"I was, and I do."

Aldus chuckled—softly. Yet another thing that Landon would not have believed possible. "I've got eight grandchildren and a great-grandbaby on the way."

"Word was that you never married."

"I let everyone believe it. It was easier than explaining."

"Explaining what?"

"Have a seat." With one hand he motioned to the sofa while supporting himself with a cane held in the other. He hadn't had the cane earlier.

"Mississippi was my childhood home. My family was poor. Life was hard, but my growing up was happy." Settling into a rocking chair near the couch, Aldus continued. "I went off to Ole Miss, made a name for myself there as a linebacker, married Dora, my childhood friend and high school sweetheart. Even played a few months in the pros."

"I knew about the football."

"Hhmph. That's what everyone says."

"There's more?'

"There's always more." Aldus set his cane on the floor and began to rock slowly. "Dora and I had settled into our new home in Chicago. I'd played a couple games for the Bears. I was walking home late one night with a couple other rookie teammates. Out of nowhere, three of the biggest men I'd ever seen attacked us."

Landon leaned forward.

"Three on three. It might've been a fair fight—but they had knives. By the time it ended, all three of us had been stabbed more than once."

"Your leg?"

"Yep. At the time, it was my least serious injury. I'd been cut in my chest and my belly, too. Spent a few weeks in the hospital."

"What about your friends?"

"One was cut real bad. Hasn't been able to do much since then. The other had only minor injuries. Recovered quick. Went right back to football."

"You stayed in football, too."

"I did." Aldus pulled himself from the rocker, motioning Landon to stay seated. Then he crossed to the fireplace and picked up a framed newspaper article. Returning to the sofa, he handed the yellowed paper to Landon. "Couldn't play anymore. Sports medicine back then wasn't anything like it is today. But one of my coaches—" he pointed to a man in the picture that Landon held— "saw that I knew the game, and I could teach it."

"You were the best position coach I ever had."

A grin crossed the leathery face. "Thank you. I wasn't fishing for compliments."

"It's true." Landon handed back the picture, and Aldus sat down again.

"You wondering what all this ancient history has to do with you and Miss Emma?" With a twinkle in his eyes, he added, "Or have you forgotten all about her?"

Landon blinked. Since leaving the kitchen, he hadn't thought of Emma at all.

"Son, you and me are alike in some ways." Aldus rocked the chair toward Landon and leaned forward. "We both had big dreams of playing pro football. We both saw success in college. We both had professional ball taken away from us."

"We both suffered leg injuries, too."

"That's right. But here's where we're different. You had the Lord when you lost football. I didn't. You've stayed away from the gridiron. I ran toward it as fast as my gimpy leg would allow."

Landon could only nod in agreement.

Aldus raised a bony forefinger toward Landon. "Listen hard to the rest, son. Football was my life. When I couldn't play it, I coached. When I couldn't find a coaching job, or after I'd just lost one, I was mean and ornery. You know that I could be."

Landon shrugged. "Yes, sir, I do."

"You got only small doses. Dora faced it every day."

Tears pooled in Aldus's eyes.

"She never loved the game. I knew that when I married her. But she loved me, and she was supportive. After my injury, she hoped I would choose some other career. I could have. I had several options. She accepted my decision to coach and was a sweet wife and mother until—" Aldus's voice stopped suddenly. His head bent to his chest. "Until she died giving birth to our stillborn son."

Landon exhaled as though he'd just received a helmet blow to his stomach.

When Aldus looked up, his cheeks were streaked with tears. He wiped a sleeve across his face. "I had two daughters, ages eight and ten, precious girls who loved me like their mama had. But I'd wanted a son—a child I could watch play football, a young man I could coach."

Once again his eyes turned toward the mantle. Gazing at the photo of him and his young family, he said, voice breaking, "After Dora died, I never let those sweet girls forget that they couldn't live up to my dream. Seeing how I treated my daughters, kinfolk eventually stepped in. Soon as I could, I moved east—alone."

Landon sat, stunned. No words climbed past his numb vocal cords.

Minutes passed. Aldus regained his composure. "Once I came to know the Lord, I wanted to find my girls. I hadn't seen either of them in over twenty years." A smile, the first Landon had seen for some time, lit the older man's face as he pointed toward the color photograph. "We shared last Christmas together."

With a deep cleansing breath, Aldus switched topics. "You've listened to an old man's tale of football woes. Now I'll explain why you needed to hear it." He leaned forward in his chair. "I don't want us to have one more thing in common—personal lives scarred by football."

The coach's gaze met Landon's.

"I gave football too much of my life. From what you've said, you're giving it too little. And another thing." Aldus poked Landon's shin with the cane he had retrieved from beside his rocker. "You say it's too hard to face being on the outside. Since when has anything concerning football been too hard for Landon Steele? The coaches used to get together and decide what to tell you you couldn't do, just so we could stand back and watch you try it."

Landon grinned.

"Focus on you and what you have to do to put football back in its right place in your life. Let the Lord worry about Miss Emma."

CHAPTER 10 ━━━━

Landon shared the entire afternoon with Aldus Spalding.

Around five, the Coach said, "You attend evening service on Sunday?"

"Sometimes."

"Will you be missing anything important if you come along with me tonight?"

At Aldus's insistence, the two arrived thirty minutes prior to the 6:00 meeting. He showed his former protege the plans for the upcoming church addition, gave him a tour of the building and the grounds, and, along the way, stopped to chat with and introduce Landon to other early birds.

They were heading toward the main auditorium when Aldus paused in the hallway. "Landon, do me a favor?"

"Sure."

"I'm thirsty. Go into the men's room and get me one of those little paper cups filled with water. I'll get our seats, since I know where I want to sit."

When Landon entered the large meeting room, he quickly spotted Coach Spalding in the section at the left. The gregarious man hadn't taken his seat, but stood deep in conversation with someone standing in front of him.

━━━━━

"I'm glad to meet you, Mr. Spalding." Emma extended her hand across the back of the pew.

"All my friends call me either *Aldus* or *coach*."

"All right, Aldus. What and where do you coach?" Emma was hard pressed to determine the man's age. He had few wrinkles, but his dark hair was generously mingled with gray.

"I'm retired now, but I did coach football."

"Football. How interesting." Sensing movement, she glanced beyond Aldus's right shoulder.

Landon stood there, extending a Dixie cup toward the older man.

"Thanks, son." While Aldus chugged the contents, crumpled the cup, and stuffed the paper into his pocket, Emma stood, stupefied. "Miss Emma, I think you already know the best Penn State linebacker I ever coached." He drew Landon forward. "We spent the afternoon catching up."

Emma hoped Landon felt the fire in her gaze. Football was taboo for her to speak of, but he could fraternize with a former football coach. What did *they* talk about? Hockey? What a hypocrite!

She focused on Aldus. "Yes, we know each other. And I'm so glad to know you, too. Now, if you'll excuse me, I need to recheck the schedule for the nursery workers. I just remembered that tonight could be my night." She gathered her purse and Bible. "I'll see you later."

Landon watched Emma leave. Then he turned back and clutched the pew in front of him. His gaze searched the carpet as though some answers might be written on it.

"My mistake, son. I'm sorry." Aldus's voice pleaded for forgiveness.

"You were trying to help."

"Guess I should have taken my own advice and let the Lord handle Miss Emma." Aldus lowered himself onto the seat. "What set her off?

"Football."

"Thought she liked the game."

"Loves it."

"Well, then—"

Aldus's comment was cut short when the service began.

"It'll work out," Landon whispered. If only he believed his own words.

Returning home later than usual that evening, Landon dialed Emma's number. As had become the norm, her recorded voice met his ears. He waited for the all-too-familiar beep.

"Emma, you don't know the whole story about Coach Spalding or about football. Please let me explain."

Before entering the church, Emma had set her phone to vibrate. She left it that way while she supervised the three years olds, and later when she stopped by her shop to double-check her needs for the morning.

Because she tried to keep as few chocolates as possible from Saturday to Monday, she had to restock the case before starting each new week. Sales had been great on Saturday. She'd sold out of several choices. After looking around, she knew she needed to be at work no later than 4:30 in order to have an assortment ready for opening.

After this day of ups and downs, Emma longed for sleep. Reaching her room, she set her phone on the nightstand, hung her purse across the chair, and headed for the bathroom. She emerged with her toothbrush in her mouth and her black pumps in her hand. On the way to her closet, she noticed the phone spinning in circles as the vibrations set it in motion. She tossed the shoes into her closet, grabbed the phone, and dashed to the sink to spit.

Landon's number lit the screen. Emma closed the phone. She finished brushing. She flossed.

She opened the phone and checked for any new messages. She saw Landon's. She closed the phone. She rinsed the toothpaste from the sink. She gargled.

She opened the phone and listened to his voicemail. She closed the phone. She washed her face. She turned out the bathroom light and crossed to the bed.

She opened the phone and hit the keypad.

"Emma?" He sounded surprised.

You haven't returned his calls all week. What do you expect?

"Make it quick, please. I've got a very early day tomorrow."

"I get panic attacks, and I have nightmares about football." He was talking fast. "Actually just one recurrent nightmare—the replay of the down that changed my life. I feel the crack of the bones. I see my twisted leg. I wake up because I hear myself yelling."

Emma fumbled for words which eluded her.

"Emma? Did you hear me?"

"I heard." Could he hear the sudden sadness in her voice? "Do you have it every night?"

"No. Usually four or five times a week."

She gulped. "That's a lot. Why didn't you tell me?"

This time the long pause came from his end. "Didn't want you to think I was crazy."

"Why would I?" Compassion surrounded the words.

"I should be over it." He sighed heavily. "I thought I was."

"When?"

"Around the Ohio State game. I settled some things with the Lord, and the dream went away for a while. Now it's back."

"Have you gotten professional help?"

"I don't need professional help."

"Who says?"

"I say."

"Are you a doctor or a counselor?"

"You know I'm not."

"Did you see a doctor after the injury to your leg?"

"Several."

"But you won't see anyone about a problem in your mind?"

"I'm not crazy."

"I didn't say you were."

"You said a *problem in my mind*. What's the difference?"

Emma searched for a connection. "Know anything about anorexia?"

"A little bit. Skinny people, usually young women, think they're fat. They stop eating."

"Exactly! They *think* they're overweight. Their minds have a problem with perception. They're not crazy, either. But they need professional help."

"I'm not anorexic. I don't need professional help."

Emma sighed into the phone. "Then why are you telling me any of this?"

"I want you to understand."

"And I'm trying to. But I really can't. Not doing something about a problem you've had for four years *is* crazy." Emma reined herself in. "I'll call you by Tuesday. Goodbye, Landon."

She heard him say, "I am doing something. Coach and I were ..." Exhaustion and frustration told her she couldn't listen to anything more tonight. She hit the red button.

Call ended.

———————

"Did you hear what I said? The coach and I ..." When silence ensued, Landon asked, "You still there?" One look at the screen gave him the short answer. She had hung up.

"Aaarrrggghhh!" If he was on his way to crazy, that woman was shoving him down the path. He snapped the phone closed and flung it onto the counter. The skidding cell slid into his nearly empty Coke glass and upended the tumbler, breaking it and spilling the sticky mess onto the surface where it ran over the edge and trickled down onto the seat of the barstool.

"No." Landon dashed for a towel to sop up the spill, all the while chiding himself. "That's what you get for acting like a fool."

He wished he could say that he felt better for having released his anger. He couldn't. He slid his feet back into his shoes and then picked up the pieces of broken glass. No sense in cutting himself as a result of this fiasco.

100

The word *fiasco* was an apt description for the last few hours. If only Coach Spalding hadn't introduced himself to Emma, Landon might have had an opportunity to explain who the guy was and what they had talked about earlier. As it was, she probably believed he had lied to her about football's effect on him. Did she trust him now that he had explained?

"Why all these problems? Things went so well at first. Why can't I get a break with Emma?" He muttered questions heavenward as he cleaned up the self-created disaster. The ceiling had no answers, and he felt that his petitions went no higher.

Monday crawled by. Landon couldn't honestly say that he thought Emma would call, but he checked his phone periodically, just in case.

By Tuesday, he was like a caged lion whose roar warned everyone to stay away. He wanted only to survive his shift and go home, where he could sit by the phone and wait.

At two o'clock, Mike called and reminded him of their plans for racquetball later.

"I can't tonight."

"You sick?"

"No," Landon barked. "I just can't make it."

"Okay, okay. What's wrong with you? Someone break the office coffee pot?"

"Sorry, Mike." He exhaled strongly. "I'm as mean as a snake today."

For once, Mike had no comeback, just a sympathetic, "Well—sure—buddy. Can I help?"

"Wish you could."

"Let me know if you change your mind, about racquetball or anything else."

By seven o'clock, Landon was pacing. By eight, he had decided he needed to run. By nine o'clock, when he returned, exhausted, and he still had no message, he contemplated driving over and confronting Emma. The fact that it was still Tuesday, and she hadn't specified a time, convinced him, instead, to hit the shower and then sit down to watch the cable news channel. He tuned in as the commentators began a debate on ways to stimulate economic growth.

He awoke to the sound of the bells in the stock market. The stock market? What was happening on the screen? He sat forward. The chimes that were his ring tone finally pierced the fog of his brain. They had clanged several times before he lurched forward.

"Hello? Hello?" *Rats!* Too late. Emma—of course—his phone log confirmed it.

He pressed speed dial. "Don't be leaving a message." He had fallen asleep. *What time is it?*

He heard the ring on the other end at the same time that he consulted his watch. Eleven fifty-eight. *Nothing like cutting it close.*

"Hi." Her voice sounded foggy.

"I'm sorry I missed your call. I fell asleep watching television."

"It's late."

"Yeah, I'm surprised you're still up." *Was that a sob?* "You okay?"

"Not really." She snuffled into the phone. "I need more time, Landon."

"Time for what?" A tourniquet of apprehension squeezed his heart.

"Time to decide if there can be an 'us.'"

"There already is." Surely she had seen that: phones calls, visits, red roses, a card in which he revealed his thoughts. "You can't let one Bowl game change that."

"You already did."

She blew her nose.

"Until you settle your football questions, you are cheating yourself. And this problem's not only about you. Unless I can think of you completely separated from football, I'm cheating you, too."

"I don't feel cheated."

"We have issues." She sounded tired. "If not, Tuesday night wouldn't have happened."

Landon punched the throw pillow. "We'll take things slower. I can do that." He knew he could, no matter how much he hated the idea.

"I'm swamped, Landon. Business has gone better than I'd hoped. I'm indebted to you for part of that success. I appreciate all you've done. But even with Sylvia's help, I can't manage alone. I need to hire someone part-time, at least through the holidays. I don't have time to sort through personal things right now."

What was she saying?

"Let's wait and pray—until after the New Year. When I come back from Florida, we'll get together and see where we are."

After New Year's? He already had her Christmas present.

His dad would have said that Landon was jumping the gun, to buy so sentimental a gift after knowing Emma only a few weeks, but it hadn't seemed so to Landon at the time. He'd found the bracelet in a quaint shop in Boalsburg.

Each of the multiple strands of silver was intricate and delicate. Together, the dainty chains formed a whole that was exquisite yet strong.

To Landon, the bracelet exemplified Emma. The various parts represented the myriad of interests, experiences, and trials of her life. She was stronger for each of them. And breathtakingly beautiful.

What would he do with it, especially if she hadn't changed her mind by New Year's?

"Say something, please." Her soft voice brought him from his quagmire.

"You mean not see each other, not talk to each other, anything—until the beginning of next year?"

"I'm reminding myself that it's only seventeen days."

Landon huffed. "Through the holidays, Em. I wanted to spend those times with you."

She sniffled. "I wanted it, too."

"Not much, you didn't, or you wouldn't have ..."

Emma burst into tears.

Landon felt like a heel. "Don't cry, honey." *Where had that come from?* "I'm sorry."

She blew her nose again.

"I'm praying that the Lord will give us strength and answers." A calm sadness permeated her words.

"So, there is an 'us'?"

"I hope so, Landon. I really do." A ragged breath. "I'll be praying hard and counting the days." She choked out a teary, "Good night."

The loneliness of silence filled the space.

Landon stared at the phone. He slumped back onto the couch. No use going into his room. He'd be out here anyway as soon as the nightmare hit, as it had for the last several nights.

He carried the smooshed throw pillow to the recliner and settled in, but sleep eluded him. Why was this happening? Didn't God see how much she meant to him?

What are you thinking? Landon's mind knew the right answers. *Of course He sees.*

But does He care? His heart wasn't as convinced. *He's let you down—again.*

God never lets us down. He's always faithful. Once again his mind urged him to be stronger than his feelings.

Without realizing he was doing so, Landon began humming. Then the lyrics, words that he didn't realize he still knew, came back to him: "Great is Thy faithfulness. Morning by morning new mercies I see. Thou changest not. Thy compassions they fail not. Great is Thy faithfulness, Lord, unto me."

Wide awake now, and singing to himself, he pondered the words. They were taken from scripture. Where?

He pulled back the blanket, set the chair upright, went for his Bible, and looked up *faithfulness* in his concordance. The verse was Lamentations 3:23. Odd place for such a comforting verse. Leafing through the Old Testament, he located the third chapter of the small book after Jeremiah and read the twenty-third verse. The idea wasn't complete without verse 22. Together the passage read: "Through the Lord's mercies we are not consumed, because His compassions fail not. They are new every morning; great is Thy faithfulness."

Glancing back at the page, Landon noticed verses 25-26. "The Lord is good to those who wait for Him, to the soul who seeks Him. It is good that a man should both hope and quietly wait for the salvation of the Lord."

Not if an entire football team had tackled him could Landon have taken a harder blow than those words delivered. "The Lord is good to those who *wait* for Him… It is good that a man should … quietly *wait*."

Wasn't that exactly what Emma wanted—for him to *wait* seventeen days? It seemed that the Lord concurred. He tried to swallow the idea, but the words stuck in his throat. He reread the verses. This time something else drew his attention: the word *good*. Twice it was tied to those who wait.

It didn't take a rocket scientist to figure out the next step. Could he carry it out? Only with Divine intervention.

━━━━━━━━

The following days confirmed Landon's suspicion: thinking about waiting was a lot easier than actually waiting. Keeping busy helped. He volunteered to do whatever extras were needed for Dave who was still with his mom. He rescheduled racquetball with Mike. He visited his parents over the weekend.

Early Monday morning Landon had an uncontrollable urge for a cup of gourmet coffee and some chocolates. Was he violating Emma's request or being a loyal patron? Her reaction would give him the answer.

When he entered the shop, she was busy with a cluster of customers. He crossed to the coffee maker and chose his favorite. With his back toward her, he sat at a table, hoping to make his presence less obvious. He wanted to approach the counter while she was alone.

After several people had purchased and departed, Landon heard, "You don't have any of those toffee chocolates this morning, Emma?"

"They weren't quite set by the time the morning rush hit, Mr. Wagner. I'll check on them, if you'd like."

"I'd like that very much." Toffee was the guy's favorite. Landon could hear it in his voice.

The sound of Emma's quick steps faded. Landon rose and stood beside Mr. Wagner at the counter. "Those toffee chocolates any good?"

"Too good, young man." The dapper fiftyish gentleman turned toward Landon. "I buy two on my way to the office. I eat one and then wrestle myself all day not to sneak the other before I can get it safely home to my wife."

Landon laughed and said, "Maybe I'll try one."

"You won't regret it—unless you plan to save it for later." The man's eyes sparkled.

"Here you go. Sorry about ..." As she stared at Landon, Emma's voice stopped short. When she'd recovered, she said, "Sorry about the delay."

"Worth the wait, I'm sure." Mr. Wagner accepted the bag Emma held out, and then turned to Landon. "Try one. Maybe you'll find a new favorite."

Emma gathered up the dollar bills and change that rested on the glass in front of Mr. Wagner. "To the penny. Thanks." She avoided Landon's gaze.

"See you soon."

Lucky guy, Landon thought as the businessman turned to go.

"I'll be here."

At the sound of the tinkling bell that signaled the man's exit, Landon said, "I had to ..."

The jingle sounded again. A group of young women entered, their giggles and chatter announcing their presence.

"To pay for this"— he held up his steaming cup—"and I'd like one caramel and one toffee, please."

The young women had gathered around the display case, oohing and aahing on either side of him as they eyed the confections.

Landon watched Emma's face as it blanched and then flushed. Was she angry? Flustered?

She set the small bag in front of him and rang up his merchandise. "That's five fifty-six."

He gave her a twenty, extending his hand for the change. Her hands trembled as she counted the money into his palm. When their fingers touched, their gazes locked.

"Thanks," he said, taking the sack.

Her eyes held the sadness of a lost puppy.

"I hope to be back soon." He stared a moment longer before heading for the door.

———

"These all look delicious. How can I choose just one?" a pudgy brunette said. She and her three companions had scrutinized the contents of the display case multiple times and from every angle.

"They're heavenly!" A tall girl with auburn hair cackled at her own pun. She craned her long neck toward the door and added, "And the scenery in here is even better. Did you see that guy?"

Laughter and bobbing heads assured the redhead of her companions' assent.

A blonde in a tailored wool coat scurried up to the cash register. "Does he come in here every day?"

"Not regularly." Emma marveled that she'd answered with such apparent detachment.

"Does he live here?"

"I don't see him around town much." Emma struggled to be both truthful and discreet. "I don't feel comfortable talking about one patron to another." She didn't appreciate the girl's barracuda-like questions or tone, especially when Landon was the prey.

"Oh." The blonde rolled her eyes at Emma and cast a knowing glance at the redhead. "Angie, I'm not so sure about chocolates today. They are so fattening."

Angie tossed her shoulder-length red hair away from her face and nodded in agreement. "If we don't have the chocolates, we won't need the gym—and we'll have more time for Christmas shopping."

The brunette, who had pined for each candy in turn as she made her way back and forth in front of the case, sighed heavily. "It's probably best. I can't decide."

The fourth young lady of the group, the only one who hadn't spoken yet, moved from her place at the back of the pack. Freckles dominated her cute features, and dark curls escaped from a beret perched at an angle. "I don't care what these three are doing. I'm having two chocolates. Have to power up for the day. This is the only time I'm fighting the crowds. I plan to shop till I drop and then go home ready to wrap, decorate, and wait for Santa."

Emma chuckled. "You still have five days. That's a lot of wrapping, decorating, and waiting."

The pixie-faced girl waved to her friends as they motioned that they were leaving. "I'll catch up to you at the car."

She turned back to Emma. "Since I'm not in classes, and I can't find a job for the holidays, I have time. Lots of it."

Her response brought another smile and an idea to Emma. "What kind of job are you looking for?"

She pointed out her choice of candies as she explained, "I can't be picky. I'm available for only a month or so, and then classes will have me too busy."

"What hours can you work?" Emma added the girl's money to the register and handed her the chocolates.

"Morning, noon, or night." The more inquiries Emma made, the more the girl's eyes sparkled. She grasped the counter top and leaned toward Emma. "Do you know of a job?"

"I need part-time help through the holidays, and I haven't had time to post an ad."

The imp's squeal hurt Emma's ears. "Seriously?"

"Seriously." When the girl stopped bobbing up and down, Emma asked, "Do you have time to fill out an application and answer a few questions?"

She looked in the direction her friends had gone. "Can I take the application and come back later for the questions?"

"As long as you come back today." Emma needed help, and if this wasn't the person, then she had to find someone else—fast.

"One o'clock?"

"Perfect." Sylvia usually arrived around 12:30 and could manage things during the interview. Emma reached below the cash register, thankful that she'd printed out a few generic applications the night before. "I'll see you at one."

"I'll be here." She folded the paper neatly in thirds and tucked it into her bag. Then she stuck out her hand. "My name's Pepper."

"Parting is such sweet sorrow." Juliet's words to Romeo ran through Landon's brain. Reading them in high school English, he'd thought them stupid. How could parting be sweet?

This morning he knew the answer. The *sweetness* of parting was the one you were leaving behind. Emma's charm magnified the sorrow he felt when they were separated. The more time he spent with her, the more time he wanted. The drive to work both heightened his desire and strengthened his resolve. Starting now, he would wait, and he would win Emma's heart.

She needs answers.

Landon started at the thought. He hadn't heard the words from the mouth of God, but in his heart he knew that they came from Him.

Have you searched for answers?

Landon hated the response he knew he had to give.

———

At lunchtime he went online and looked for information about nightmares. He found a number of experts who agreed that nightmares which recounted a traumatic event were extremely common. He wasn't crazy after all.

Further research, however, made him rethink his assessment. Everyone he read agreed that nightmares of this type were usually short-lived. If they persisted for more than a few weeks or months, the dreamer should seek help. Weeks or months. No one mentioned a year or longer. According to the experts, Landon was long overdue.

He rose from his desk, wandering as he pondered. Eventually he boiled all his thoughts down to one conclusion: he'd start with his pastor.

———

"I'm not a trained psychologist or an expert on nightmares and their treatment," Pastor Murphy said, "but I have read several sources over the years. I've also worked with many people who've suffered from bad dreams." He handed papers back across the desk to Landon. "What you brought me concurs with my research." He offered Landon a glass of water before pouring one for himself and taking a drink. "Here's what I know. Most experts agree that suppressing a dream is not helpful. There is often a correlation between it and real life."

"Mine is so real I can see people and colors and feel pain." Landon winced.

"What do you do when it comes?"

"Wake up yelling."

"And then?"

"Try to calm down and go back to sleep."

The older man leaned back in his chair, placing his hands behind his head. "Have you heard of any of the techniques for dealing with the dream itself?"

"You mean writing it down, drawing or painting it, imagining a more pleasant ending?"

"Those and others."

"I read about them earlier today."

"So you haven't tried any of them?"

"Didn't know about them." Guilt hit Landon. He could have known. "Do you think they really work?"

"Most people I've counseled say so."

"Writing down a bad dream helps it go away?" The idea seemed ludicrous.

"The techniques go back to the idea that suppressing the dream is detrimental. Humans naturally avoid the uncomfortable or scary. It's understandable—but not helpful."

"Give me a pen."

A half smile lit the older man's face. "I'd suggest writing it after you have the next one. See if you sleep better."

"I'll do it. Thanks for your help." Landon started to rise.

"Mind if I ask you a couple questions before you go?"

Feeling obligated after seeking the pastor's help, Landon perched on the edge of the chair. "I guess not."

"What about football?"

"What's that got—"

"Suppression and nightmares go hand in hand." The pastor's loving but firm gaze bore into Landon. "You've blocked out the nightmare and eradicated football. I think there could be a strong connection."

"But you're not an expert." Landon's sarcasm was pointed.

Pastor Murphy shook his head. "I'm not an expert on dreams." He sat upright in the chair, lessening the distance between himself and Landon. "But I know people pretty well."

Landon had no rebuttal. The man was highly respected as a counselor.

"For the first twenty-one years of your life, I watched you run toward football. For the last four, I've seen you bolt in any other direction."

Landon avoided the man's direct stare.

"Why, Landon?"

Pastor Murphy was the fourth one in less than a month to ask the same question. By now, Landon knew the real answer. He met his pastor eye to eye. "I feel robbed." He waited for a response of surprise. None came. "God gave me ability. I worked hard to use it to honor Him. Then He stole it."

"And if you can't use that ability in the way you want, you won't use it at all?" Pastor's analysis was brutal but accurate. "Were you really using it to honor Him?"

———————

Landon respected his pastor and had always admired the man's dedication to both the God he served and the flock he led, but that Tuesday, Landon was more than peeved with him. He'd practically accused Landon of being dishonest with himself and others.

He spent the drive home and the rest of the evening justifying all that he had done since that terrible day. Who wouldn't be angry to have God strip away his dream? Anger was a natural response.

"Be angry and sin not." The verse blasted his brain. What was his sin? He moved on with his life. He kept going to church. He tried to do what was right. That was enough. At least he could tell Emma—whenever he saw her—that he was looking for answers. He hoped she didn't push him too hard as to which ones.

CHAPTER 11 ══════

On Friday, December 24, Landon left the office party early. He couldn't be jolly, couldn't get into the holiday spirit, couldn't say "Ho! Ho! Ho! Merry Christmas" to any of the employees milling around in their festive garb.

Hoping that Emma hadn't decided to close early on Christmas Eve, he drove to Bellefonte. The *Yes, We're Open* sign still hung in the window of Heavenly Chocolates. "Thank you," Landon said skyward. He tucked a small box into his pocket, walked across the street, and opened the door. As he entered, two impressions greeted him: the alluring smell of Emma's creations and the disappointing lack of her presence behind the counter.

A stranger stood in Emma's usual spot, a thin girl with dark curly hair, black plastic-framed glasses—the ones that always reminded Landon of the serious brainiacs he knew—and a Santa hat that made her look certifiably elfish.

Santa's helpers would have been proud of her. While Landon stood in line, she scurried from here to there, answering questions and filling orders. She had a pleasant comment for everyone and an answer for each question.

"Hi, Pepper," a middle-aged woman said as she approached the glass case. "Where's Emma?"

"On her way home, I hope."

That answers my question. Landon stepped closer to the lady.

"Leaving you here to finish up while she rests at the Sawyers'? That doesn't sound like her."

"She's on her way to Pittsburgh where her dad lives. Wants to go to the Christmas Eve service with her brother."

Pepper handed the woman a large bag. Landon hadn't even heard the lady place an order.

"Emma filled this for you before she left, Mrs. White. She told me to be sure to wish you a Merry Christmas."

Mrs. White beamed. "Why, thank you, Pepper." She hefted the sack and handed Pepper some cash. "She's such a sweet young lady—and so are you, my dear. I think that's why this place is so busy."

"That—and the chocolates." Pepper wiggled her eyebrows at the plump woman.

With a small chuckle, Mrs. White agreed. "Yes. The chocolates."

While Mrs. White collected her change and maneuvered the bag and her purse into their respective places, Landon contemplated his next move. He didn't feel right about leaving without purchasing something, but his whole reason for coming centered more on Emma than on candy. Pepper was quickly finishing with a customer beside him. He'd buy a few of his mom's favorites and include them with her Christmas gift.

The chocolate-peddling elf stepped in his direction. He waited for her pleasant, "How may I help you?"

Instead she said, "Hi, Landon. Emma hoped you'd stop in."

While he picked his jaw up from the floor, Pepper moved to the register, pulled something from the shelf beneath it, and extended a white envelope to him. "Is there anything I can get for you?" He shook his head, and she moved to the next customer.

Landon stood like an unmanned blocking dummy wondering what was in the envelope and how the girl knew him. Eventually he relinquished his place in line and sat at a table. He tore the envelope open.

The front of the light blue greeting card embossed with silver held only one word: *HOPE!* The inside read:

> *To a world of sinful men,*
> *He brings peace on earth;*
> *To a heart burdened with care,*
> *He brings peace within.*
> *Celebrate the birth of the Savior!*

She had signed her name underneath the verse. Opposite the sentiment Landon read:

Dear Landon,
> *If you're reading this, you did what I'd hoped, and Pepper remembered you as she said. Merry Christmas! I pray that you and your family share a wonderful day together rejoicing over Christ's birth. Think of me as I spend the weekend with Dad and Bud.*

Not a chance he *wouldn't* do that.

*I'm praying for you and about us. I hope you're doing the same.
I'm also counting the days. I miss you—even more than I knew
I would.
Emma*

Landon read her words three times before he looked up. By the time he set the card down, his eyes felt moist. He longed for God's peace, but didn't have it. He knew he should be praying diligently, but he wasn't. He hoped for a Merry Christmas, but he didn't expect one.

A tap on his shoulder made him jump and look up. Pepper, complete with fuzzy red hat, stood beside him.

"Do you want some chocolates before I close up?"

Embarrassed, Landon sprang to his feet. "It's closing time?"

"For today it is—four o'clock."

"I'd like some to take to my parents."

Pepper moved toward the counter, and Landon followed her. By the time he'd stuffed the card back into the envelope, she had grabbed a bag and was waiting to fill it.

"Start with caramels, and then give me an assortment—ten or twelve, please."

"Is caramel your favorite?" She pulled her head from the display and deposited the candies into the sack.

"Yeah. My mom's, too."

"One of our most popular."

"How long have you worked here?"

"Four days. I was in here on Monday with some friends. We walked in just as you were ready to leave."

"And you remembered me?"

"You made an impression."

He didn't ask what she meant, but he did notice the slight flush on her cheeks. "This time, I'm glad I did."

"Me, too. Emma really wanted you to have that card."

Landon pulled the small box from his pocket. "I'd like her to have this. Would you put it some place where she'll find it as soon as she returns?"

"Sure."

"Are you closing up by yourself?" How could Emma trust someone so much after only four days on the job?

"No, Sylvia will be here any minute."

She rang up his sale and handed him the candy.

"Nice to meet you, Pepper." When she opened her mouth to speak, he added, "You make quite an impression yourself. I'm sure Emma's glad you're here."

"She says she's pleased."

Landon turned toward the door but managed only one step before looking back. "Does she mention me?"

Pepper surveyed something on her shoe while rocking back and forth on her heels. Then she glanced up. "Landon, I don't want to—"

"Does she?" He wouldn't let her shrug him off.

"She does."

"Is she still angry?"

This answer was immediate. "No."

"When did she leave for Pittsburgh?"

"She left here at noon. I don't know what time she actually hit the road."

"When's she coming back?"

Again Pepper hesitated. "I'm not sure I should say."

"I have her cell phone number. I can call and find out."

"She doesn't have to tell you."

Landon returned to the counter and bent so that their eyes were dead even. "You've talked to her. Do you think she would mind my knowing?"

"Oooohh." Pepper strode for her coat and hat. "Emma told me not to fall prey to those blue eyes of yours," She yanked a sleeve onto her arm.

Landon laughed out loud. He could imagine Emma saying the words.

"It's not funny." She stomped around closing things up, storing items for the long weekend, but Landon sensed that she wasn't really miffed, just embarrassed.

"Tell you what I'll do. I'll look out the window, and you answer my question." He turned his back to her. "Would she mind my knowing when she's coming back?"

"Emma's leaving Pittsburgh after lunch on Sunday," she blurted.

Landon spun and faced her. "Thank you."

"Don't thank me. You weaseled it out of me."

Landon laughed again. This girl was hilarious. "How old are you?"

She glared at him. "Don't you know it's impolite to ask a woman how old she is?" She drew a very small green purse with an extremely long skinny strap over her shoulder. The bag hung almost to her knees.

More laughter erupted from inside him.

"Why are you laughing?"

"You look like an elf. I've thought so since I walked in. Now I'm sure of it."

"An elf?" She stamped her foot. "A twenty-year-old pre-med student does not look like an elf."

"That one does," he said, pointing. "Short black boots, red wool coat, green purse, and Santa cap. Definitely an elf. Somewhat taller than average, but an elf for sure."

"Merry Christmas, then, from one of Santa's finest." She curtseyed slightly and crossed the room, reaching the door just as Sylvia did. Pepper threw it open and hugged the older woman as if the two hadn't seen each other in forever. "Have the best Christmas, Sylvia. I'll see you on Monday." Pepper donned red polka dot mittens. "Bye, Landon." With a flip of her red cap, she was gone.

Landon laughed—again. He'd chuckled more since he walked in than he had in days. "She's a character," he said to Sylvia.

"That she is." Sylvia wiped her feet on the mat and removed her gloves. "And she's a godsend. Emma was nearly ragged, and I wasn't able to help as much as I'd hoped. Mort's father is ill. We've made several trips to visit him in the hospital." Sylvia began emptying the register and filling a cash bag. "I'll be glad to have this deposit made. Handling money makes me nervous."

Good thing she'd never started a business. "Is Emma doing well?"

"You're her accountant. Don't you know?"

"We haven't spoken in a few days."

"Why not?" Sylvia finished securing the bundle and tucked it inside her coat. Landon walked with her to the entrance.

"She needs time."

"For what?"

He opened the door and held it for her. "Hasn't she told you?"

"I'm asking you what you think."

He had never seen this direct side of Sylvia. "She says I have issues about football."

"Do you?"

The two stood on the sidewalk while Sylvia locked up. Christmas carols filled the brisk afternoon air.

"I guess so."

"Want some advice from an old woman?"

Landon recalled Emma's description of Sylvia as an "incurable romantic." He grinned. "I don't see an old woman anywhere, but I'm listening."

Sylvia beamed. "Solve the issues—whatever they are." She put a hand to his shoulder and brought his ear close. "That girl cares for you." She released him, but pointed a finger at his chest. "Don't you dare tell her I said so." She waved and then walked the few feet to her car, calling "Merry Christmas" just before she climbed in.

An hour and a half earlier, Landon had wondered how he would survive the next twenty-four hours. When Emma hadn't been at the store, he'd felt even worse. Then, in the last few minutes, a Christmas card, an elf-girl, and an old woman had given him hope. God had a sense of humor.

━━━━━━

Christmas Eve service was tradition with the Steeles. Landon could remember only a few instances interrupting their routine: Great Grandma's death three days before Christmas, a journey to Florida for the holiday, Dad's earning a trip for him and the family to Germany.

Each year the congregation sang heart-stirring Christmas carols, the pastor reminded them of some aspect of the miraculous birth of Christ, and the service concluded with the whole group gathering around the perimeter of the sanctuary, each person holding a small unlit candle.

As they began the much-loved "Silent Night," the pastor would light his candle and the candles of those on either side of him. Those two would then pass their lights along to the ones standing at their other sides, and the process would continue until the entire circle was aglow.

Landon's thrill as a child was the first time he had been entrusted to carefully handle his own lighted candle. As he grew, he enjoyed the simple yet soul-stirring melody of the Austrian hymn and the voices of those singing it from their hearts. Christmas Eve was a treasure.

This year the occasion would be different. Pastor Wood had retired. A younger man, with his wife and small daughter, had arrived in November. Landon had never met him or his family.

As the service began, Landon looked around for people he knew. He was more focused on the crowd than on the proceedings. When a clearly nervous young woman stepped to the microphone, he wondered if she would survive her part in the service. Then she opened her mouth and began to sing. A hush cloaked the room.

> "I wonder as I wander out under the sky,
> How Jesus the Saviour did come for to die
> For poor orn'ry people like you and like I;
> I wonder as a wander out under the sky."

Like everyone else in the auditorium, Landon sat up and listened. It was a Christmas carol he'd never heard. The words simply yet powerfully proclaimed the reason for Christ's birth. And the soloist's voice was beautiful: clear, sonorous, and perfectly pitched. Her sincerity emanated from her eyes and resonated in each note. She wasn't singing for an audience; she was worshiping the Lord.

"Who is that?" Landon leaned over and asked his dad.

"Karyn Newman," he whispered. "The pastor's wife."

Landon's mind returned to the words. The second stanza spoke of Jesus coming to earth as a lowly baby, born in a cow's stall. The third focused on Christ as God. The stanza closed with the reminder "He was the King." Then once again Mrs. Newman sang:

> "I wonder as I wander out under the sky,
> How Jesus the Saviour did come for to die
> For poor orn'ry people like you and like I
> I wonder as a wander out under the sky."

As her voice faded away, Landon could feel the words sink deep within. She stepped toward the edge of the platform, and her husband rose from his seat, offering her his hand and an encouraging smile as she descended. Not until that time did Landon notice the scars. One long pinkish line ran from her left eyebrow to her chin, and the hand she extended also bore several scars.

Landon turned again to his father who only mouthed, "Later."

Landon's dad took notes on the sermon and nodded enthusiastically several times. Landon could focus on nothing other than the Christmas carol and the woman who sang it. The haunting words of the song and the mystery behind the soloist nagged at him. Even the candle-lighting ceremony lost some of its enchantment.

———

Back at his parents' house, he wasted no time before speaking to his dad. They were in the kitchen making coffee. "What's Karyn Newman's story?"

Landon leaned his tall frame against the counter and watched his dad run water into the carafe. "She seemed scared to death to be in front of everyone, until she started singing. Incredible voice."

"She trained at Juliard. Wanted to be an opera singer. At the start of her senior year, she was already being sought out." Dad paused while he measured the grounds.

"But—"

"But she went with some friends one night to celebrate the successful stage appearance of one of her classmates. Everyone knew she didn't drink, so they didn't try to convince her to, but most of them were drinking."

Landon didn't like where this was headed. Why hadn't she had more sense than to be in a car with a drunk driver?

Pulling out a chair, Dad sat at the table. Landon did likewise. "When it was time to leave her friend's home, Karyn knew that no one in the car she had come in was fit to drive. She volunteered, but the owner of the car wouldn't give up his keys."

"She was smart to refuse." Landon furrowed his brow at the troubled look on his dad's face.

"When Karyn couldn't find a safe way home, her friend's boyfriend volunteered to drive her to the dormitory."

"He was drunk, too?" Landon anticipated his dad's next words.

"No, he wasn't drunk." Dad bowed his head. When he looked up, a grimace contorted his face. "He was lustful."

Landon groaned. He thought of an old saying his grandfather had often repeated. "Out of the frying pan; into the fire." Poor Karyn. He hated to ask, but he had to know the rest. "What happened?"

"He attacked her in the car. Slashed her with a knife when she fought him."

That explained the scars. "Rape?"

"He tried, but Karyn managed to unlock the car door. She fell from the moving car and rolled into a ditch."

"He gave up then?"

"He skidded to a stop, grabbed her from the ditch, and began dragging her back."

Landon couldn't believe his ears. All of this because she didn't feel secure with the other driver.

"He was ready to shove her in, when a car approached. He threw her back off the road, jumped into his vehicle, and sped away."

"Of all the low things to do." Landon heard the tone signaling that the coffee maker was finished and got up to pour two cups. "What happened then?"

"She seems frail now, but she was strong that night. She crawled back to the highway. Eventually a family stopped to help."

Landon was silent for a moment. After setting the cups on the table, he sat down and looked hard at his dad. "Why would God allow that?"

"He had a purpose."

"You're sure?"

"Absolutely."

A retort flew to Landon's lips, but his dad's reproving look made him cut it short.

"Karyn Newman is, too."

"How do you know?"

"The family who stopped to help were Daniel and Susan Newman, and their son, Daniel, Jr., a seminary student."

"Your pastor?" Landon's voice portrayed the surprise he felt.

Dad nodded. "More than once I've heard Karyn refer to Dan as her 'knight in shining armor.' He was there for her that night, and he's been with her through everything since then."

"What's *everything?*"

"Sutures galore, three reconstructive surgeries, one cosmetic surgery, counseling, physical therapy. You name it."

"And Juliard?"

"She graduated with honors a semester later than scheduled."

Landon tried to imagine the timid young woman facing a cheering yet critical crowd. "She sings professionally?"

"No, that part of her dream probably won't ever come true."

Yep. That's the way it works. Have your heart set on something and watch it die.

"She started giving voice lessons last month. She already has as many students as she can take." Dad's eyes became soft and warm. "You should hear their daughter. That little girl sings beautifully, and she's only three."

"But teaching wasn't Karyn's dream."

"It is now." Marshall stood, taking his mug with him. "Good night, son. I'll see you in the morning." He clapped Landon on the shoulder. "I'll pray you get everything you need for Christmas."

Emma had hoped Landon would call—on Christmas Eve, early Christmas morning, after Christmas dinner, or following the official Christmas Challenge chess game that he and his dad always played. He didn't call, and she was miffed. Not that she should have been. She had set the ground rules: wait until after New Year's. *Stupid rules.*

Pepper sent a text saying that she had delivered Landon's card and adding that he had sat for a long time reading it. Emma could call him. But should she?

A loud crash from below broke her reverie. She dashed from her room and flew down the stairs.

Her dad sprawled on the floor just inside the entryway, his shoulder plastered against the stand on which he kept his car keys and spare change. The lamp that usually lit the small table lay shattered on the throw rug.

"Dad, are you okay?" Emma hurried to help him up.

Bud's strong hand grabbed her arm, and he planted himself between her and her father. "Get up, Dad."

Emma's head swiveled toward her brother. She had never heard that tone from Bud.

"Too—dizzy." The garbled words told Emma everything she needed to know about where her father had gone after Aunt Chloe and Uncle Jack left. Dad needed help. She took a step toward him. Bud blocked her path.

"Dad, get up."

"Gimmee a hand." Dad's attempt to reach for help ended with his hand flopped on the floor beside him.

"I'll get him to bed." Emma bent to help.

Bud didn't budge. "Get up and go to bed, or stay on the floor, your choice, but no one's going to help you."

"I am." She tried to shove Bud aside.

"No, you're not." He grabbed her by the shoulders and pulled her to him. "We've always covered for him. First Mom, then you, then me. We all hoped he'd get better." Bud's eyes softened briefly. Then hardness stole into his gaze. "He's getting worse, and we're helping him do it."

A thud drew their attention back to their father. His torso had slipped to the floor where he now lay, out cold. "Oh, Dad." Emma's heart wrenched, and she looked away, burying her head in Bud's T-shirt. Tears streamed down her face.

Her brother wrapped his arms around her. "He's okay. He'll probably have a bump on his head where he hit the floor, but that's all."

Emma brushed tears from her face. "Will he stay there all night?"

"Maybe, maybe not. He might sober up enough to find his way to bed. I'll check on him later."

"Can we at least cover him? Make him more comfortable?"

"No! He has to feel the consequences." Bud pushed her away from him but kept a hand on each shoulder. "I know it sounds mean, but it's necessary."

Emma glanced over her shoulder at Dad, oblivious to anything or anyone around him. She shuddered. Pressure on her shoulders drew her attention back to Bud.

"Come and watch the football game with me."

"Football on Christmas?"

"Just one game. C'mon."

Emma reluctantly followed him. At least the game might take her mind off her dad.

She twirled her phone on a pillow and feigned interest during the first half. She made popcorn at halftime. In the third quarter, she filed her nails and spread her fingers across her phone to paint her nails. At the start of the fourth, she pushed her phone between the cushions, removed her socks, and reached for the file.

Bud muted the television. "Call him, already."

Emma looked up from the pink color she was applying to the nail on her big toe. "Call who?"

"Call who?" He imitated her. "You know who."

"I can't talk now. I'm watching the football game."

Bud covered her eyes with his hand. "What's the score?"

Emma hesitated. "Dallas is ahead by a touchdown."

"That's not a score." He lowered his hand. "And Dallas hasn't been ahead by a touchdown since the end of the first half."

She shoved him against the sofa. "You tricked me."

"It wasn't hard. You're not paying attention." He reached between the cushions and handed her the phone. "Call Landon."

Emma slugged her brother and grabbed the cell. She could ask Landon about his day: what family he'd seen, what his mom had cooked, who had won the chess match. Or she could wait one more week and pray that she had an answer by then.

Bud's hand waving frantically in front of her brought her out of her haze.

"Are you in there?" He knocked his knuckles gently on her skull. "Call the guy, Emma. I want to wish him a Merry Christmas."

"What? Are you out of your mind?"

"He's my favorite college football player, and I have the chance to meet him—sort of. C'mon, be a sport."

"I'm not calling him."

Bud snatched the phone from her hand. "Then I will." He darted behind the couch and zipped down the hall. "Bet Landon's number's in speed dial," he said and punched the buttons. "Aha, just as I suspected." Trapped at the end of the hallway, he paused long enough to smirk at Emma who was within a step of him.

She lunged toward him. At the same time, he lurched forward, trying to evade her. The result was a head-on collision that sent them both sprawling and the cell phone skittering across the carpet. Each sat against the wall, laughing and rubbing bruised body parts.

Bud recovered first. "You okay?"

"I think so." She stared at him. "You're—sturdier—than you used to be. I think I bounced off you." She punched his abs. Nothing moved.

"I've been working out."

Emma reached over and squeezed his upper arm. "My little brother is all grown up. When did that happen?"

"While you were off starting a business and meeting Penn State linebackers."

She raised an eyebrow. "Just one linebacker."

"The best one."

Every part of her agreed, but she didn't say so. Instead she asked, "Do you really want to talk to him?" Emma grew serious. "Remember, you can't talk about football."

"I want to talk about you. And him. You and him."

"No way!" She grabbed both his hands in hers. "I mean it, Bud."

"I want to hear what he thinks about the two of you." He freed himself from her grasp and then clutched her fingers in his. "You *are* my sister."

"And you're my brother, not my father. And you ruined my nails."

"That's right. I'm not." Bud's voice held more than a hint of exasperation. "But Dad's soused—and I'm the only brother you've got. It's up to me to have a man-to-man with this guy."

Thirty seconds earlier, Emma would have choked at her brother's audacity. Now she clamped her mouth shut and studied her younger sibling. His normally laughing eyes were clouded by concern.

"You're worrying over nothing. Everything will be fine."

"I'd feel better if I heard him say that."

Emma wrapped her arms around her bent legs, resting her chin on her knees. For several seconds she stared at Bud. Then she pointed to the phone a few feet away. "Call him. We've talked about you. He'll know who you are."

"You mean it?"

"I think so."

"You going to listen in?" He elbowed her in the ribs.

"You bet." And after he hung up, she intended to pump him for any information she hadn't heard.

━━━━━━━

Landon's Christmas had been a letdown. He'd seen the same people that usually brought him joy. He'd shared the same chess game with his dad—and won. He'd received some gifts that he truly appreciated. He should have been making the Saturday night trip back to State College with a happy heart. But he wasn't.

Emma was part of his discontent. He had daydreamed about this "first Christmas" with her, only to wake up to the reality of her in Pittsburgh and him in Philipsburg.

At the core of his being, however, he knew her absence wasn't the primary problem. *He* was his number one issue. He felt like a coward concerning football, a failure as a Christian, and a dud at winning Emma's heart. The only place he felt confident was at work.

He had to settle things, but he needed help. Whose? His dad would be more than willing, but Dad had never played college sports, never been so close to a pro career. Mike would listen, but he kept God at arm's-length and wouldn't be able to understand Landon's desire to grow closer to the Lord. After the way Landon had dismissed Pastor Murphy at their last meeting, he felt uncomfortable asking for more advice. Who else was there? He ransacked his brain for possibilities.

Coach Spalding! The answer screamed out to him. He knew football, understood what Landon had been through, had experienced problems because of sports, and had found the Lord in spite of everything.

Landon pulled his cell phone from his pocket. It rang as he was opening it. Emma's number lit the dial.

"Merry Christmas, Emma." It had suddenly become one. "I hoped you'd call."

Silence. Then a throat cleared. A male voice spoke. "Hi, Landon. This is Bud Porter, Emma's brother. I'm on her phone."

"Uh—hi, Bud." Fear seized Landon's heart. "Is Emma all right?"

"She's fine."

Releasing the stranglehold on his cell, he asked, "How was your Christmas?"

"Mostly good. Dinner was great. Emma did the cooking and kept Aunt Chloe out of the kitchen."

"Left her to keep an eye on the weather?"

"That's right! Emma must have told you about Aunt Chloe." Bud paused. "Did you have a good holiday?"

Landon thought about the glib, *Just fine*. What he said was, "It would have been better with Emma."

"We needed her here."

Landon appreciated the kid's honesty. "I volunteered to come with her."

"You did?"

"Yep. Would I have been welcome?"

"If it was my decision, sure. If my sister made the call, I don't know."

Landon heard a voice in the background. Emma. She was eavesdropping. What was up?

"You called just to wish me a Merry Christmas?"

"No." The response was quick. The explanation came more slowly and with deep conviction. "My dad's not available to talk, but I—we—want to know—about you—you and Emma. She seemed pretty excited at first—" Landon heard a puff of air as though someone had punched Bud in the stomach. Emma, no doubt. "Now she seems—confused."

Landon hadn't missed Bud's reference to his dad's unavailability, and he could guess the cause. He also had to admire this younger brother's grit. Protecting the heart and reputation of an independent young woman was hard enough for any father. This kid was shouldering a responsibility that shouldn't have been his.

"I can understand that. I'm confused about some things myself." The bluntness of his own statement surprised Landon. "But I'm clear about others. I care for your sister. I'll do my best not to hurt her." He cleared his throat. "She's there with you, isn't she?"

"Yes."

"Turn the phone toward her, please." He waited a few seconds. "I'm searching for answers, Em."

CHAPTER 12 ===

"**C**oach Spalding, it's Landon."

"Hello, Landon. Merry Christmas."

"Same to you." The coach sounded groggy. "I know it's 10:30, and I hope I didn't wake you. I'm wondering if we could meet again and talk."

"Don't worry about it. I'm still up—waiting for a call from my grandson in California. It's early there." He cleared his throat. "I'm surprised you're speaking to me. I messed things up good with Miss Emma."

"You meant well." Landon could almost laugh about the debacle now—almost.

"I did, but I sure 'laid an egg' as my mama would have said."

"I'm guessing that's not a good thing."

"Not unless you're a hen."

Landon chuckled. "You do have a way with words."

"My mama said that, too. She didn't always mean it kindly. Seems I was prone to stretch the truth at times."

Before Landon could think of a response, Aldus said, "Must be pretty important, this thing on your mind, if you're thinking about it on Christmas."

"It is."

"I wish we could meet tomorrow after church like we did last week, but I'm being treated to dinner by some coaching buddies. Hope to be able to speak to them about the Lord."

"You still keep in touch?"

"With most of the guys from Penn State, I do."

"That's good."

"It's my ministry." He paused a moment. "How's Monday night?"

"Sounds great." Hopefully nothing would come up at the office. Dave was back, and things were somewhat normal. "Where should we meet?"

"You up to coming here again? I could whip up some more barbecue."

"I'll be there. What time?"

"Does 6:00 suit you?"

"Sure. See you then. Thanks, coach."

"No problem, son. See you Monday."

For Emma, Christmas night had been a play in many acts. The first was her dad's dreadful stage appearance in the doorway. Like many a court jester, he had become the fool that most people laughed at instead of with. Those who loved him most pitied him for his folly.

Dad's exit—lying in a stupor on the floor—stabbed at Emma's insides.

Bud had taken the lead role in the next act of the evening. He entertained Emma and filled her in on family news. He handled Dad and all the complications surrounding their father. He gave his estimation of Landon shortly after Emma shut her phone.

"I like him." Her brother's three short words were high praise, since he tended to be skeptical about people and reticent in stating his opinion.

"You like him because …"

"Because he seems honest. Seems like he's telling me the truth, not just what I want to hear." He stood and extended his hand to her. "Why didn't you tell us that he offered to come here?"

"He didn't offer to," she said as she accepted his help. "We never—oh—yes—he did."

Bud's creased brow said it all.

"We were arguing. He said he'd do whatever I wanted for Christmas: come here, stay in Bellefonte, or visit his parents. I didn't think he was serious."

"He was." Bud slung his arm over her shoulder and took her with him down the hall. "Too bad you didn't bring him."

"And have him see what happened earlier with Dad?"

"You can't keep it a secret."

"I haven't tried. Landon knows about Dad's drinking."

"Then he would have understood."

"*I* don't even understand." She stopped abruptly and turned on him. "How can we let him lie there?" Nearly three hours had passed, and their father remained on the hardwood floor. "He's so—so—pitiful."

Her brother clenched her shoulders, making her wince. "That's just what he wants you to think. Go ahead. Have pity on him. But don't expect him to thank you or even remember what you did."

Bud released her and turned toward his bedroom.

Emma hesitated, her heart aching to help her dad, but her head knowing that everything Bud had said was true. Dad wouldn't acknowledge any help they gave him. Maybe this "tough love" approach was best.

She found her brother sitting on his bed. His shoulders slumped. His eyes focused on the floor. When she sat next to him, he turned toward her. "You're right," she said. "I know that. It's just ..."

"You hate seeing him like that." Bud finished her sentence. "I do too. But the people I've talked to say ..."

"What people? You haven't been telling everyone?"

"Not *everyone*, Emma." His tone made her feel like a child. "I've spoken to Pastor Jacobs and to Paul Inman. Mr. Inman runs a mission center for men with addictions. Both say the same thing: Dad will never face his alcoholism until he's forced to."

For the next hour, the two sat on Bud's bed and talked. He explained his counselors' ideas and what he had done over the last few weeks to implement them. He also related the triumphs and disasters. "Some days I think he's closer to realizing his problem. On others, I'm convinced he never will."

Emma leaned her shoulder into Bud. "How did you get to be so smart?" At his shrug, she asked, "And when did you become the man of this family?"

"When I finally realized Dad wasn't and probably wasn't ever going to be."

His frank assessment stunned her, and she hugged him tightly. "I'm sorry for what you go through. I would have stayed here. You know that, don't you?"

He pulled away from her. "I know you would." His face became somber. "But I won't let you. You came back for Mom. Now you have your own life."

"What about *your* own life?"

"My time is coming." The statement carried a steely resolve. "Pastor and Paul both make time for me. Their encouragement helps." His eyes suddenly lit up. "I'm ready to send for my driver's permit again. Those two are going to help me get the driving time I need."

Emma's heart welled over. "I'm so excited for you. Landon and I prayed about your driver's license."

Bud shouldered Emma this time. "I knew I liked him. Maybe I'll have my license before I graduate."

Emma hugged her brother and whispered, "We'll keep praying."

Landon had been the star of the last act of Emma's Christmas. His words, "I'm searching for answers, Em," echoed through her mind into the wee hours of the morning, no matter how hard she tried to silence them.

With each audio replay came snapshots: his muscular body sheltering her from the wind as they walked outside, the smile that lit his face when he handed her the roses on her opening day, and those captivating sapphire eyes that sparkled when he laughed.

The image that surpassed all others was his spur-of-the-moment kiss. She could still feel his strong hands on her shoulders, his warm, commanding lips as they silenced hers. As the memory replayed, her heart rate surged. Then she recalled his coffee "proposal" and laughed into her pillow. Flustered and funny and fabulous he had been at that moment. The kiss had started it all. There was so much to love about the man.

Was she in love with Landon? During her sophomore year at PSU, she thought she loved him every time she stared at his photo. She would sit and dream about somehow meeting the guy. What would it have been like to know him then? Maybe she would understand the struggles he faced now. Maybe she could have helped him avoid them. Emma was pondering those possibilities when sleep finally overtook her.

━━━━━━━

Landon couldn't remember being so sick. Not long after he went to bed Christmas night, he woke up shivering. He added an extra blanket. Later he threw off the covers and lay sweating. By three in the morning, he had begun making trips to the bathroom. His stomach retched. He vomited and felt some relief, only to have the whole ordeal start again a short time later. Over and over the cycle repeated itself.

At some point he heard himself plead, "The nightmare, please, Lord. Not this."

After making numerous trips from bed to lavatory, Landon slumped against the wall and dozed right in the bathroom. He was close when he needed to be. When he woke later, his neck felt ready to break, but at least his stomach had given him some respite. He had no idea how long he had camped near the commode, but the thought of a soft bed instead of a hard floor compelled him to make the trip to his room once again.

Lying on his side, with a pillow lightly cushioning his belly, he shut his eyes and was dead to the world.

Sparkling water cascaded down the falls right in front of him. He stretched out his hand to touch its coolness, to bring a sip of refreshment to his parched lips. Only a few more inches to go. Just a little farther.

Thud! Landon jumped and the vision vanished. In place of the cooling cascade was the spilled glass that lay on the floor. His attempts to reach the waterfall had evidently knocked the tumbler off the nightstand. With a groan, he hung one leg over the side of the bed and pulled himself to the edge. He needed a drink. The spill on the floor would have to wait.

A few minutes later he crawled back into bed and looked at the clock—11:45. Nearly twelve hours had passed since he went to bed. His head felt as if an elephant were sitting on it, and his stomach rumbled—from hunger or something else, he wasn't sure.

Good thing Coach Spalding was busy today. The mere thought of pork barbecue made his insides roil, and he stifled a gag. He should get up. He would get up. He fell asleep.

Shortly after 2:00 he opened his eyes again.

What time is it? What day is it?

Memories of the horrible night came back. He needed to use the bathroom, and he needed some mouthwash—badly. A few minutes at the sink revived him. His hair protruded in all directions, but he felt human again.

Grabbing a clean pair of shorts, he shambled to the kitchen. A drink of water eased his thirst but what could he do to dislodge the elephant from his skull? The thought of medicine on his sick, empty stomach nauseated him. Caffeine would help his head, but coffee sounded horrible. He had to eat something. But what?

He was snatching a steaming piece of toast from the toaster when his phone rang. "Unknown caller" filled the screen. "Hello," Landon croaked into the device as he buttered his bread.

"Landon Steele?"

"Yes." Landon didn't recognize the voice.

"This is Ed Mickle. How was your Christmas?"

Ed Mickle was the head of all the department heads of all the accounting departments at Penn State. He had never spoken to Landon, much less called him. "Until the middle of the night it was okay, sir."

"Your lady friend leave your bed then?" He sniggered.

Landon's wan face blushed scarlet. Ed Mickle was a notorious philanderer who entertained multiple female companions and expected others to do the same.

"I was sick. Spent much of the night in the bathroom."

"Did she join you?" Again the lecherous laugh.

Landon barely controlled his seething anger. "I was alone all evening, sir. May I ask the purpose of your call?"

Mickle's tone turned brusque. "You're due for a review in June, but we're moving it up, and I'll be handling this one."

Landon gulped and steadied himself against the kitchen counter.

"I'm headed to Maui first thing tomorrow morning. I won't be back in the office until January 6. I've scheduled your review for Friday, January 7, at 1:30. Be sure to confirm the time with Stewart. He's asked to be there."

Questions bombarded Landon's brain. Had he made a colossal error that had cost the university? Was the department being downsized? What did Stewart know? He forced composure and replied, "I'll tell him, sir. We'll see you on the seventh."

"Be prompt, Steele."

"Yes, sir. I will."

Two elephants plodded around in Landon's head as he closed the phone. Could his life be any more chaotic? Before he fell asleep again and forgot the date and time of his review—little chance of that—he found his briefcase and day planner. On Friday, January 7, he wrote. *Review: Edward Mickle, 1:15.* Better safe than sorry on the time.

Of all the people to have to deal with today. The man was arrogant, rude, and downright lascivious. Everyone knew it. But the Mickle name was big on campus. Ed's father, grandfather, and great-grandfather had all played crucial roles in the development of programs at PSU and had donated substantial sums to the college's endowment funds.

Everyone also knew that Edward Mickle had a shrewd mind and a nose for business. From an accounting perspective, he had earned his place at the top. The man understood his job and deserved the renown he enjoyed. But he could be ruthless, and he had been known to backstab associates as readily as he discarded girlfriends. What lay behind Mr. Mickle's sudden interest in Landon?

The cold toast stared up at Landon, and at the idea of eating, his stomach suddenly revolted. He chucked the golden bread into the trashcan and headed back to his room. So much for a restful day after Christmas. Tomorrow looked iffy too. He hoped Stewart and Coach Spalding had some answers.

━━━━━━━━

The seven days between Christmas and New Year's loomed large for Emma. Family issues, business concerns, and personal dilemmas fought for her attention as she drove the two hours back to Bellefonte late Sunday afternoon.

She didn't know how or when Dad had gotten himself to bed last night, but she had heard him in his room as she made a pancake breakfast for Bud and herself. By the time they returned from church, he had roused himself, showered and shaved, and was nearly back to normal. He kidded Bud about some girl in Bud's class at school and quizzed Emma on how her business was doing.

Her departure had been tearful. Dad was stoical, as always. Bud hugged her so hard he squeezed the breath out of her.

"Don't worry about us," he'd whispered as he clenched her in his arms. His eyes looked so confident, that she'd had a moment's relief from her anxiety. Her brother was amazing in his resilience and fortitude.

This workweek promised to be just as busy, if not busier, than the previous one had been. Some of Betty Steele's leads had paid off, and Heavenly Chocolates was to be the confectioner for two large shindigs: one in Altoona and the other in State College. Emma anticipated spending very little time with customers at the shop because her days would be consumed in the kitchen, making candies as fast as she could.

Pepper could cope with the counter and register. The girl was a quick study, and her wit and quirkiness made her a crowd favorite. She had also accepted the challenge of handling the day of New Year's Eve by herself since Mort, Sylvia, Hailey, and Emma were flying out mid-afternoon on Friday for the Penn State-Alabama Bowl Game on New Year's. With Mort's dad on the mend, Sylvia hoped to be more available this week, as well. Emma would need all the extra hands she could find.

And then there was Landon. Her heart ka-thumped excitedly at the mere thought of him. This was it, the week she must decide what to do. She knew Landon's desire—to spend time together and let their relationship develop. More than ever, her heart echoed his. If only she knew the Lord's wishes as precisely.

━━━━━━━━━━

"You don't look so good." Aldus swung the door open.

"Don't feel the best, either." Landon rubbed his stomach. "I caught something late Christmas night. Spent yesterday in bed and took today off work."

"You up to barbecue?"

"Not really." Landon retched at the thought. "You go ahead."

"One of the best parts of good barbecue is the smell." Aldus surveyed Landon's face. "By the looks of you, even that is making you green around the gills. Do you feel like eating *anything?*"

"Not at the moment."

"Well, settle yourself in the living room. I'll be in directly."

Landon made himself comfortable on the couch. He could hear the clinking of dishes and the refrigerator door opening and closing.

"You sure you can handle a serious talk?" Aldus's voice floated into the living room.

Landon's answer was emphatic. "I need some advice."

"What makes you think I'm the one to give it?"

"You understand football, you love the Lord, and you know Emma."

"Let me set you straight," Aldus said, carrying his plate and glass from the kitchen. "I do know football, but I've only recently settled things with the good Lord, and I've talked to Miss Emma for only five minutes—and stirred up a hornet's nest when I did."

"But you were married. You understand women."

Aldus chortled, throwing his head back so far that he tipped his glass, nearly spilling the milk from it. "Son, no man completely understands any woman, not even the one he's married to. They're as different from us as a tabby cat is from a pole cat." Landon smiled at the image, and Aldus beamed back. "The contrasts are what hit you." He set both his plate and his glass on the seat of the rocker, clapped Landon on the shoulder and grinned. "Besides, from what you said the other day, your daddy's been married to your mama for a lot longer than I was to Dora. Why not ask him?"

Landon pondered a moment. Was he wrong not to go to his dad?

Waiting for the conversation to resume, Aldus set up a TV tray, moved his supper onto it, and then seated himself in his rocker.

"My dad and I are—at odds with—each other on some things. I want another opinion, one from someone more objective than either of us."

Aldus paused, his sandwich in mid-air, before returning it to his plate. "The last place I want to be is between you and your daddy." His piercing stare penetrated to the back of Landon's skull. "There's no safe place in the middle."

"I haven't told Dad about coming here. Didn't want you to feel pressured."

"Except from you."

"I won't push you."

"You already have." Aldus sipped his milk. "What if I tell you something that makes you mad as a wet hen?" He wrapped both hands around the glass, looking over the top of it at Landon.

What if? Landon couldn't guarantee the answer.

Each man gazed at the other. In his mind, Landon was transported back to the PSU practice field. He envisioned Coach Spalding crouched in a lineman's position, eyeball-to-eyeball across from him just before the snap of the ball. "What you made of, Steele? Can you live up to your name?"

The taunt had stirred Landon's resolve. When the ball left the center's hands, he had surged forward and knocked Coach backward, discarding him and several others on his way to the quarterback.

Landon knew the man's grit, and Coach Spalding knew his.

The standoff ended when Aldus said, "I'll listen. That's all I can promise."

Landon's shoulders relaxed. He leaned back into the couch. Aldus once again raised the sandwich.

"I've told you about my nightmare, about how I've stayed away from football, and about how Emma doesn't understand my avoiding the game."

"Yep, last time you were here." Aldus nodded.

"I didn't tell you that my dad agrees with Emma about football, but for a different reason."

"And that is …"

"Dad ties my avoidance, the dream—everything really—to God."

"Everything in life is tied to Him. I learned that the hard way."

"I spent my football years trying to show those around me how important He is."

"You did a great job." Aldus paused. "Your life had a whole lot to do with my accepting the Lord."

Landon gulped. "I—didn't know. I'm glad."

"I am, too, more'n I can say. Some time soon I'll tell you the story." Aldus wiped his mouth and leaned back, setting the rocker in motion. "Go on. What's your daddy's concern?"

"He says I'm mad at God for taking football from me. That's why I can't forget things and move on."

"And you say …"

"I haven't forsaken God. I go to church. I stay away from sinful things. I've forgiven Him for ruining my plans."

Aldus remained motionless for several seconds after Landon stopped speaking. Then he silently moved the tray to the side, rose from the chair, and stepped next to Landon. Without warning, he sank onto the cushion, while at the same time grabbing a small pillow and slamming it into Landon's mid-section.

Landon groaned, his stomach shooting with pain. "What're you doing?"

"Did I hurt you?"

"Only my sick stomach."

"Oh, sorry."

"It's okay." Landon straightened, shifting slightly away from Aldus.

In a heartbeat, the coach's hand stretched behind Landon's head and cuffed him at the nape, delivering a blow reminiscent of the ones Landon received when he'd muffed an easy play.

"Coach, cut it out."

"Sorry, son. Forgive me?"

Landon stared at him. Had the guy lost his mind? "Yeah, sure."

Aldus extended his right hand. Landon slowly clasped and shook it.

"I forgive you, too."

Landon's jaw fell. What was in the coach's milk?

Aldus again flummoxed Landon by asking, "What's the matter?" A lazy grin crossed his face. "Looks like you've seen a ghost."

"Why are *you* forgiving *me*? I didn't do anything wrong."

Aldus's smile fled. "Neither did God, but you decided that He needed your forgiveness." Coach reinforced his words with a rock-hard glower.

Time ticked by. "He took my dream."

"Which you had because of Him."

"He robbed me of football. He—"

"No, son." Aldus's leathery hand clamped the younger man's shoulder. "God took you out of the pros. You sidelined yourself."

While Landon stared at the carpet, Aldus rose and left the room. Before long, he returned, holding a small paper sack. He tapped Landon's shoulder and nodded at the bag.

Taking the package, Landon looked inside. A single CD case. He pulled it out, gasping as he did. What he held wasn't a CD. It was a DVD, the one he had made after his recovery. The DVD no one had believed in.

"That's one mighty good linebacker," Aldus said, resuming his seat in the rocker.

"He used to be."

"That guy still is."

"Too bad nobody but you believed that."

Landon remembered the day he put thirty-two DVD's in the mail, certain that more than one coach or GM or team representative would respond. In the weeks that passed, his hopes had oscillated but never died. Then came the rejection letters—some short, some long, some terse, some flowery, all with the same message: no position for Landon. The would-have-been Butkus Award winner wouldn't be on the roster.

Aldus's voice beckoned Landon to the present. "You okay?"

"Yeah."

"Where'd you go?"

"Back three years—all those rejection letters."

"What keeps football going?"

Somewhat surprised at the change of topic, Landon still answered quickly. "Fans, players."

"Nope. Football feeds on money. You know that."

Landon did know. No amount of sugarcoating could change the ugly reality: men were drafted because owners and coaches believed they could help the team win and could, therefore, create revenue. The players were commodities. Injured players were useless commodities.

"Those coaches were in a tight spot. Even if they wanted to take a chance on you—and I know some who did—they were squeezed by the odds." Aldus rocked the chair forward and slid to the edge of the seat, resting his elbows on his knees and his chin on his knuckles. His dark eyes gleamed with determination. "Those rejection letters convinced you that you're not good enough." When Landon nodded, Aldus said, "You've let others sell you short, not only in football but also in life."

"Only one guy gave me a chance."

"That's what I'm talking about." Aldus slapped his knee and nodded vigorously. "Is a lightning-fast filly any slower because she's scrawny and undersized or because she's never won the Kentucky Derby?"

Another of Coach's colorful word pictures. "No. But nobody will notice or care about her speed."

"She will." Aldus blurted. "So will the boy who cons his friends into betting against her." He cackled at his joke.

"I'm not a horse."

"Then don't let others treat you like one." He snatched the video from Landon's hand and held it up. "You know what you're capable of. You have a say in how your football story continues—and when it ends."

Landon's eyes dilated. "You can't be saying I can make the NFL."

"With God, nothing is impossible. I've learned that."

Flabbergasted, Landon gasped, nearly swallowing his gum. He choked and sputtered.

Aldus clapped him on the back. "Nothing is impossible. But some things are pretty unlikely—and probably foolish." When Landon had recovered, Aldus said, "And there's so much more to football. Think how many people helped you along. You could be one of them for someone else."

"Not if I can't be around the game."

"Nothing is impossible with God. Remember that."

Landon wondered what it would be like to mentor young kids. Finally, he smiled.

"Something tickle your funny bone?"

"If I didn't know better, I'd swear you've been talking to my dad, my pastor—and Emma."

"Ah, yes, Miss Emma." Aldus sat and rocked silently for a space. "She remembers your glory days?"

"She went to all the home games. Even cut out my picture from *Sports Illustrated*."

"Oohoo!" Aldus chortled "She's kept it all this time?"

Landon's eyebrows puckered. "I don't know. She said she hung it on her dorm room door. Never told me what happened to it after that."

The trademark twinkle lit the coach's face. "You think maybe she's set her cap for you?"

"Her cap?" Another colorful phrase Landon had never heard. "I know she has a cap, but …"

Aldus snorted, reached over and thumped Landon's arm. "You are too young. When a young lady 'sets her cap for you,' she has romance in her head and you in her sights." The older man's eyes shone with mischief.

How Landon wished his coach were right. "If Emma ever set her cap for me, it blew off two weeks ago—about the time she learned the whole truth."

"What truth?"

"I'm a has-been and a coward."

"Her words—or yours?"

Landon paused. Did Emma see him the way he pictured himself? More than once, she had referred to the linebacking records he still held and the fabulous plays she'd seen him make. When it came to his nightmares and obsessive behavior, her answer was, "If you weren't such a—a—man—you'd realize you need help." She didn't seem to view him as cowardly—just stubborn. "My words, I guess."

"I thought so." Aldus rubbed his chin between his thumb and index finger. "I didn't figure that little lady as cruel. Feisty, definitely. But not cruel."

"You hardly know her."

Aldus slapped his hands on the arms of the rocking chair. "A few minutes ago you called me an expert." He cast a skeptical glance at his former protege.

Snared by his own words, Landon gulped. "I wanted your opinion."

"Do you still?"

A niggling sense of foreboding dashed through Landon's brain.

"Are you willing to hear—and heed—my advice?" The coach's voice was soft and undemanding. His stare, however, was like a white-hot scalpel that laid Landon's conscience bare and chiseled at his hardened heart.

Landon gripped the couch cushion. He could feel the cold sweat creeping over his body. He blinked twice, trying to evade the searing glare. Still Aldus scrutinized him, his dark orbs never looking away..

A heavy sigh punctuated Landon's words. "I am."

"Give up." The words swirled in the air between the two men.

"Is that a question?"

"It's the answer." Aldus leaned far back in the rocker. "Sounds strange, doesn't it? Especially from the guy who always said, 'Want to win? Never give up.'"

Landon managed to nod, but his face must have registered bewilderment.

"Give up everything to God." Aldus paused. "Against Him, you can't win until you do."

CHAPTER 13 ━━━━━━

Knowing she was behind schedule, Emma crossed the threshold of Heavenly Chocolates earlier than usual on December 28. Ensconced in her own chocolatey world, she melted and molded at break-neck speed.

Nearly three hours later, Pepper skipped into the kitchen and past the row of filled trays. "You've been busy." The nimble sprite stopped at the dome-shaped peanut butter-filled creations that were one of her favorites. "How do you stay so thin? If I could make these things, I'd be popping one into my mouth each time I walked by."

Emma grinned, stretching her back as she stood. "Should I be checking for chocolate on your breath?"

Completing her circuit of the room, Pepper stood in the doorway and quipped, "No, but you might want to survey my purse each night." She ducked out. Emma chuckled. The girl was a gem.

Mere seconds had passed before Pepper reappeared, wearing a grin of impish delight. Silently, she placed a small box next to Emma, raised her eyebrows, and scooted away.

Emma wanted to ignore the package. She had so much to do, and she was not in an opportune place to pause. After all, it was just a belated Christmas present, probably some silly trinket Pepper had found or created. But the enigmatic gleam in her assistant's eyes triggered Emma's curiosity. The absence of a card also intrigued her.

You might as well open it. You won't concentrate on anything else till you do.

Setting aside the tray in front of her, Emma removed her plastic gloves and picked up the box with its shimmery red and green paper and white ribbon. As she drew it closer, her nose caught the scent of something "un"chocolate but clearly familiar. Definitely cologne. Not the drugstore variety. The expensive type that delights a girl's nose without deadening her olfactory nerves. Definitely Landon's.

Her heart simultaneously soared and ached. He had remembered. She had forgotten. Not forgotten, exactly, but bypassed.

With trembling fingers, she lifted the box higher and inhaled. Even the scent of him excited her, increasing her anticipation. A few seconds later, she lifted the cardboard lid and removed the cottony layer underneath. While tears pooled in her eyes, she raised the silver bracelet.

The gasp from the doorway overshadowed Emma's.

"Sorry. I shouldn't be spying." Pepper pivoted to leave.

"Stay."

The girl turned and edged forward.

"When did he bring this?" Emma asked.

"Christmas Eve, in the afternoon. You'd already gone."

"Where was it?"

"Underneath the cash register. Way in back on the shelf." She slid nearer and touched the gift. "It's beautiful. The guy has great taste. Angie would be green. She wanted to get her clutches on him the day we came in."

"The blonde?" Emma remembered her nosy questions.

"No, that's Sophie. Angie's the red-head."

"I thought both of them seemed—predatory."

Pepper had lifted the bracelet from Emma's fingers, admiring it up close. She grinned devilishly. "Jealous?"

"Yes." Emma couldn't keep the red from her cheeks. "But you never heard me say so."

Pepper crossed her heart and handed the gift back. Emma chortled.

"Don't forget the card" were the co-ed's parting words.

"What card?"

"Taped to the bottom." Her voice wafted from the other room.

Emma set the bracelet on the counter beside her. Turning the box upside down, she located the miniature envelope and removed the tiny card. *Delicate but strong, simple but exquisite. This bracelet—and you. L58.*

Ten words and his abbreviated signature. Emma stood, mesmerized, studying first the beautiful gift and then returning to the enchanting message.

"Emma, are those ..." Pepper's rapid-fire question halted at the threshold, as did her scurrying feet. She stared openly at her boss. "I don't believe it."

"Believe what?"

"You." She gestured toward Emma's face. "This starry-eyed, dopey-grinned, puppy-dog look. It's the same one he wore when he read *your* card." She rolled her eyes as she walked past, on her way to collect some coffee supplies. "When you return to earth, you can show me what else goes into the display case. It's almost time to open."

Landon bolted upright on his bed. He clutched his lower right leg. He panted furiously. He surveyed his surroundings.

The dream had resurfaced after nearly a week's remission. Fumbling for the light switch, he grabbed the notepad and pen next to his clock. For the next ten minutes, he scribbled vivid details: Iowa's smudged black and gold uniforms intermingled with Penn State's mud-stained blue and white ones, the precise route the receiver had taken, surging pain followed by gasps of horror. He could recall a hushed silence and envision players huddled around him. One of them was Jordy. Tears streamed down the lineman's abundant cheeks as he repeated over and over, "You didn't have to do it. The Butkus was yours."

Not once in four years had Landon remembered Bernard Jordan's mournful black eyes and tortured words. For a half hour longer, Landon struggled to capture on paper every bit of minutiae. Then, as minute after minute ticked by, he lay wide-awake, marveling at how clear the image had been.

In the wee hours of Tuesday morning, Landon made a decision. He wasn't going to the office today. He had vacation days. He needed time alone.

―――――――

At ten o'clock, having waited as long as he could, Landon dialed Stewart's number. Moments later, Stew's secretary transferred his call.

"Hello, Landon. You still sick?"

"Not so much. I needed a personal day."

"Trouble?"

"I hope not." The January 7 meeting loomed in Landon's mind. "Ed Mickle called me the day after Christmas. Told me about my review."

"I wondered how long he'd wait."

"What's up, Stew?"

"I have no idea. Mickle was tight-lipped. I couldn't badger anything out of him."

"Have I done—or not done—something?"

"I honestly don't know, but I want to."

"Thanks for offering to go along."

"Purely selfish reasons, Steele. I don't want to have to replace a good accountant."

"So there's no problem with you?"

"If I had a problem, you'd know it."

Landon smiled into the phone. The man spoke truth. "Thanks again."

"Don't spend your day off worrying about Ed Mickle."

Good advice. Landon hoped he could follow it.

————

An hour later he rang the doorbell at 111 Cherry Lane. His mom opened the door.

"Landon! What are you doing here on a Tuesday morning?"

"Scrounging." He leaned to give his mother a hug. "You gonna let me in?"

"Of course." She preceded him inside. He shut the door. "What are you scrounging?"

Landon removed his sweatshirt, tossing it onto the sofa. "First, some old albums or scrapbooks. Later, some lunch."

"Albums or scrapbooks?" She didn't conceal her surprise, but she recovered quickly. "Spare bedroom closet. Help yourself."

Landon advanced in that direction. Would he find what he sought? Could he really look for it? Before he found out, Mom's voice reached him.

Hands resting on her hips, she stood a few feet from him. "You took a day off work to glance through albums and scrapbooks?"

"And get food."

"Hmmm" was all she said before disappearing into the kitchen.

She's suspicious. If he were successful, she'd understand soon enough.

Landon opened the closet door and marveled at the neat array in front of him. His apartment closet was tidy, with items grouped together so that he never had to sift to find things, but his mom's was organization plus. She had dedicated hours to gathering and arranging the family keepsakes. He began skimming the labels on the album spines. His breath caught when he came to the third one: *Youth Football, Age 10.* He shivered. Then he extended his hand.

The cover featured an inset frame with a picture of a tow-headed boy decked out in a blue and gold uniform. The pads extended several inches beyond his narrow shoulders, and the faded helmet he clutched no longer matched his jersey. His grin, however, couldn't have been broader, nor his eyes more excited.

Landon involuntarily smiled at his likeness. He remembered kneeling on the football field that scorching July day, exuberant to be wearing a real football uniform. Without warning, his mind raced in turbo speed through the years that had followed that photo. The magic of the uniform, whichever one it was, had never faded. Every time Landon suited up, the spell was cast.

A stranglehold clutched Landon's trachea. Gasping, he flipped open the cover and raced through page after page, oblivious to everything he passed. By the time the imaginary fingers loosened from his throat, he was mid-way through the book. "I can't do this!" He slammed the album shut and shoved it into the open slot on the shelf. He retreated from the closet, heading for the bedroom door.

"Think of all the people who helped you." Coach Spalding's words rose like a barricade to impede his escape. He halted. They replayed, adding height to the invisible wall.

Landon slowly retraced his steps and reclaimed the album. Numb, he carried it to the bed. He flipped open the cover without a downward glance and skimmed through five pages, never even looking. Then he let his gaze lower. There it was. The team photo.

Nearly thirty nine- and ten-year-olds squinted into the bright sunshine. Some wore stoic stares. Others grinned openly. Landon avoided his own face in the picture. Instead he searched the coaches who flanked both sides of the team. Where was Coach Matt?

He scrutinized each man's face. None matched the features he remembered: coal black hair, a beak-like nose, and eyes that flashed with pleasure each time a player followed his instructions.

Under Coach Matt's guidance, the scrawniest kid could at least budge the tackle dummy. The boy with two left feet eventually learned to navigate the tires. Matt hadn't cursed or berated, and he was always the one to suggest ice cream at the end of an especially hot afternoon. Landon turned to the caption below. Of the four coaches listed, none was Matt. Under "Not Pictured" were two additional names: Donald Norman and Carl Mathys.

Even after sixteen years, Donald still resided in Landon's memory: a big, clumsy, ten-year-old bully who delighted in tripping people and laughing as he watched them nosedive. When Donald contracted chicken pox and had to miss the last two weeks, his teammates quietly cheered his calamity.

Whereas Donald was indelible, Carl Mathys seemed invisible. Landon didn't recall anyone by that name. Sighing, he closed the album and rose from the bed, moving to return the book to its assigned space. A few seconds later, he jerked to a stop.

"Mom," he yelled, jogging from the bedroom, "is your computer booted up?"

"Yes."

Retrieving the album, he hurried to the den, plunking the book onto his mom's computer desk and flipping to the team photo. Then he Googled *Carl*

Mathys. Several responses appeared instantaneously. He scanned the page, grimacing when no image accompanied any of them. A Seattle entrepreneur dominated the first entries, a schoolteacher from Kentucky the next few.

He kept reading. The last item on page one was an obituary notice from the *Centre Daily Times* dated September 21 of this year. Landon's heart catapulted to his feet. The subject was a man of 57, who "died suddenly at his Milesburg home on Tuesday." The details were few but poignant: the man had a massive heart attack during the night, never woke up, left a wife, three sons, and a daughter, loved hunting, barbecuing—and coaching youth football. The deceased's name was Carl (Matt) Douglas Mathys.

Landon plopped his elbows onto the desk and covered his eyes with the base of his palms. Carl Mathys was Coach Matt, one of the few football memories that had never betrayed Landon. Even when thoughts of Landon's high school team and the Penn State squad brought nausea and cold sweats, Coach Matt's replays remained friendly. Landon ached to let the guy know. Now he never could.

He carefully reread the article. "In lieu of flowers, the family asks that donations be made to the youth football program." He hit the print button, closed the Internet, and gathered the two pages from the machine. At least he could send a card to the coach's widow and a donation in his honor.

He had returned the album to the closet and was shutting the door, when he spotted two storage boxes on the floor in the corner. On the end of each box, Mom's neat handwriting proclaimed "PSU items." Icicle clutches seized his lungs. Specters of the contents paraded before him. He squeezed his eyes shut.

Then Emma's image appeared. Surely the boxes held some keepsake he could give her. She loved Penn State as much as he did. He reached for the lid. His mom's voice drifted from the kitchen. "I've whipped up some lunch."

"Be right there."

Landon grabbed both boxes, dashing them to the car before he could change his mind.

―――――――

A deluxe cheeseburger and a dish of home-canned pears from their neighbor awaited him in the kitchen. His mom chattered, updating him on family and friends but never asking about what he had looked for or if he had found it. She had to be curious.

There was something else about her. Almost as if she, too, had a secret. Not wanting to pry or be questioned, Landon dined with his thoughts. Apparently his mom felt the same.

When he'd eaten, he gathered his sweatshirt and the obituary. After hugging his mom goodbye, he slid a note from his pocket. "Give this to Dad, will you?"

Looking up at him, she accepted it. "Should I ask?"

"Let Dad tell you." The message was short, but Landon knew his father would understand. "Not my will, but Yours, Lord. I give up." He smiled slightly, hoping to ease her mind. "Thanks for everything, Mom."

━━━━━━

Landon needed a sympathy card. State College had several places to find one. He'd buy a card before he went home and put it in the mail this afternoon. Coach Matt's wife might receive it tomorrow. He reached for the obituary to be sure of the address. Milesburg.

A new idea sprang up. The coach's home wasn't far away. A simple change in Landon's route was all it would take. He could stop in Milesburg and deliver the card. From there he could drive through Bellefonte and on to State College.

Bellefonte. The new route would take him within one block of Heavenly Chocolates. After he stopped at Coach Matt's house, he would drop by to surprise Emma.

First, a quick stop a few blocks from his parents' home. Rite Aid sold greeting cards.

━━━━━━

The Mathys home was a split-level ranch on a side street, just outside the tiny town of Milesburg. Landon drove up the winding asphalt path, parking near the front door.

"Sure you want to do this?"

Since purchasing the card that lay on the seat beside him, he'd asked himself that question several times.

"Get going."

Reluctantly, he opened the car door and pushed himself forward. He pressed the doorbell. Time elapsed. He was looking for a place to stick the card when a lady appeared in front of him.

She looked to be about his mom's age. Gathering her cardigan more tightly around her, she spoke through the storm door. "May I help you?"

144

A deep growl reached Landon's ears. Behind the woman, a mammoth Rottweiler rested on a rug.

"Quiet, Hank." She waved a hand in the dog's direction, and he laid his head on his paws. His eyes remained alert, his gaze fixed on Landon.

"I'm Landon Steele. I played—your husband was my—"

"Carl was your youth football coach?" she finished for him.

"Yes, ma'am, when I was ten." Landon shifted his weight and momentarily surveyed the porch beneath him. "I just learned of his death. Sorry for your loss."

"Thank you."

Landon held out the card. "I know it's late, but I …"

Mrs. Mathys discreetly unlocked the door. Hank stood, a rumble once again thundering in his throat. "Drop," she repeated. The dog lay.

Turning back to Landon, she added, "He was Carl's constant companion. Since my husband's death, Hank's become my protector."

"I don't doubt that." The dog's keen eyes followed Landon's every move as he slipped the card through the slit of space and placed it in the woman's outstretched hand. "He'd make anyone think twice before entering."

A trace of a grin lit the widow's face but never quite reached her sad eyes. She extended a hand in the dog's direction, and he immediately rose to stand beside her. "Hank's been more of a comfort than I ever would have guessed." She patted his head without seeming to realize.

"I wish I could thank Coach Matt— He was the best—" Landon's voice cracked, and he felt moisture in his eyes. "I better be going."

"I appreciate your thoughtfulness." Her earnest look cemented her words in Landon's mind. "Tell me your name again."

"Landon Steele."

Again the sad smile. "It sounds familiar. Did you continue playing football?"

Landon's face warmed. "Yes, ma'am, for twelve years."

"Twelve years. You must have played in college."

"At Penn State."

"Really."

Landon couldn't tell whether he heard surprise or respect in her tone. "Linebacker."

"Did you start?"

Coach Matt's wife had football perception. "Four years."

"You must have been good."

Landon shrugged his shoulders.

"Do you really need to go, or could you come inside for a minute? I'd like to check on something."

"Maybe I'd better not." He motioned toward Hank.

"Oh, he'll be fine." She patted the dog's head. "Hank. Rug." The dog strode to the rug he had occupied previously. "Drop." Hank lay down. "Stay." He shifted to make himself more comfortable.

With that final command, Mrs. Mathys opened the inner door and motioned Landon inside. The Rottweiler's dark eyes still scrutinized him, but the dog never moved his head or emitted a sound.

"I'll be right back."

She walked down a hall. Hank stared at Landon. Landon avoided the dog's gaze. Mutual distrust hovered in the air. "Should've mailed the card," Landon whispered. "That's what I get for finagling to see Emma."

He gave serious thought to going back outside to wait. Before he could retreat, Mrs. Mathys returned. A bulging manila folder filled her arms.

"My husband was a better collector than an organizer, but he did manage a semblance of order with this football assortment." She held up the file. "Would you mind sitting?" She motioned to a bench along the wall of the foyer. She sat. He joined her.

"What year was Carl your coach?" she asked, settling the folder in her lap.

At Landon's answer, she fingered through years of history, quickly retrieving a paper-clipped bundle.

She held up a half-page brochure with numerous slips and scraps escaping from it. "Is this it?" The same team photo he'd seen earlier graced the cover. A program similar to the one she held had been circulated to the spectators at every game.

"That's it." A lump blocked the rest of his words.

"Let's see what's here." She removed the paper clips, slipping them into the pocket of her sweater.

Just inside the cover was a collection of Sticky Notes. Wide-eyed, Landon nodded. "The last game. Someone's mother handed those out and told us to write something for one of the coaches. Looks like Coach Matt got most of them."

"I remember reading them with him. Both of us laughed—and cried." Picking up the cluster, she asked, "Shall we find yours?"

146

"No, please." If only she knew how close he was right now to bolting out the door.

She seemed surprised but moved the notes aside. Greeting cards, a few photos of individual players with her husband, and various stat sheets passed quickly through her hands without any remark. Then Mrs. Mathys's pace slowed.

"Here they are." She held up a stack of medium-sized pages torn from a notebook. "Carl wrote one of these about every player, every year that he coached. When he finished, I'd alphabetize them so he'd be able to find one quickly if he needed it. Sometimes high school coaches would ask about players as they got older." She hesitated. "Are you curious?"

Petrified was more like it, but he had to admit that Coach Matt's opinion mattered. One nod, and she began leafing through the stack. Landon's page was near the bottom.

She pulled it from its spot. "Landon Steele, Age 10: Great raw talent. Team player. Perfect size to play several positions, especially linebacker. And teachable. Best player on this team. A kid every coach dreams of."

When she stopped reading, Landon couldn't speak. His hostess didn't seem to expect him to. Both sat in poignant silence for some time, while Carl Mathys delivered his message to each of them.

She recovered first. Folding the paper in half, she handed it toward Landon. "I want you to have this."

"I can't."

"Carl would want you to." She pulled Landon's envelope from her abundant pocket. "You gave me something in memory of him. I want to return the favor."

Croaking a barely audible "Thank you," Landon accepted the paper.

━━━━━━━━━

Reaching his car a few minutes later, Landon looked toward the house. Coach Matt's wife waved goodbye. Hank stood beside her. Landon raised his hand before climbing in. Turning his Camry around at the top of the drive, he wound his way back to the street, pausing before entering traffic.

Leaning to look in both directions, Landon heard the crinkle coming from the front pocket of his sweatshirt. He removed the paper, opened it, and reread the coach's words—noticing the ones written in different colored ink at the bottom of the page. The ones that Mrs. Mathys hadn't said earlier: "State College

High School star, four-year starter at Penn State, two-time All-American. The best I've ever coached."

Landon replayed the words, somehow hearing them in his coach's voice.

Then he heard another voice. A ten-year-old's as he recited the words he'd written on a sticky note to his favorite coach: "You're almost like my dad, only in football."

For twenty years Carl Mathys had mentored young men, volunteering his time, sacrificing his summers. What had he received? Before today, Landon wouldn't have known what to say. Now he knew the most important answer. Coach Matt had gotten the pleasure of seeing others succeed. He had done his best so that they could achieve theirs. And he'd loved doing it.

"Think of all the people who helped you." Aldus Spalding's words resurfaced. This time they conjured an unspoken and unsettling question. *Who have you helped?*

As he drove, Landon searched for the answer. He hadn't found it by the time he pulled to a stop in front of the chocolate shop. He got out, locked the car, and stepped inside the store.

"Your timing stinks." Pepper wiped the counter top as he entered.

"What?" He blinked at the audacious girl.

"You came to see Emma, right?"

"Yes."

"She just left. Making a delivery." Pepper moved farther down the display case. "There's some fancy gala in Altoona tonight."

"That's almost an hour from here."

"Yeah, but she wasn't going that far."

Landon trapped her cleaning cloth between his hand and the glass. "What are you saying?"

Her progress halted, Pepper turned to the wall behind her and removed a clipboard. She rattled off the particulars. "Seven o'clock tonight; banker's dinner; Ramada Conference Center, Altoona."

"You said she wasn't going to Altoona."

Pepper looked up from the page. "She wasn't. Only part way—the contact lady was taking them the rest of the way tonight."

"Then where *is* Emma going?"

"Some little town—had a man's name in it." She glanced back at the paper. "Here it is. Philipsburg. 111 Cherry Lane."

CHAPTER 14

By the end of the day, Landon took stock. He knew nothing more than he had that morning about his upcoming interview with Ed Mickle. He had waited too long to thank Coach Matt, and he had missed a colossal opportunity to see Emma. Not what he had hoped for.

But he had met Mrs. Mathys—and received the special gift from her. He sensed that he'd given her something, too, something much more important than a card. He'd helped her relive treasured memories. All in all, it had been a good day.

Around six o'clock that evening, the phone rang.

"Hi, Dad."

"Hello, Son. Your mom says she had an unexpected visitor today."

"Yeah. She still takes me in, gives me the run of the house, and feeds me."

"And enjoys every minute."

"That's what she says."

His dad's chuckle had barely ceased when he added, "Thanks for the note."

Landon heard the catch in his father's throat. He didn't have to imagine what the short message had meant to the man who had been praying for years that Landon would surrender.

"When I tried to read it to your mom, the page seemed blurry." Tears. They had evidently returned, for Landon could hear them as his dad spoke. "You can explain everything the next time you're down."

"Sorry it took so long."

"God is a patient God."

"And you and mom are patient parents."

"We can't do what God can't do. If you weren't ready to listen to Him, we had no choice but to wait."

"I love you both."

"And we love you." Landon heard whispers. "Your mom says she's so happy for you."

"Put her on the phone, will you?"

"I'll go get ready for the big dinner. Bye, Son. I'm proud of you."

"Bye, Dad."

"Hello, Landon."

"Hi, Mom." No sense beating around the bush. "How was Emma today?"

A laugh erupted. "Fine. When did you find out?"

"About ten minutes after she left her shop headed in your direction."

She chuckled again. "Sorry." She cleared her throat. "It's probably not funny to you."

He wished it weren't, but he could see the humor.

"When I opened the door and found you there, I was sure I knew why you had come. Then you stumped me by hibernating in the bedroom, never even asking about Emma."

"Why didn't you say something?"

"You were pretty tight-lipped."

He had been. "I'll ask next time."

"I probably won't know anything then." He could hear the smile in her voice. "So I'll divulge this tidbit now. She really wishes you were going with them."

"Did she say that?"

"She did."

"Anything else?"

"No."

"Thanks for telling me." At least it was something.

———

Landon's Wednesday, the day to try to catch up on everything he missed Tuesday, was a whirlwind. Thursday was nearly as hectic. By Friday, when everyone began anticipating the New Year's Eve celebrations, he wished he had made different plans.

Several young adults from his church had agreed to meet at the home of Tim and Beth Rhodes, a couple about Landon's age. The idea had seemed fine when they'd suggested it. Landon's parents had already made arrangements to entertain some of Dad's business friends. Landon could go down on New Year's Day if he decided to, or he could stay at the apartment and avoid the holiday football fest. Maybe catch part of it if he felt confident enough.

But the more he realized what would be involved Friday night—a whole evening of seeing couples while avoiding certain single ladies, and enduring the "ball drop" and the inevitable kiss, without Emma—the more he wished he could opt out. Still, he'd said he would go, and he felt obligated.

At eight that evening he arrived, chips and salsa in hand, smile pasted on his face. By eleven, his self-appointed departure time, he was engrossed in a cutthroat game of ping pong with Mike, who claimed the victory ten minutes later. Assuring everyone that he'd enjoyed himself—and he had—Landon wished all a Happy New Year and left.

He'd survived over two weeks without Emma. Now just over thirty hours remained. He didn't know her flight times, but his plan was set. He would begin his New Year by meeting her at church Sunday evening. There would be no sneaking up on her in the parking lot, no Aldus Spalding to misspeak and make her angry, no letting her run off and hide in the nursery during the service. He'd be settled next to her from the moment she arrived until the second she departed. If she hadn't gotten back by Sunday night, he'd see her at the shop on Monday morning.

What if she ended things between them? He couldn't go there—wouldn't.

What to do in the meantime? He stuck his DVD of the original *Stars Wars* into the player. The trilogy would occupy at least six hours. Add in time to sleep and maybe take a trip home, and he would have conquered over half the dismal minutes.

After two hours of watching Luke, Leia, and Han battle the Dark Side, Landon adjusted the pillows on the sofa, grabbed the throw, and settled in. The Empire could strike back later.

When he opened his eyes, a bright, frosty New Year greeted him, and the clock informed him that it was nearly noon. He had successfully consumed over eight hours in sleep.

After a piece of toast and some coffee, he called his parents.

"Happy New Year."

"The same to you." His mom sounded perky. "Do you have any big plans for the day?"

"Not sure yet. I just woke up."

"Dad said we might drive your way after we watch the Penn State game on TV. Will you be home?"

"I should be."

"We'll plan on it, then."

After he hung up, he headed for the shower. Ten minutes later, refreshed and ready to face the Siths, he settled on the floor in front of the couch, his bare feet stretched out in front of him, T-shirt and socks at his side. The doorbell rang. He snagged his shirt and pulled it over his damp torso.

New Year's morning. Mrs. Goldberg!

Heading to the door he recalled the conversation from two days earlier when his neighbor had met him as he picked up his mail.

"And, hello, young Landon. How are you this cold day?" Mrs. Goldberg always addressed him as if he should still be carrying his lunch to school.

"Fine, Mrs. Goldberg. And you?"

"As well as can be expected for a widow of my age."

"Your son well?"

"Yes, Isaac and his family, with the children and grandchildren, will be arriving tomorrow. We will welcome the New Year together."

"Sounds like fun."

"And you will be away already on January 1?"

"Not in the morning."

"Ah, this is very good. I will bring the honey cake."

A twinkle lit his eye. "I should tell you not to bother."

Her gnarled fingers clutched his wrist. "But you won't disappoint a lonely old woman, eh?"

"Or myself."

"You are a good young man." She'd clasped his fingers briefly and then toddled down the sidewalk.

Until he heard the doorbell, Landon had completely forgotten about her and her honey cake.

"Happy New Year," he proclaimed, throwing the door wide.

"Happy New Year, Landon."

"Emma!" There she stood, wearing the same marshmallow coat he'd seen before, holding a small bag in front of her.

"May I come in?"

"Y-y-yes!" He clasped her arm and nearly pulled her inside. Then, without wasting another second, he engulfed her, reveling in her softness, savoring her scent.

"I—can't—breathe."

Her choked words beckoned him from his trance. Loosening his hold slightly, he asked, "Why aren't you in Florida? The game's almost ready to start."

"I was too busy. I have a huge event on Tuesday. And I couldn't leave—Pepper—by herself."

Landon heard her slight hesitation, saw her gaze shift toward the floor. Did her words mean what he hoped they meant? His heart pounded like he'd been running sprints for time trials. He relaxed his grip, clasping his hands behind her, leaning back to see her face more clearly. "Pepper seems competent to me. Knows everyone's name. Starts a conversation as soon as anyone walks in."

Emma cast him a cynical glance. "How many times have you been in lately?"

"When you weren't there, you mean?" He cocked his head to one side and grinned.

Mouth gaping, she slapped his arm. "I guess I'll take these." She held up the silvery bag trimmed in bright blue. "And go on a chocolate binge." She wriggled in his grasp.

Landon clamped his arms around her. Then he leaned close and whispered, "I don't think so."

Emma giggled. "You're tickling my neck."

"Am I?" His lips nearly touched her just above her coat collar.

She shivered. "You know you are." Again she laughed.

He pressed a kiss into her neck, and she wilted in his arms. "Why," he asked, "did you give up the Capital One?"

She opened her mouth but snapped it shut.

"Emma?"

"Hailey's younger sister is studying abroad. She had only three days to be here, and she really wanted to spend time with Mort and Sylvia."

Landon drew away from her neck and searched her eyes. "Mort asked you to give up your ticket?" It didn't sound like him.

"No—I—volunteered."

"Oh, Em." He squeezed her tightly. "That game meant so much to you."

"But I'm not family." Her words were muffled as she spoke into his chest. "They needed to be together."

He took her face in his hands and turned it upward. "You are so sweet."

Her eyes glistened with tears, but she smiled. "You're not saying that just so I'll give you chocolates, are you?"

Her eyes were too intent, her hair too soft on his fingers, her lips too close. He bent forward.

The doorbell rang.

"Urrrhhh." Landon couldn't suppress his growl. He lowered his arms from around Emma, pulled her to his side, and opened the door.

Dressed in a bright blue wool coat and a fur-trimmed hat, his neighbor held out a delicate plate on which sat two round cakes.

"Hello, Mrs. Goldberg. Happy New Year." With a smile he accepted the gift.

"A happy one to you, too." Her eyes turned toward Emma. "And to your young lady."

"Mrs. Goldberg, I'd like you to meet Emma Porter. Emma, this is Mrs. Goldberg who lives three doors down." He gestured toward her home.

Emma extended her hand. "Nice to meet you." The two shook hands, and then Emma asked, "Have you brought Landon a special treat?"

The elderly lady's eyes glistened. "A honey cake for the New Year."

"Yum."

"You know the honey cake?"

"No, but I'd like to. It looks wonderful." Emma's smile brought one to Mrs. Goldberg's face.

Landon spoke up. "Emma knows sweets. She owns a candy shop in Bellefonte."

Before his words had faded away, Emma held up the gift bag. "Would you like a sample? I'm sure Landon would love to share."

"Do you worry about the kosher?"

Landon gulped at his neighbor's blunt question, but Emma said, "I use pareve ingredients almost exclusively." She pulled out a plastic zipper-seal bag. "These will be just fine."

Mrs. Goldberg focused on her neighbor. "Young Landon, this is a rare woman: polite, smart, and generous." Grasping the cane that hung from her wrist, she planted it firmly on the walk. Then she accepted the chocolates from Emma. "I must go. We are just now headed to visit Sol's grave. Mazel Tov to you both." Seconds later she turned back, pointing at Landon. "Share the honey cakes with this sweet one."

As soon as Mrs. Goldberg was out of sight, Landon closed the door once again. Emma took off her coat.

"You gave away my present." He reached for the bag, but she avoided his grasp and set it on the table.

"Only part of it." She stepped into his arms. "Are you going to?"

He grinned. So she hadn't forgotten what he'd been about to do. He resettled her in his arms and teased, "Going to what?"

"You know." Her gaze held his. Then she stretched up to whisper near his chin. "Share the honey cakes with me." With one hand she grabbed the plate. With the other she shoved Landon's chest and ducked away, heading for the kitchen.

He laughed where he stood until he heard kitchen drawers opening and closing. Dashing around the corner, he saw Emma leaning against the far wall, delving into the cakes. "Leave one for me." He hurried toward her.

"This is great." She handed him a fork. "I just remembered I didn't have breakfast."

In no time at all, the soft cakes were a memory. When Landon went for a glass of milk, Emma moved to the sink. As she ran water over Mrs. Goldberg's plate and squirted detergent on it, Landon hugged her from behind.

She relaxed into him, resting her head on his chest.

"You haven't told me why you're not in Miami."

"Yes, I have."

He spun her around and placed her wet, soapy fingers on his shoulders. "Tell me the other reason." When she looked at her shoes, he tipped her chin up. "Why, Emma?"

"Because if I was in Florida, there couldn't be an 'us' on the first day of this new year." The earnestness in her eyes squeezed his heart like a vise. "I want there to be—even if we have things to work out."

"Me, too." His arms enfolded her. "I was afraid you'd break my heart when I had finally turned it over to God."

———

The intensity of Landon's blue eyes befuddled Emma's tongue. But if she was never able to speak coherently again, she could at least stand and stare, which was what she was doing when the quick pressure from his biceps drew her back from floundering in the depths of his gaze.

"You in there?" He hunched so that they were eye to eye. "Did you hear what I said?"

Not daring to look away, she nodded.

"You going to say anything?"

Emma pulled him to her, tucking her head under his chin. "It's what I've been praying for—but—I almost—can't believe it. How terrible is that?"

Landon sighed. "Terribly normal."

"It shouldn't be. 'Pray in faith, believing.'"

"But when you want something so much ..."

She raised her head. "And you don't see how it can work ..."

"You pray only because you know you should."

"What happened, Landon?"

"My dad, you, my pastor, and Coach Spalding happened—all at once." Emma gave him a look so filled with confusion that he had to laugh. "I'll tell you all about it."

"Now?"

"I could." He glanced at his watch. "Or we could find some lunch and be just in time to watch PSU clobber Alabama."

Emma squealed as she jumped from his arms and headed for the refrigerator. "What do you have?"

———————————

Landon marveled as he watched her work. She scanned everything available, finally declaring, "Cheese omelets. You're in charge of toast."

Away she went, cracking and whipping, slicing and flipping. The end result was two golden, fluffy omelets worthy of the front cover of any woman's magazine and having a flavor that more than equaled their visual appeal.

"You can come over any day and cook lunch for me." Landon reached for her empty plate. "Or breakfast."

When Emma only smiled, he took her hand. "I mean that."

"I know." It was a breathy whisper. She held his gaze briefly and then scurried to wipe off the stove. "The game's going to start in about ten minutes and—oh, fudge." She swatted the range top with her cloth.

"Fudge?"

"I didn't bring my Penn State stuff. How am I going to enjoy the game without my blue and white?"

"You're wearing blue jeans. I'm sure I can find—"

"Not my special game-day ones." She looked at him as if he'd asked her to go skydiving without a parachute. "And I don't have my PSU sweatshirt or hat or gloves."

"Are you cold?"

"No, but—"

"I'd be glad to warm you up."

She left the cloth where it was, crossed the room, and clutched Landon's arms just above his elbows. "Focus! I don't need the clothes because I'm cold. They're tradition."

Every ounce of Landon longed to chortle at her obsession. Instead he pulled away from her and clasped both of her hands. "Let's shake up tradition." Leading the way, he headed from the kitchen.

"It isn't tradition if you change it," she sputtered, trailing after him.

Arriving at his bedroom, Landon released her hand and knelt by the bed. "Stand back."

As Emma complied, he pulled two cardboard boxes from under the bed, setting each on top of the comforter.

He lifted the lids and turned to her. "My Penn State store."

"No way!" Stepping forward, she raised a fleece throw from the top of the first box, cuddling the blanket's softness against her chest. "Where did you get all this?"

"Most of it from friends and family, beginning when I was recruited by PSU. I used a lot of it before—the accident. Until a few days ago, it was at my parents'."

Emma glanced longingly at the treasure trove in the boxes. Then she studied Landon. "Are you okay with this?" Returning the throw to its place, she stepped close to him and wrapped her arms around his waist. "We could start a new tradition. Me in my not-game-day jeans and white coat, and you cuddled next to me."

Landon knew she meant it, and he loved her generosity. Could he equal it? After all, *Emma* would be wearing the clothes. Emma. Sharing his sofa, holding his hand, probably screaming in his ear. Would he be worried about the memories the clothes evoked as long as he had her?

"I'm okay." He kissed her forehead. "Everything will be way too big, but have fun." Moving to the doorway of an adjoining room, he said, "Bathroom's right here. You better hurry." He squeezed her hand as he walked past her on his way toward the television.

Like a geologist on a dig, Emma began her adventure. Under the throw, she found T-shirts: white ones, blue ones, long sleeves, short sleeves. Setting the stacks on the bed as she went, she grabbed a long-sleeved white one and continued her quest. Hoodies rested at the bottom of the first box. She pulled one out.

"Can I wait till half-time to put all this back?" she yelled.

"You better. They're introducing the Penn State starting line-up."

"Yikes!" She was going to miss the kick-off. When she opened the second box, Emma gasped. "You have a PSU toothbrush."

She heard his deep laugh from the other room.

"I do."

"And a toothbrush holder and Christmas ornaments and—a garter!"

Louder laughter. "A buddy got married. I have long arms." The laughter died away. "The Alabama starting line-up."

His play-by-play had her rattled, but she delved on. Among the miscellaneous items, she found a small stuffed Nittany Lion. She added it to her pile. A pair of socks and some printed navy blue pajama pants—the kind with both elastic and a drawstring—were enough to complete her wardrobe. "Do you have a rubber band?" she yelled toward the living room.

"What?"

"A rubber band. I need one." She gathered up her collection and stuck her head out the bedroom door. "Put it on the dresser, please."

Dashing for the bathroom, she heard, "The anthem, the commercial break, and then the kick-off." She prayed for lots of advertisers.

Inside the bathroom, she removed her own clothes. Then she began donning Landon's PSU garb. The heels of the socks went up past her ankles, but her pants would hide that fact. By cinching the waist of the pants tightly and rolling it down a few times, she managed to situate the crotch nearly accurately. Rolling the legs up, she found she could walk without tripping. So far, so good.

The sleeves of the shirt also required major upward adjustments. Once she had made those, she dashed back to the bedroom. Pulling the hem of the shirt up and to one side, she adjusted the length and width to fit her much smaller frame, holding the fabric in place with one hand. Then she snagged the rubber band and twisted it tightly into the spot where her hand had been. The result was a "tail" of T-shirt that extended beyond the band at the now-smaller-and-higher waistline. She tucked it up inside the shirt and sneaked a glance in the mirror just before grabbing the stuffed animal and the throw.

With the agility of a track star, Emma sped from the room, slid the last few feet as she neared the couch, and plopped down next to Landon. By the time the kicker's toe connected with the football, she had thrown the blanket over both of them. Clutching the Lion in one hand, she claimed Landon's hand in the other. "Go Penn State!" she yelled as the ball sailed toward the end zone.

━━━━━━━

Landon had looked up when he heard the "whoosh" coming toward him. Emma's short brown hair bobbed as she ran and flew back when she slid. The thud of her landing made them both laugh.

"Perfect timing." He removed his nearer hand from her grasp, replacing it with the other so that he could reach around her shoulders and draw her closer.

"Don't panic when you see the shambles I made of your room."

During the first quarter, Emma looked in his direction several times, especially during tense moments. When a player went down and had to be helped from the field, Landon could feel her watching him. Each time he read concern on her face, he would squeeze her hand to reassure her. And pray for strength.

During the second quarter, Emma seemed to relax and have less trouble concentrating on the game. Landon, however, had more trouble. He'd expected to be spending another lonely day without her. Instead, he was caught up in her nearness.

Alabama dominated the first half and, at the end of thirty minutes, led by the score of 14-3.

"How about some popcorn?" Landon asked.

"Sure." Both headed for the kitchen "What do you have to drink?"

"Diet Coke, juice, milk—or coffee."

He chuckled at the wry expression she gave him.

"Juice sounds good."

While Landon located the popcorn and manned the microwave, Emma got a glass of juice for her and a Coke for him. Their food foray complete, they returned to the living room, settling the bowl between them and placing both glasses on the end table near Landon.

"Can they come back?" Nodding at the television, Emma drew her feet up onto the couch and clutched her knees.

"They can." Landon had recognized some weaknesses that the Lions could exploit. "They'll make adjustments at half time."

"You really think so?"

"Yes." He could tell she doubted.

Sighing, she added, "Good. I was beginning to think that breaking tradition had jinxed them."

He allowed himself the pleasure of scanning her body. "In that great outfit? No way!" He had no idea how she could look so cute in clothes at least three sizes too big, but she did. "Where's the rubber band?" He'd been curious since she asked for it.

"Do I have to tell?"

Landon couldn't decipher her look. Was she embarrassed because of where the band was, or was there some other explanation?

"I'm afraid I'm going to owe you a shirt."

Now he was really confused.

Handing him the popcorn, she jumped to her feet and stood in front of him. When she flipped up the hem of the T-shirt, the tail became obvious. "Without the rubber band, the shirt looked like a dress. With it, the hem gets stretched out."

"Pretty clever idea." He set the bowl on the end table, reached toward Emma, and grabbed the protruding fabric. "I like it." In one tick of the clock, he pulled her forward, and she was sitting on his lap. In another, he was kissing her—not to stop her frustrated ranting—but to reveal his heart.

She gasped. Then her lips responded, and her arms closed around his neck. As he increased his pressure and intensity, the kiss leaped from warm to smoldering. Feeling Emma's magnetism in every nerve of his body, Landon pulled her closer, his hands clutching the narrowness of her waist. The more his lips and hands discovered, the more of her he wanted to experience.

All too soon she shoved herself backward and scrambled to her feet.

"Emma?"

She didn't respond.

He rose. "I'm sorry—I—I got—"

Finally she looked up. "Don't apologize." A deep blush lit her face. "It was wonderful—but—"

But risky. Landon knew how risky. Ever since seeing her at his door, he'd been barraged by images of her in his home: in the kitchen sharing a meal, snuggled against him on the sofa, experiencing a kiss that left both of them flushed and breathless. He'd won her heart. More than ever he wanted the rest of her.

"Maybe this wasn't …" Sidestepping him, she grabbed the Lion and the throw. "I'll put these—"

"Don't, Em. Please." Resisting the titanic urge to hug her, Landon positioned himself between Emma and the bedroom, where he knew she was headed.

"Landon, we—"

"I'll keep my distance." Watching Emma's face, Landon recognized her struggle. "I promise."

"We'll watch the game?"

"And see Penn State come back."

She gave him a half smile, and he knew he was gaining yardage.

"No more of me on your lap."

Reluctantly he nodded. "But not too far away." His tone was more confident than he felt.

She sighed and evaded his gaze.

He'd scored points. Were they enough? How he found the strength to stand still and wait while she deliberated, Landon had no idea. But he did both for what seemed like an eternity.

She finally turned her brown eyes back toward him. Wordlessly, she stepped back to the sofa and sat down.

Landon breathed deeply for the first time since they'd kissed. He, too, resumed his original position. He grabbed the popcorn and handed it to her. Then he extended his hand.

Her fingers slid between his.

CHAPTER 15 ═══════

L andon felt the clench of Emma's fingers as the game clock ticked down—
:04—:03—:02—:01—:00. She screamed.

She bounced up and down on the couch. She threw her hands into the air and yelled again. Then she jumped to her feet, pounding rapid steps into the wood beneath her.

Stopping abruptly, she tumbled back to the sofa and planted a quick kiss on his cheek. "They did it! How did you know they would come back?"

Shell-shocked, he shook his head and laughed. "I didn't know they would. You asked me if I thought they *could.*"

"Three touchdowns in the second half!" Without leaving her seat, Emma stomped on the floor. Then, ceasing the commotion, she sprang up again. "I need a drink." She bounded toward the kitchen.

"No caffeine for you," Landon called to her. "You're high enough already."

He heard the water running in the kitchen and recognized the sound of ice cubes as she filled her glass.

She reappeared a moment later. "This would be the perfect time for me to make candy. I'd get so much—" As her words halted, the glass nearly slipped from her hands. "I need to go. I'm so not ready for Tuesday."

"I'll come with you. I can help."

She coughed, nearly choking on an ice cube "No, you can't."

Landon slumped his shoulders and pooched out his lower lip.

"Ah, did I hurt your feelings?" she bantered, closing the distance between them.

"Yes."

She eased in close and turned her face upward. The teasing had left her eyes and voice. "I wouldn't be able to concentrate on chocolates with you there."

Wrapping both arms around her, he said, "I guess I can let you go then— until tomorrow. I'll meet you at church."

"Yours or mine?"

"Your choice."

She hesitated. "Mine. I think Aldus Spalding will be relieved that we're together."

"He will." Landon's heart suddenly clenched. "But not as relieved as I'll be."

She grinned and hugged him tightly. "I really have to scoot. I'll go change my clothes."

"Don't." He didn't relinquish his hold. "Wear mine home. You can bring them back next time."

"What if you need them?"

He gave her an obvious "duh" look.

She snickered.

"I have others."

"And lots of—interesting—things to go with them." She wrinkled her nose at him.

"That garter still bothering you?" He couldn't squelch a grin.

Crimson stole to her cheeks. "You do know what catching the garter means, right?"

"Yeah. Single women try to catch *you* and rush you to the altar."

Placing her palms flat against his chest, she asked, "Why didn't you let someone else have it?"

"And be deprived of a spectacular interception when the best man thought the thing was his? Couldn't do it."

Her face had incredulity written all over it. "What is it with men and competition? Even when they don't want the prize."

"I did want it."

"I'm not talking about the garter itself."

"Neither am I." Landon caught the gleam in her eye and the smile on her face. He beamed. "I was beginning to think that thing was a dud."

She smiled into the back of her hand. "And now?"

"Not so sure. Maybe I'll hang it in the windshield of my Camry."

She laughed and walked out of his grasp. "I'll go grab my things and close up your 'store.'"

Within five minutes she stood at the door poised to greet the cold afternoon.

"Sure you can't stay long enough to say hi to Mom and Dad?"

"I can't. Besides, I saw your mom earlier this week." She laughed. "Wait till you see Pepper's imitation of the way you looked on Tuesday when she told you I was headed to 111 Cherry Lane in Philipsburg. It's hysterical."

"I bet." He rolled his eyes.

"Nine-thirty tomorrow morning."

Landon reached for her at the same time she reached for the doorknob. In a show of superior strength, he grasped her shoulders securely and kissed her briefly but thoroughly. "Thanks for staying. This is the happiest New Year I can remember."

––––––––––

After shutting the door, Landon headed for the coffeepot. His dad would definitely share a cup of French roast with him. His mom might even join them.

Carrying his coffee with him a few minutes later, he entered his bedroom. When he emerged, he had the garter in his hand. He probably wouldn't display it in his car window, but the reaction it stirred in Emma was too great for him to leave it hidden away.

He was pondering where to hang the thing when he noticed the silver bag on the table. He still didn't know what was left of her gift. Laying the garter down, he looked inside the bag and removed the tissue paper. In a zipper-seal plastic sack like the one she'd given Mrs. Goldberg, he found three caramels. He popped one into his mouth. There were definite perks to having a special someone who was also a chocolatier.

Looking into the bag again, Landon found a small white box. His heart sank. The bracelet. "Why didn't you keep it, Em?" he agonized aloud while he lifted the lid. A folded note drew his attention. He set the box down to take up the letter. As he lifted the paper, he found not a silver bracelet underneath it, but a single piece of candy. The top of the milk chocolate square was absent any decoration except for a lion's paw done in white. On a tiny tag next to it, Landon read these words: *The premiere piece in my new "PSU All-Star" collection. The Linebacker: 5 kinds of crunch; 8 layers of smooth.*

Tears stung his eyes. The Linebacker: L58. She'd created a chocolate inspired by him. Even if the candy had the taste and texture of a football helmet, he'd still think it was great. He couldn't believe what she'd done.

When he took a bite of the treat, his eyes rolled back, and he licked his lips. Whatever the five kinds of crunch were, they were a perfect compliment to the chocolate and caramel layers that surrounded them. This was his bona fide new favorite, and that designation had nothing to do with its name. Overwhelmed, Landon plopped into the nearby chair and turned his attention to the other paper.

Dear Landon,

I've been praying for God's peace concerning us. Your "I'm searching for answers" gave me hope on Christmas night. On Tuesday, your mom's news that you'd been looking through football memorabilia increased my optimism. On Thursday, when this "PSU All-Star" idea struck, I was convinced that the Lord was speaking. Then Hailey's sister returned, and I felt that she should go with Mort and Sylvia, and I should stay with you.
Was I right?

> *Happy New Year,*
> *Emma*

P.S. The bracelet is gorgeous. I love it. Thank you.

He read the note again, wiping his eyes as he finished. She was right; they belonged together.

After only a few weeks, she had learned so much about him, had reached deep into his soul to understand who he was. Did she recognize that he was in love with her? Surely she could read his feelings in his eyes, his words, his touches. The memory of that passionate kiss stirred him, and he wondered if she knew the extent of his desire.

Landon's mind transported him back to ninth grade, the year that his tall body had evolved from lanky to muscular, the season that he began playing on the varsity football squad. For the first time, he'd noticed, in a positive way, the admiring stares and grins from the girls in his class. One of them, Ivy, the younger sister of a junior on the football team, began appearing at the door of the locker room each night after practice. For a week she had accompanied him on his way to the car where his dad waited.

At first, Ivy's attention had made him blush and stutter, but after a few days he had beamed and swaggered when she approached.

As they covered the path from the school to the parking lot, she had created opportunities for their bodies to connect: her hand resting on his biceps when she laughed, her side brushing against his as they walked, her eyes boldly assessing him as he moved.

One evening Landon had put his backpack and duffel into the trunk and settled himself onto the front seat next to his dad.

"Beware of any girl who teases you with her body." His father's candid words had brought an instant flush to Landon's face. "She's tempting you with something more valuable—and far more powerful—than she knows."

That had been one of the nights that Landon thought his dad was a relic from the Stone Age. For a week he had seethed, becoming angrier each day. Dad had no right to talk about Ivy the way he had. He didn't even know her.

The following Friday, an away game for the football squad, Landon had carried his bag onto the bus, excitement welling inside him as it always did on game night. Hearing a familiar giggle, he looked out the window. Across the parking lot was the girl he'd seen so often lately—arm in arm with the second-string quarterback as they headed toward the other bus. Her body collided with his several times along their way, and her hand stroked the quarterback's arm just as it had Landon's.

At that moment, Landon had felt used. He'd been such a chump. He had slouched in his seat and pulled the hood of his sweatshirt as far over his face as it could go, ignoring everyone during the bus ride. Later, he'd played horribly, so badly that the coach had even threatened to demote him to the JV squad.

Ivy had taught him a valuable lesson. Over the next few years, several co-eds had been more than willing to give him a refresher course, especially at the height of his Penn State career. With his dad's admonition echoing in his head and the Lord's strength in his heart, Landon had managed to resist. Then he met Emma.

She wasn't a tease like Ivy, but she was a temptation. Her sweetness, vivacity, and love for the Lord brightened his day and made his life more fun. Those qualities alone were hard to resist. But the woman was also beautiful. Landon couldn't think of anything about her that he'd change. Her face—from the dainty nose to the inviting lips—captivated him as soon as he saw her. Her chocolate eyes expressed volumes in a glance, and her thin body accentuated her delectable curves.

He was almost afraid he would scare Emma away if she knew how much he desired her. She seemed pure. And careful to stay that way.

He headed to the kitchen for his phone to make a thank you call for the priceless gift. On his way, he glanced out the window into the still-bright sunshine. His mom and dad were pulling into the drive. He snatched the garter, gathered the pieces of the gift, and stowed everything in his room, just in time to swing the door open before his mom rang the bell.

"Happy New Year!" In spite of his bare feet, he stepped out, enclosed his mom in a hug and swung her in a full circle before setting her back on the ground.

He'd surprised her so much that her mouth hung open without emitting a sound. When both his dad and he began to laugh, she sputtered, "Are you feeling okay?"

"Better than that." He stepped back inside and motioned to them.

His mom hesitated. "You heard about the game?"

"We watched it." He laughed again at his mom's incredulous smile.

"We?" his parents said in unison.

"Emma and I."

His mom had returned to sputtering. "But she's in Florida."

"Nope. She didn't go." Landon's grin grew as the truth hit him again.

"I talked to her on Tuesday. She never said—"

"The shop's too busy." He winked at his mom who'd played a major role in the event on Tuesday. "And Hailey's sister came home for only a few days. She wanted to spend time with the Sawyers. Emma's not family. She gave up her ticket."

His mom sent him a look which said, "Nice try," and he was sure she knew there was more to the story.

"Your mom's waiting for the part that explains why you can't stop grinning."

Dad was right. He couldn't stop. "She wanted us to be together on the first day of this new year."

His mom gasped before clapping her hand over her mouth.

His dad said, "That's what we wanted to hear. I'd shake your hand but—"

Landon finally noticed the small Crock-Pot his dad held.

"What's in there?"

"Spicy sausage dip, and the tortilla chips are right here." He flapped his arm. A plastic bag hung from his wrist.

Landon rubbed his hands together. "Put it on the table. I'll get the plates."

"It will taste better if you warm it up."

His retreating footsteps nearly drowned out his mom's voice.

"It'll be great as it is."

Casting him a wry grin, she said, "I'm not sure you'll taste it."

———————

After church on Sunday morning, Landon and Emma sat in a booth at the family restaurant near his apartment. Noticing her hand waving in front of him, he blinked.

"Something bothering you?" She lowered her hand but leaned toward him. "What?"

"You stopped eating. You're staring into space."

He stretched his arm across the table. "Sorry." How could he be thinking of anything but her? He'd waited for weeks for a moment like this.

"What is it?" Her nut-brown eyes searched his face.

"My yearly review."

Her brows furrowed. "Did something happen at work?"

"I can't think of anything, but the review's been moved from the middle of June to this Friday at 1:30."

"This Friday? As in five days from today?"

"Yeah."

Her eyes widened. "Wow." She exhaled. "At least it's not your first one."

He tried to mask his concern while he nodded. "It's not my first, but it's not like the others." Landon knew he had botched his explanation. He breathed deeply and started over. "The head of all the accounting departments at Penn State called me the day after Christmas."

Emma listened attentively. When he had finished, she stretched her other hand out to him. "I'll be praying and trying not to worry."

"Me, too."

"And you'll call me as soon as you know anything?"

Landon's heart swelled. She cared—a lot. At least that's what he was reading on her face and in her voice. Sliding his hands up her arms and grasping her elbows, he rose slightly from his chair, leaned over the table, and brushed a quick kiss across her lips. Emma's fingers caressed his forearms, and her softness once again overwhelmed him. Against his will, he sat back down. "I'll call you."

She rewarded him with her beaming smile. "Good."

"Speaking of good—" Her nearness had almost made him forget. He cleared his throat and held her gaze. "The Linebacker is better than good."

Instantly, Emma's face blanched.

"Em?"

Her voice trembled. "You really like it?"

"Best of all."

"It's not too—silly? Candy named after football positions."

Reaching out, he cupped her chin in his hand and spoke from his soul. "Are you kidding? In the heart of Lion country? It's incredible."

"Nor too personal? People will ask what the name means."

He raised one eyebrow, grinned and leaned closer, his voice just above a whisper. "How much do you plan to tell them?"

Finally, Landon felt her relax, and she giggled.

"Nothing more than your phone number."

———————

Even with the hours she had worked on New Year's Day and a twelve-hour Monday, Emma chased herself to get everything ready for the Tuesday night banquet in State College. By noon she recognized a terrifying truth: she needed more hands. Since Pepper's were nearby, Emma called Sylvia and begged her to come and man the store. When Sylvia arrived, Emma snagged the younger woman by the arm and whisked her to the kitchen, quickly giving her an apron and a crash course in the chocolates that were on the evening's menu. By four o'clock they were nearly finished.

"Do you plan on fitting all of this into your car?"

Emma looked up from the tray in front of her. Sylvia stood, hands on her hips, just inside the kitchen door.

The question hit Emma like a stampede of horses. She glanced around, and her shoulders sagged. "I will—somehow."

"Take my SUV," Sylvia said. "Come and get the keys when you're ready."

Less than an hour later, Emma pulled away from the curb, headed toward State College. Amazingly enough, she was on schedule, but one drawback had arisen.

Snow. It began falling in fluffy puffs as Emma and Pepper carried tray after tray to the SUV. By the time Emma left Bellefonte, the flakes had accumulated, and more were being driven by a sharp wind, strong enough to push a person around as he walked along the street.

Night had fallen, and visibility was limited. Having decided not to take the Interstate because of the weather, Emma drove slowly on Route 150, making her way cautiously out of town and along the more rural path to her destination. As she rounded a slight curve, two large eyes reflected in her headlights.

Her hand hit the horn. Her foot slammed the brake. The white-tailed deer darted from her path, but not before the car's anti-lock brakes pulsed repeatedly. Though Emma tried to negotiate the curve, the SUV slid from the roadway. Hitting the gravel shoulder, one tire finally found traction, but not before the vehicle came to rest with its right wheels in a shallow ditch.

Scared and shocked, Emma sat gasping for breath in the tilting vehicle. When she could think clearly, she located the switch and turned on the interior lights. Patting her arms and legs, she assured herself that she was okay.

A moment later she flung off the seat belt and threw open the door. Sylvia's SUV! The chocolates! Had they both survived?

Leaving the door ajar, she had enough light to see a portion of the driver's side. She inspected it as closely as possible and then ran her land lightly over the frigid metal. She couldn't see or feel any sign of dents or dings, but she hadn't really expected to find any on that side. She scurried to the other side and grasped the door handle, but the edge of the door was lodged in the gravel. Her hands shook uncontrollably, and her feet slogged in muddy ooze.

Frantic about the chocolates, Emma retraced her steps, shielding her eyes from the headlights as she passed. She was headed toward the rear when she noticed the approach of flashing lights—not the red and blue hues of a police cruiser, but the amber shade of a highway vehicle. The mammoth truck lumbered to a stop behind her on the shoulder where Emma's tracks had left the road.

A chill raced up her spine. She hurried to the open front door and lunged for her purse and phone—in case. She had just emerged, when an overalls-clad man approached.

"You all right?" His voice was direct but not gruff.

"I—I—think so."

He turned his attention to the tire tracks. "What happened?"

"A deer in the road."

"Did you hit it?" He glanced around as if looking for any sign of the animal.

"No, it ran. But I couldn't make the curve, and I ended up here."

"Anyone else with you?"

"No, thankfully. I'm making a—" Mindless of the man standing there, Emma scrambled toward the back hatch. With the help of the interior light, she surveyed all the trays. Empty space gaped at the back and left part of each, while jumbled candies spilled out at the front and on the right.

"My candies!"

"You spilled a bag of candy?" The man had followed her.

"Not a bag—a banquet." She reached for the nearest tray and then yanked her hand back. Her hands were contaminated, and she was late. She shut the hatch with a thud and, turning toward the front of the car, ran smack into the highway worker.

"Where you coming from?"

Did the man not see that she needed to hurry? "Bellefonte, my candy shop."

"Is your name Emma?"

"What?" Were the shocks of this night never going to end?

"Your name. Is it Emma?"

She was sure she'd never met this man. "Yes, but—"

"You know a guy named Landon Steele?"

Emma hesitated. "Yes."

He held out his right hand. "I'm Mike Reynolds. Landon and I have been friends since high school."

Mike. Landon had mentioned him a few times. "You're the guy he plays racquetball with."

"And you're the candy lady, his swee—" He choked off the rest. "Nice to meet you, but not this way." He pointed toward the candy. "Where are you going with these?"

"State College." She gave him the hotel's name.

"This thing have four-wheel drive?"

"I think so. It's not my mine. My friend Sylvia let me borrow it."

"Slide into the passenger seat from the driver's side, and I'll see if I can get you back on the road."

While Mike ran to his truck, Emma climbed in. By the time she was settled, he had returned. He engaged the four-wheel drive and carefully backed the SUV out of the ditch and onto the shoulder. Jumping to the ground, he jogged around and inspected the passenger's side.

Emma lowered the window a bit to hear the news.

"There's mud and snow in the wheel wells, but no damage that I can see."

He crossed in front again and opened the door. "You okay to drive?"

Emma's trembling knees and shivering arms begged her to say "No," but her head knew she had to climb back behind the wheel. Over two hundred guests would be waiting at the banquet.

"I hope so."

Mike looked as though he wanted to argue, but he eventually nodded. "I'm headed toward State College, too. You can follow me."

Emma sighed her relief. "Sounds good." She managed the first smile since the trauma began. "You can face the deer."

A wry grin crossed his face. "They don't have a chance against that thing." He motioned to the thick-bodied vehicle. "My route ends before we get into town. I'll pull into the municipal building parking lot. You know where that is?"

Emma nodded. "I'll wave as I go by."

This time he did take issue. "I'd rather you stopped so that I can see how you're doing. You'll be back on your way in no time."

The determination in his eyes, and the fact that he had been so helpful, convinced her to relent. "Okay, I'll stop, too."

"It'll only take a minute."

Heading toward his Camry after work, Landon heard his phone and reached into his pocket. "Hello."

"Landon, it's Mike. Where are you?"

"Just leaving work. Where are you?"

"Driving the salt truck. I met the candy lady."

"What?"

"Emma. Your candy lady."

"Where?"

"Heading south on 150 toward State College. She had a little trouble delivering chocolates." Mike hurried on. "She's okay. Get in your car and meet us at the municipal building outside town."

"Is Emma with you? Did she wreck her car?"

"She's following me. The car's fine. I just thought you might want to come to her rescue."

Landon imagined the grin he knew was on Mike's face. "I'm leaving the parking lot right now. I'll see you there. Thanks, buddy."

"No problem. See ya in a bit."

Following behind the PennDOT truck, Emma clenched the steering wheel so tightly that her fingers began to ache. Her back stiffened, and she could feel a cramp in her right leg. Surely, they must be nearing their turnoff. She hadn't wanted to lose precious time, but now she longed to stretch her muscles, if only for a few seconds.

At last she saw a turn signal flash in front of her. Mike pulled to the right, and she followed. She had just slipped the car into park when a form loomed at the window. She jumped, and her hand flew to her chest.

Landon whipped the door open, his face white with concern. "Are you okay?"

Her whole body relaxed, and she slumped into him as he reached for her. "How'd you know?" she mumbled into his chest. It was a silly question.

He answered it anyway. "Mike called as soon as he got back into his truck."

She clung to him a bit longer before pulling away. "Some of my candies are ruined, and I'm so late." Reaching for her phone, she said, "I should have called earlier, but I had to concentrate on my driving."

She found the number and punched it into the keypad. While Emma explained, Landon walked around the vehicle. He returned just after she closed her phone.

"How about I leave my car here and drive you into town. I'll help you set up. We can get the Camry on the way back."

Relief flooded through her. "Great idea."

A honk from the road truck drew their attention. Mike stuck his hand out the window and waved goodbye.

Both Emma and Landon yelled, "Thank you." Another blast from the horn, and Mike maneuvered the truck onto the snowy highway.

"Let's go." Putting his one arm more tightly around her shoulders, Landon placed his other beneath Emma's knees and lifted her from the car.

"What are you doing?"

Carrying her toward the passenger door he asked, "Can't you tell?"

Her first response was a giggle. "Yes, but why are you doing it?"

He placed his lips next to her ear. "The truly noble reason is that I don't want your feet to get wet."

Snuggled against his chest, she ignored the fact that they were already soaked. "Is there a less noble reason?"

"Uh-huh."

"What is it?"

"If you have to ask, something's wrong."

She sighed contentedly. "Nothing's wrong."

At that moment, in spite of blowing snow and troublesome deer and spilled chocolates, Emma was telling the truth. Absolutely nothing was wrong.

CHAPTER 16 ═══════

Entering Ed Mickle's anteroom, Landon found a friendly face. "Hi, Stew." He shook his supervisor's hand before settling himself into a nearby chair. Leaning forward so that Mickle's executive assistant couldn't hear, he said, "Do you know what's up yet?"

"Not yet," Stew responded under his breath. "I hate being held hostage by Mickle. You never know that guy's next move."

Landon pondered a response but never got to it. The trim assistant had left her office and was heading in their direction.

"Mr. Mickle is ready for you now." She turned on her heel and briskly led them down the tiled hallway, her shoes tapping out her movement till she reached the door at the other end. Rapping twice in quick succession, she grasped the silver knob and swung the door wide. "Mr. Greer and Mr. Steele."

After Landon and Stew stepped forward, she disappeared. Landon heard the click of the latch. Only then did he notice that two other men were already seated in chairs in front of Ed Mickle's massive desk.

By the time a slender black man had unwound himself completely from one of the chairs, Landon found himself looking up a few inches into the stranger's serious face. The man's companion, an older, shorter, stocky, red-haired gentleman, smiled slightly.

Ed Mickle's sharp voice cut in. "Randall Key, George Newsome," he said, motioning first to the taller and then to the shorter man, "This is Landon Steele and his supervisor, Stewart Greer." He waved his hand toward two other chairs. "Have a seat. Let's get this thing started."

The four men exchanged handshakes. Key and Newsome resumed their seats, while Landon and Stew took the two to their right. All four turned their attention to Mickle, who sat behind the desk in front of them.

"Landon, you've been in your position almost four years now." He adjusted his reading glasses on his nose and scanned the page in front of him before looking back at Landon. "Everything I read here is positive. Stewart wants to keep you in his department, and Rosalee Potts—is that woman ever going to retire—nearly gushes in praise of you."

Prickly heat crept up the back of Landon's neck. He tried to focus—and breathe.

Mickle released the page and leaned forward, his forearms resting on the desk, his eyes peering into Landon's. "I have to agree. You should stay, but—"

Landon tried to swallow his anxiety, but his gulp neither settled his nerves nor cleared any of the dry pastiness from his throat. Somehow he managed to maintain eye contact with Ed Mickle. The older man stopped speaking but stared intently.

"But—" The word came from Landon's left. George Newsome caught his glance and continued. "I'm sure you know that Penn State hires many accountants to oversee the athletic programs here."

Landon did know that. The bigger programs even had their own accountants within the department.

"Mr. Greer may want to keep you," George Newsome said, "but the football department has a place for you, if you want it."

"And if I agree," Ed Mickle interjected.

"Yes," Newsome said.

Landon couldn't move. Football memories blitzed through his brain. Panic bombarded his heart. A football-sized obstruction lodged in his trachea. "Why me?" he finally croaked.

"Because you know what it takes to win, you're a stickler for details, and you can stand up to people. You've done it before." George Newsome's eyes shone when he looked at Landon.

"Accountants notice details. It's what we do." *Why am I arguing with the guy? He just paid me a compliment.*

"Maybe Randall can explain." Newsome leaned back in his chair as Key leaned forward in his.

"I grew up in Charlotte, North Carolina. From the time I was in grade school, I dreamed about going to North Carolina University and being a Tar Heel. The day I got my scholarship to study accounting was the best day I'd ever had."

Pictures of smiling faces flashed through Landon's mind. He could relate.

"Being an accountant, working a white-collar job was my dream, but a few weeks after I mailed my acceptance letter, the university called and wanted me to come and audition for the basketball team. I was shocked. I'd played basketball in high school but had seldom started. I went down anyway, and the coaches liked me."

Basketball player. The height and the toned physique certainly made sense. Landon bet that Randall still played.

"They said I'd see some court time, and my academic scholarship would be supplemented and protected by an athletic one. They offered a tutor to help if I got behind because of the travel. I couldn't refuse."

"I can see why." Landon was intrigued by Randall's story but also baffled by it. How did it relate to this meeting?

"At first I played sporadically. Then team injuries and transfers took their toll, and I was on the court every game. By my junior year, I was a starter, and my whole perspective had changed. Basketball was my life."

Landon's heart lurched. He'd uttered that exact sentiment about football scores of times.

"Somehow I hit the books hard enough to earn my degree, but after graduation I headed to the NBA. My star was flying high."

The man's words should have brought jubilation to his face. Instead, Landon read a hollow regret in his eyes.

George Newsome, who hadn't spoken since the story's beginning, cast a sympathetic look in Randall's direction. "Tell the rest."

"Within a few months, so was I, as high as the drugs that I'd always avoided could take me. My habit and my new 'friends' leached me dry. In less than two years, basketball was a thing of my past."

Tragic. Stupid. Unnecessary. The words trailed each other around in Landon's mind. He could think them, but he couldn't say them. He couldn't say anything.

But Ed Mickle could. "Get to the point, Key. I have another appointment in a few minutes."

Landon glared at the rude man. He wasn't alone in doing so. He could see a defiant glower on Stew's face. Disgust emanated from George Newsome.

If Mickle noticed, he didn't care. "Steele's waiting to see what this has to do with him," he barked.

"After I hit the zero point, a buddy from back home—a true friend since the first day of first grade—rescued me. He convinced me to move back to Charlotte, found an excellent rehab program for me, and after I could think again, helped me to study for the CPA exam."

Landon had spent weeks studying for each grueling portion of his tests, and he'd started right after graduation. He didn't want to consider all he would have forgotten in two years, especially if he'd been doing drugs. His respect for Randall skyrocketed.

"Not long after I landed a job in the field that had for many years sounded like my dream come true, I saw an ad for a position in the basketball department at Penn State. The description said they were looking specifically for accountants with NBA experience. Even though my NBA time was limited, I applied for and got the job. A year earlier I thought I had lost both accounting and basketball. This job brought both of them back."

George Newsome's smile lit up his ruddy face. "As a test case, Randall has far exceeded our expectations. His accounting skills are excellent, and his basketball experience gives him insight as to expenditures that may be out of line one way or the other." Newsome patted the arm of the man next to him before turning his focus to Landon. "We'd like you to be our second experiment, this time in the football department."

"I never played in the NFL." The words hurt Landon far more than just as a liability for a job.

"Barring your injury, you would have. We're confident that your football savvy is more than adequate, and we know that your accounting skills are top notch."

"Besides that, the choices are few." Ed Mickle's snide comment interrupted Newsome. "The vast majority of professional football players don't even have degrees."

"Actually, about half do." Landon felt compelled to defend the players. "And the NFL has a program to help those who don't to continue their education."

"Most in sports broadcasting, athletic training, and other mindless professions, I'm sure. Nothing too taxing on their concussion-racked brains."

Landon squeezed the arms of the chair and mentally began counting to ten.

Stewart spoke for the first time. "We're not here to denigrate or defend NFL players. We're here to find out if I'm going to lose an accountant from my department." He turned to Landon. "What do you think?"

Continuing to clutch the chair, Landon said, "I'm not sure what to think. I had no idea this was coming. I need time."

"Will a week be enough?" Newsome's mellow voice caught Landon's attention.

"I'd say so."

"Then I'll call you next Friday if I haven't heard from you before then."

Landon nodded, and Newsome and Key rose simultaneously.

"Steele can let *me* know of his decision." Ed Mickle glowered at Newsome. "I'll determine *my* answer, and then *I'll* call you."

Placing his hand on Mickle's desk, George Newsome leaned forward, his cheeks glowing even more brightly than they had been at the outset of the meeting. His stare penetrated the electric air. "Since you know so few intelligent football players, maybe you'd better not let this one get away."

For once, Ed Mickle had nothing to say.

Out in the hallway, the four made their way from Mickle's office. Randall Key clutched Landon's shoulder, detaining him momentarily. "I know your story, Steele. It's a tough one."

The understanding he saw in Randall's eyes both surprised and unnerved Landon.

"This could be your answer." He clapped Landon's shoulder. "It was the one I needed."

Landon heard Emma's voice just after the third ring.

"Hi. How did it go?"

"Well, I think."

"You think?"

"I learned some things."

"What things?"

"Ed Mickle is a bigger jerk than I thought."

Emma gasped. "Landon!"

"He is, Em, really."

"From what you told me earlier, you shouldn't be surprised."

"Probably not, but that guy gets under my skin."

"What did he do?"

"Insulted the intelligence of football players. Treated the four of us as peons. Tried to impress us all with his power."

"Wait a minute. Back up." Emma's excited voice interrupted his ire. "Did you say 'the four of us'?"

"Yeah."

"I thought only you and Stew were going."

"So did I." Landon paused. "I really don't want to talk about this on the phone. Can you meet me for dinner—someplace where we can talk?"

"I'd love to." Her answer was quick and her voice bubbly. "Where do you suggest?"

"If you're up to it, my parents' place. You and I can talk on the way down, and then the four of us can discuss it after supper."

"It must be important."

"It is, but it's not bad."

She exhaled into the phone. "So, it's safe to assume you didn't lose your job?"

For the first time since Landon had entered Ed Mickle's office, he smiled. "It's safe to assume that."

"And your mom won't mind if we come on short notice?"

"She was expecting *me*. She'll be thrilled to have *you*." He chuckled. "I think you're her favorite these days."

Emma's laughter floated across the miles. "I keep wondering when she's going to get tired of all the phone calls we share." Her laugh seemed cut short, and a pause ensued. "At first she made me miss my mom so much. Now she fills the void a little."

A twinge pulsed through Landon's heart. "She'd be glad to know that."

––––––––––––––––––

Emma zipped through the living room, sliding to the coat rack where her jacket waited. Headlights told her that Landon had just pulled in. Why was he always so prompt? She stretched her arm into the first sleeve. "The candies for Betty and Marshall," she exclaimed before bolting up the stairs, her other coat sleeve flapping behind her. On the top step she rapped her foot against the unforgiving hardwood tread. In pain she mumbled, "Why can't you ever slow down? He'll wait." She forced herself to walk the rest of the way to her bedroom.

There on the dresser sat the box. Shrugging her other arm into the dangling sleeve, she stole a look in the mirror, settled a strand of hair that had flown up during her whirlwind flight, and breathed deeply. She could hear Sylvia's and Landon's voices from below.

Sweeping the box into her hand, she made her way out the door and back to the steps. She was silently congratulating herself on her composure when she looked down and saw Landon.

He wasn't wearing his leather coat. Instead, he stood in a silver-gray suit, sophisticated enough to be professional, trendy enough to be eye-catching. Even unbuttoned, the tailored jacket hung impeccably, and the slacks came to rest on a pair of highly polished, sleek, black shoes. A purple shirt and striped tie completed his look. With one hand in his pocket, and his weight shifted to one leg, he could have stepped from the page of a men's fashion magazine. Emma's composure took a nosedive, and so—nearly—did she.

Gazing at him, she had missed one step and slid on another before she clutched the banister and halted her downward motion. By the time she righted herself, Landon was leaping up the steps, two at a time.

"What happened?" He extended his hand and held hers securely while she descended the few steps to meet him.

Emma supposed that her glowing face told the story, but Landon didn't seem to suspect. "Just being my normal, graceful self."

He laughed as they took the last few stairs together.

———

Emma shut the front door behind them and took Landon's arm, not wanting to give a repeat performance on the porch steps. "I must have missed the memo."

"What memo?"

"The one about appropriate attire for the evening." She looked down at her jeans and sneakers. "I'm woefully underdressed."

He covered her hand with his. "Five minutes once we get to Mom and Dad's."

They had reached the car, and she turned to face him. "I'll be kind of sad."

"Sad?"

"You and that suit are a devastating combination."

After laughing and hugging her briefly, he said, "You're good for my ego."

"But you're bad for my equilibrium." She didn't know if he grasped her full meaning, but she knew the words were true.

———

"Mickle's secretary walked us down the hall. When she opened the door, two other guys were already seated in his office." Landon had begun his explanation as soon as they were on the road.

"Who were they?"

"Randall Key and George Newsome. Both are accountants at PSU. Randall works in the basketball department. George heads it up."

"Why were people from the basketball department at your interview?"

"They want to use me as a guinea pig."

The creases that wrinkled her forehead were visible in the light from the dashboard.

"A guinea pig for what?"

Landon summarized Randall's story, ending with, "I'd be Randall's counterpart, but working in the football department rather than in basketball."

"Oh, Landon, how exciting! What a ..." She stopped as if sucking the words back into her mouth.

"What a ..." He cast a fleeting glance to his right. "What were you going to say?"

Her hand squeezed his upper arm. "What do you think of the offer?"

Landon sensed the earnestness in her voice. Though he would have been more comfortable hearing her thoughts, he pressed ahead. "I can see pros and cons."

Emma angled to face him. "You name them off. I'll keep score." She held one hand up in front of her. "Pros first."

Her direct approach made him smile. "Okay. Pros first. Doing a job I already know how to do." He paused while she held up one finger. "A new position without having to switch companies or change addresses. Being a little farther up the food chain."

"That's two more."

"I do enjoy football. At least I want to."

"Now you've confused me. Is that a pro or a con?"

"Good question. One I've asked myself all day."

Emma scrunched her brows and pursed her lips. After a few seconds, she said, " Let's come back to that one in a minute. Anything else?"

"Yeah. My doing well would show Ed Mickle a thing or two. I'm almost willing to take the job just to prove him wrong."

She laughed. "Sort of like tackling him from his blindside."

"There's a thought." Landon imagined the arrogant womanizer in a heap on the grass.

"Better not dwell on it." She punctuated her words with a chuckle and a pat on his shoulder. "Now the cons."

"The added pressure to do well, especially because of Mickle."

Emma raised one finger on her other hand.

"Leaving the team I work with. They're good guys. And Stew was really supportive today."

"You sound surprised."

"Stew's hard to read. He can be very demanding, and he rarely praises anyone."

"Did he praise you?"

"Evidently whatever he wrote in my file did. Mickle said so."

Emma reached for his hand. "I'm proud of you."

"For doing my job?"

"For doing your best." She squeezed his fingers. "And for even considering the new position. It has to be hard in some ways."

"Now we're back to football." He groaned.

"The pro that could be a con—and vice versa."

Landon smiled at how well she understood his dilemma. Emma entwined her fingers with his. Her soft smile brought neon brightness to his soul.

She sighed. "Are there any other cons?"

"I'll miss Rosalee."

"Couldn't you take her with you?"

"I could. I doubt she'll go. She's been in that building since she started."

"She's a gem, isn't she?"

"She saved my job the first few weeks."

Emma's laughter bubbled over. "What did you do?"

"I forgot about meetings, couldn't remember names, left things undone."

She snatched her hand away and rolled her eyes. "You did not!"

He sighed heavily. "By the second week, I started finding Post-It notes everywhere. Names. Dates. Times. Responsibilities."

"You owe all your success to Rosalee and her sticky notes?" Emma still seemed surprised.

"Enough to dread an office without her."

Nearing his parents' home a few minutes later, Landon said, "I've got time to think and pray about the job."

"We could start praying now."

"We could, but since I'm driving—"

"You drive. I'll pray." She placed her hand on his arm. "Lord, you know this opportunity surprised Landon. But it didn't surprise You. Help him to see Your plans. Guide him as he explains everything to his mom and dad. Thank You for Your blessings. In Christ's name, Amen."

Her voice faded away just as Landon turned into the drive. Shutting off the car, he unbuckled his seatbelt and turned to face her. "Thanks for coming tonight."

"My pleasure."

"Mine, too." Gently grasping her shoulders, he pulled her close and kissed her. As her lips clung to his, he leaned nearer and wrapped his arms around her. While desire prodded him to linger for a few minutes in the car, prudence reminded him that his parents were expecting them. Mom had delayed supper so that all of them could eat together. He backed away and whispered, "I don't want to go inside, but—" Another quick kiss.

"We'd better." She finished for him. A second later she started to giggle.

"What's funny?"

"Look." She pointed out the windshield.

Landon's gaze followed. His mom stood on the deck, looking in their direction. A moment later his dad joined her.

Landon groaned. "Definitely time to go in." Feeling like a teenager caught out past curfew, he opened his door and hurried around to get Emma's.

She must have sensed his agitation, for as soon as he closed the door after her, she placed her hand on his neck and whispered, "I think it's cute they're concerned."

Another giggle met his ears.

He smiled a half-hearted smile. "Yeah, I suppose."

"Come on, Grumpy. Let's go in." Holding the box of chocolates and her purse in one hand, she took his arm with the other, and they began the jaunt up the asphalt to the sidewalk.

Not until he and Emma were nearly to the deck, did Landon catch a clear look at his mom's and dad's faces as they gazed into the night. Their smiles seemed strained, his mom's especially. Was he imagining things? He quickened his pace. Emma matched his speed.

By the time his foot hit the deck boards, Landon could see the glimmering in his mom's eyes.

"What's wrong?"

Unshed tears pooled instantly.

His dad answered. "Have you heard the evening news?"

Apprehension sneaked into Landon's voice. "We didn't have the radio on."

The look his parents shared portended the ominous.

"What happened?"

"Scandal at the university. The football program."

CHAPTER 17 ═══════

Scandal involving Penn State football? How could anything have happened and Landon not know? "I've been on campus all day. I'd have heard."

His dad's solemn stare smothered Landon's retort and buckled his knees.

"Come inside." Dad urged Mom ahead of him and then motioned for Emma to follow her.

Taking her hand as she passed him, Landon trailed behind Emma. Her fingers trembled and were as cold as though she'd been playing in the snow without wearing gloves. What catastrophe were they about to discover?

His mom headed straight for the living room, never pausing at the kitchen. Landon and Emma sat on one section of the sofa. His parents settled nearby on another.

Landon's dad spoke first. "Do you want to watch the news report we recorded, or would you rather hear it from us?"

Landon turned to Emma.

She shrugged. "Whatever you want."

Landon looked to each parent. His mom's grief was palpable. His dad's expression, grim. "Let's watch it."

Raising the remote, Dad clicked the power button. Seconds later he pressed another button, and the six-o'clock news anchor filled their screen for the second time that night. "The Nittany Valley reeled today as the grand jury released its report on a child sex abuse case stemming more than fifteen years. Indicted in the scandal was former Penn State football coach ..."

Landon processed the name—that of a well-respected, long-time coach, beloved by many. The accusations alleged that he was a man worthy of scorn, a person guilty of committing and covering up heinous crimes involving boys he was supposedly mentoring.

Having entered Penn State well after this man's tenure as coach, Landon knew little more than his name, but he had seen the former leader around campus and had been introduced to him at a football function. If Landon had known then what he'd just learned, he might have taken the guy down with a brain-rattling tackle.

"Identities of victims are being withheld." The newsman's next words jolted Landon. "Penn State's president, its athletic director and others, including football legend Joe Paterno, are also being investigated as to what they knew and when."

"What!" Landon leaped from the couch and shot toward the television. "No way! No way Paterno knew."

The reporter wasn't finished. "Pending further investigation, the possible dismissals of the university president, the athletic director, and even Paterno himself, hover over State College."

Landon had heard enough. He strode back across the room and yanked open the front door, slamming his fist against the doorframe. He grabbed the handle of the storm door and flung himself outside. Tromping to the railing opposite the door, he pummeled the cold, damp wood, before leaning forward and yelling his frustration into the night. Then he attempted to breathe and think.

His alma mater was the object of a grand jury investigation, and Joe Paterno might somehow be involved! This couldn't be happening.

Coach Paterno—long time advocate for PSU, beloved mentor for hundreds of players, proponent of hard work and team play—was being questioned about his knowledge of sordid crimes. Crimes that allegedly occurred on or near the Penn State campus during Paterno's tenure. Landon's imagination couldn't wrap itself around any part of the story.

After over four decades at the university, Joe Paterno was an institution. He'd led the Lions to two National Championships. He'd once been named Sportsman of the Year by *Sports Illustrated*. He'd been memorialized by a statue that stood near Beaver Stadium. He had a Penn State Creamery ice cream, Peachy Paterno, named in his honor.

The door opened behind Landon. He turned.

Without saying a word, his dad stepped up and draped a coat over Landon's suit jacket. Moving to the railing, he stood shoulder to shoulder with his son, looking out across the yard.

"How could any coach do that to kids?"

"You're assuming he did?"

"You're not?"

"I'm trying not to assume anything."

"Innocent until proved guilty?" Landon couldn't keep the sarcasm from his tone.

"That's supposed to be how it works."

Landon knew that in theory his dad was right, but this coach's actions had smeared the name of Penn State football and had cast a pall over thousands of

PSU alumni supporters. It was hard not to believe the worst. "What about Coach Paterno? There's no way he's involved."

"We don't know much yet, but we will soon, I expect."

"The university can't fire him." Landon desperately wanted to believe his own words.

"Depends on what it finds." His dad looked toward him. "No matter what happens from here, Penn State is tarnished."

"Maybe sanctioned by the NCAA."

"The least of its troubles, I'd say."

Did his dad have no concept of what an NCAA reprimand would mean? "Sanctioning is huge."

"Not compared to the human suffering."

Thoughts of the innocent victims aroused fury in every part of Landon. "God could have prevented all this."

"He could have."

His dad's words of confirmation only fueled Landon's rage. He pivoted in Dad's direction. "Then why didn't He?"

Dad winced, but he held his ground. "Men can choose. Adam chose sin. Humanity bears the consequences of his action. We're sinners by nature and by choice."

Landon pounded his palms onto the railing in front of him. "This guy used his position to prey on his victims." The thought repulsed him.

"It appears that way if the allegations are true."

"And people let this go?" Landon couldn't include Coach Paterno in that group. "How could they? We trusted them, admired them—"

"They're just men." His dad cut Landon's words short. "At his best, man is flawed. At his worst, he can devise horrendous evil."

Disbelief surged within Landon. "But Joe Paterno's always preached what's right about college sports—get your degree, play by the rules, work hard." Landon had heard or read hundreds of Paterno accolades over the years—and having played under the man's coaching, he believed them. "He wouldn't have let this go."

"We'll know more soon." Dad stared hard at Landon. "No matter what else surfaces, this is a sad day for everyone associated with the university, especially those involved with the football program."

"Or those who might have been."

Dad's brows furrowed. "Did I miss something?"

"I had my yearly review today at work, six months ahead of schedule." Landon waited for a response. When none came, he continued. "With Stew—and Ed Mickle."

His dad's face registered surprise. "What did Mr. Mickle have to say?"

"He didn't say anything about a scandal." Could Ed Mickle not have known? "What he did say was that he thought I should stay right where I am."

"Were you planning a move?"

"No, but two accountants from the basketball department are planning one for me." Landon clenched the rail harder than before.

His dad waited.

"One of the two guys played briefly in the NBA. He's done so well in the basketball department that his boss wants me to take a corresponding position for the football team."

Dad's heavy sigh punctuated the silence. "And now this." Extending his arm to the side, he pulled Landon toward him briefly. "I'm sorry. I wish I knew what to say or do to help."

"Why can't God let me be happy?" Landon paused long enough to shove his arms through the coat sleeves. "I finally have football back. I've been offered a job as an accountant in that department, and today, hours after my meeting, the bottom falls out."

"You're assuming, once again, that this is God's fault."

Landon jerked his head toward his father.

"I didn't hear His name mentioned in the indictment." Dad allowed his words to fade into the night. Then he leaned one side against the wooden slats. "Those allegations are against a sinful man. We may not understand how God works, but we have to allow Him to work in His own way—a way that is perfect in His ultimate plan."

Landon couldn't argue. His dad would use the Bible to prove his point, and he had all the biblical ammunition in his favor. "What am I supposed to do now?"

"About the job?"

Landon nodded.

Dad hesitated. "What would you have done before all of this?"

"Thought about it. Prayed about it." Landon faced his father. "I told them to give me a week."

"Sounds like a good plan. How has the last twenty minutes changed it?"

Landon's mouth gaped. "I'd be working in a scandalized department."

"You're working at a scandalized school, no matter what the department."

"You think I should take this job?" His intensity had risen with each word.

"I think you should do exactly what you said a moment ago, think and pray. About the job. And about how to glorify God in this travesty."

As it often did, his dad's faith stunned Landon. "You really think God can be glorified in this?"

"I know He can." Dad's firm hand grasped Landon's shoulder. "We can bring Him glory by doing what's right, no matter what." Placing his other hand on his son's remaining shoulder, he added, "Penn State University is more than a football team. More than a handful of sinful, corrupt men. Recovery won't be easy, but PSU can survive, and so can those who have been hurt in this."

Those who've been hurt. The words clanged through Landon's brain. Emma. He'd been so absorbed in his own misery, that he'd forgotten about her. He dashed inside.

When Landon entered the living room, his mom glanced in his direction. Traces of tears streaked her cheeks. Like mud beneath a football cleat, his heart squashed under the anguish in his mom's eyes.

Emma slumped next to his mother, one hand wedged under each leg, her stare riveted to the floor. She never looked up, not even when he knelt on one knee in front of her.

"You okay, Em?"

Her head lifted. A glassy stare met his eyes. "All the happy football memories. All the Penn State pride—gone."

He longed to agree, but he wouldn't let himself. He had to help Emma even though he felt himself floundering. "Not the memories. No one can take those. They're still here." He raised a hand to his heart before inching toward her. Then grasping her forearms, he drew her hands from beneath her legs and clasped her fingers. "No one can steal the memories of the day we met at a football game."

A glint flickered momentarily in her grief-clouded eyes, only to be extinguished by her words. "I trusted them. We all did." Defeat reverberated in each syllable. "Now we hear the university president might be involved. Maybe even coach Paterno."

From the corner of his eye, Landon saw his mom rise. He heard her pass behind him on her way to the kitchen.

He couldn't deny what Emma had said, but he hated to see such torment on her face. Pulling himself to the sofa, he began stroking her hands with his thumbs. "I know you're hurting."

Her head jerked up. "People lied."

"I think so."

"They abused their power."

"They did."

"They destroyed young lives."

"That's the worst part."

She pulled her hands from his and buried her face in them. "One man did evil," she said, her voice muffled, "and maybe others let him get away with it."

Landon slid close. He gently wiped away her tears. He put his arm around her. He pressed her head to his shoulder, rested his head on top of hers, and said softly, "That's what hurts the most."

A gasping sigh shook her body. "My heart is breaking." Sobs chased the words from her throat.

Should he urge her to stop crying? Should he tell her things would be okay? Landon had no idea, so he did neither. He simply sat and held her close, absorbing her shudders, handing her tissues, kissing her hair, and wondering how long she'd need to come to grips with her sorrow.

Minutes passed. Mom peeked in and then shrugged, mouthing, "Supper?"

Landon wasn't hungry, but the meal would be a welcome diversion. He nodded ever so slightly. Mom returned to the kitchen.

A short while later, Emma emitted several choppy cleansing breaths. She raised her head and moved out of his grasp, turning her red, puffy eyes toward him.

"Your job offer."

He tightened his hold on her shoulder. "Not the best day for it, huh?"

She almost smiled. "It's so unfair."

When a loud crash emanated from the kitchen a moment later, Landon released Emma and went to investigate. "What happened?" He found silverware scattered across the floor and his mom kneeling to pick it up.

"Unloading the dishwasher. I spilled the basket." Her grin lightened the moment. "Guess I'll put everything that hit the floor back into the basket and start over."

"Let me help."

"I'll help, too."

Landon turned to see Emma retrieve a fork from the floor.

"How are you feeling, dear?" his mom asked.

"Better, I guess. Maybe *numb* is the best word."

"That's exactly what Marshall said after we first heard the report." Gently squeezing Emma's hand she asked, "Do you feel like eating?"

"Not really, but I am thirsty." She patted her flushed cheeks. "Could I use your bathroom?"

Betty pointed toward the hallway. "First door on the left, remember?"

———

Gazing into the mirror of truth, Emma groaned. She looked horrible—worse than she felt, and that was saying something. Crimson orbs had replaced her cheeks. Her brown irises now had red spider-like veins emanating from them. Why hadn't God made a woman to be beautiful when she cried?

That's easy. We'd have no incentive not to succumb to tears if we looked good when we cried.

If deterrence was the Lord's plan, He had accomplished His purpose. No woman wanted her face to look like Emma's did at the moment.

A few splashes of cold water, several deep breaths, and some time for composure helped measurably. She repaired as much damage as possible, before hazarding one more glance. Encouragement trickled into her heart.

Then she remembered Landon with his breath-taking good looks and that exquisite suit. Wilting, she gripped the vanity in front of her. "Of all the days for him to look so—so—perfect."

Emma squared her shoulders, left the bathroom, and headed toward the kitchen. Nearing the doorway, she heard the amazement in Betty's words as they drifted into the hall.

"Landon, this candy is named for you."

Betty opened the chocolates.

A sorrow strong enough to cement Emma's feet to the floor halted her immediately. Earlier in the day she had put the finishing touches on samples of the second piece in the PSU lineup—the Coach—dedicated to Joe Paterno.

"The Linebacker is the first in the Penn State All-star series." The sorrow in Landon's voice echoed the ache in Emma's heart.

"Oh, Landon, that poor girl. Of all the times for this to happen."

Betty's sympathy made mush of Emma's resolve. The heat of tears stung her eyes. Before the first drop fell, Emma was on her way back to the bathroom. She would not let them see her cry again—not tonight, anyway.

———

After five minutes, Landon expected Emma's immediate return. After ten, he began to wonder. When everything was ready in the kitchen, and Emma still hadn't reappeared, he took action. Confirming that she hadn't returned to the living room, he glanced outside. No sign of her on the deck. He headed down the hall.

At the bathroom, he stopped and knocked. "Emma?"

In a simultaneous motion, she swung the door wide and stepped into his arms. A smile brightened her mouth but did little to cheer her troubled brown eyes.

Landon hugged her. "Everything okay?" He flinched. *Dumb question.* "Don't answer that," he whispered.

She backed away from his embrace. "It's a good thing I *know* that the Lord has a plan for everything because right now I want to doubt."

The frank admission was so "her," a testimony of her reliance on God even in difficulties. "Me, too." He pulled her against himself. "My mom has a favorite verse for days like today. 'Weeping may endure for a night, but joy comes in the morning.'"

Wrapping her arms around him, Emma said, "Maybe I ought to go to bed early so that morning can come quickly."

He chuckled. "I've thought that more than once. I want to take the words literally, but troubles don't usually go away over night."

"This one certainly won't."

She was right, but Landon didn't want her to dwell on that thought. He tried diversion. "Mom has drinks and snacks on the table. You still thirsty?"

For a few seconds, all Landon heard was a significant silence.

Emma stepped back before casting him a melancholy but determined stare. "I can't talk about the lineup."

"I know." He cupped her chin in his hand. "They won't ask."

CHAPTER 18 ═══════

True to their word, neither his mom nor his dad mentioned Emma's chocolates except in praise of the family favorites she had included in a separate container from the Linebacker. His mom brought the package out as dessert.

"Emma, these peanut butter candies are fabulous. Look out Reese's."

Surreptitiously glancing toward Emma, Landon chuckled along with the rest. She was holding up well, it seemed, so he plunged ahead. "Mom, I told Dad while we were outside, and I want you to know, too. Today, just a few hours ago, I was offered a different accounting job at Penn State—in the football department."

Emma clutched his hand.

Landon's mom gasped. Her jaw slackened. "A new position—were you looking—in the football department—but how can they?" She sputtered to a halt.

The grin that Landon had kept corralled finally escaped and galloped in his mom's direction. She had succinctly, if not eloquently, asked many of the same questions that had been troubling him.

His smile seemed to draw one from her, and within seconds she chuckled. "I must sound like a babbling idiot." Her glance went from Dad to Emma. "You won't want to come back. First we lambaste you with terrible news even before you can take your coat off. Now I'm jabbering as though I've lost my brain."

Emma's infectious giggle filled the room, and Landon could have hugged his mom. Her self-effacing comment had called forth some humor. Humor that had been missing since their arrival.

═══════

The job offer and its nuances filled the next two hours. Then Landon noticed that Emma was wilting. Instead of asking questions and making comments as she had earlier in the evening, she sat glassy-eyed and still, occasionally succumbing to a head bob that startled her back to semi-attention.

"We'd better go. Emma's exhausted, and we've discussed my employment opportunity from almost every angle. The only thing I can do is pray and wait to see what happens."

"Don't leave because of me." Emma's earnest eyes pleaded with Landon's. "I'm okay."

You're way better than okay. You're fabulous. Even when you're fighting to stay awake and struggling with devastating news. The words didn't leave Landon's mouth, but he hoped he conveyed them through his eyes. "It's getting late, and you have to work tomorrow. I stole you away early as it was." When she looked ready to argue, he added, "I'll get your coat."

"Let me run to the bathroom before we go."

She took off down the hall. Landon's mom rose to place the coffee cups and Emma's water glass into the dishwasher.

"Watch out for her, Landon. This Penn State scandal hit her on so many levels."

"I know, Mom. I will."

"She may need a hug just to survive the bad days ahead."

Landon didn't miss the glint in her eyes. "I think I can handle that, too."

"I figured you could."

"And would." His dad's voice held a note of humor.

"Any chance I get."

"Watch out for yourself, there. Be comforting, but not too close."

Landon searched his dad's face and understood his dad's concerns. "I'll try."

The weekend was a blur of accusations and investigations. Students rioted in support of Joe Paterno. Headlines from all over the country lashed out against him. The university's Board of Directors met.

The next week began with the firings of three university officials, including Joe Paterno. Some declared the football icon a scapegoat. Others demanded that every vestige of the Paterno era—even the bronze statue in front of the stadium—be rooted out. Landon shuddered every time he thought about the Nittany Lions without their storied leader.

His thoughts about the job offer swirled in the upheaval. Thursday arrived, and he hadn't called George Newsome. Landon needed an epiphany from the Lord—and fast.

It came early Friday morning.

"Mr. Steele, George Newsome's on the line." Rosalee's voice floated over the intercom.

"Thanks, Rosalee." Landon clutched the receiver, his heart pounding.

"Hello, Mr. Newsome. I'm sorry I haven't gotten back to you with my answer. With everything that's happening—"

"That's why I called." Newsome's voice throbbed with tension. "Given all that's occurred, Ed Mickle's been instructed by the Board of Directors to withdraw the job offer, for the present time."

The Lord had spoken.

"I'm sorry, Landon. I really wanted you in our department. As soon as things settle, I'll be lobbying Mickle to bring you on."

Oddly, Landon felt both enormous relief and deep regret. His befuddlement delayed his response for so long that Newsome's voice interrupted Landon's thoughts.

"I hope you're not disappointed—well—not too disappointed. I'm not giving up. I see this as a temporary setback, not a permanent situation."

"To tell you the truth, Mr. Newsome, I see it as a clear answer to a perplexing question."

"I understand your thinking. Right now, the PSU football department doesn't top the list of 'Best Places to Work.'"

Landon admired the guy's candor.

"If the job becomes available in the future, I'd be honored to have you offer it to me."

"Good enough. Keep your chin up. PSU can withstand this."

"That's what my dad's been saying since last Friday."

"I don't know your father, but I like his philosophy—and I respect his son. I'll be in touch."

Long after Newsome had hung up, Landon stared into the receiver, amazed at how decisively the answer had come.

After a quick call to his parents and a longer one to Emma, Landon felt freer than he had in a week. His euphoria uplifted him throughout the busy workday and buoyed his sagging mood when thoughts of the scandal bombarded him.

Then he stepped outside the shelter of his office building and into the mayhem that accompanied the demise of a bigger than life athletic program. Gone was the respite. In its place was a chasm of grief, a void engendered by the fact that football at PSU was forever changed, and Joe Paterno would never again be the head coach of the Nittany Lions.

Landon's thoughts often centered on how the players would respond to another coach, how the student body would behave under scrutiny from the media, and how Paterno himself would react to being removed so abruptly from a position he clearly loved.

But Landon never envisioned the changes in Happy Valley. Reporters from every imaginable venue swamped the campus looking for a person to interview or a picture to take. Hoards of alumni came from across the United States in support of their alma mater, while countless others spoke of hiding their PSU logos and withdrawing their donations. Life for those associated with Penn State felt like a nightmarish virtual reality that Landon hoped to escape soon.

By now he thoroughly understood his plight. Penn State University was forever tainted. Its reputation tarnished. Its standing lowered. Its records suspect. And Landon, as a graduate and employee of PSU was lumped in with myriad others as a part of "the Penn State Scandal." His blood seethed when he remembered that one man—one wicked man—was the root of all the chaos.

In his calmer moments, Landon pondered God's provision. What if he had been offered the accounting position earlier and had taken the job? How would he have coped if he had been thrust into the pandemonium?

Aldus Spalding had been a blessing throughout the ordeal. He called regularly. His upbeat personality always made Landon's outlook brighter. Aldus practically bubbled over each time he spoke of Emma, whom he called "Little Sunshine." He had invited Landon over for dinner that night. Pork barbecue was on the menu.

At lunchtime Landon's cell phone rang. Emma.

"Hi, honey. How are you?"

"Terrible."

She sounded terrible, but he hated to say so.

"I have a fever and a headache. And I'm vomiting."

"Ugghh. Sounds like what I had on Christmas night." *Poor girl.* Landon still shivered when he remembered that terrible ordeal. "Where are you now?"

"I just walked in the door at Sylvia's. I'm going to bed."

"Good idea."

"But I can't sleep long."

"Why not?"

"Too much to do. I still have December's month-end bookkeeping to finish and tax records to gather. For my accountant."

Her spunk hadn't suffered any because of her illness. "Maybe you can talk him into helping you out."

A heavy sigh, tinged with relief, drifted his way. "Oh, Landon, you're the absolute best."

Happiness surged through him. "That's not true, but thanks. I'll see you right after work. Go to bed, and stay there."

"Yes, sir." Her words rang with a snap-to-it force that probably took more effort than normal for her to muster. "Goodbye, love. Thanks."

Was it her fever that had her calling him "love"? Did she realize she had? Day's end couldn't come fast enough. He could be at the Sawyers' before 5:30 if he stopped on the way to pick up something for supper.

Supper. Aldus. "Rats." He punched the coach's speed dial number.

"Hello."

"Coach, this is Landon."

"So it is. What's new?"

"I hate to do this, but I have to cancel tonight's supper. Emma's sick with a fever and upset stomach. She has accounting that needs attention."

"If Little Sunshine needs your help, you better scoot on over there. Give her my best." Aldus's cackle blasted Landon's ears. "You been swappin' germs with that girl? Sounds like you might have shared your Christmas ailment with her."

The tell-tale heat crept up Landon's neck. "Yeah, maybe."

"Maybe? Germ swappin's not a 'maybe' event."

Good thing Landon's phone didn't have video. If Coach could have seen Landon's face, the scarlet in it would have egged him on. "The germ swapping is definite. The sickness, I hope, is coincidental."

Another chortle split the airwaves. "I hope so, too."

━━━━━

Landon plowed through the rest of the day, torn between calling to check on Emma and not wanting to interrupt her sleep. The more he watched the clock, the slower time crawled. At five o'clock he grabbed his briefcase and locked the door.

"'Night, Rosalee."

She looked up so quickly that her reading glasses slipped from the top of her head and landed somewhat askew across the bridge of her nose. "Aren't you the punctual one tonight?" She adjusted her spectacles. "I don't think I've ever seen you dash out of here so quickly."

"Emma needs my help."

"And what kind of help would that be?" The glint appeared in her eye—the same glint that usually came when she spoke about him and Emma.

"Accounting and tax help for a sick client."

"Didn't know you made house calls." The glint had become a beam.

"Only for special people." He winked.

"I thought as much."

"See ya Monday."

———————

Hitting a fast-food drive thru, Landon stashed his sandwich on the front seat and his Diet Coke in the cup holder. He pulled into the Sawyers' driveway a few minutes earlier than he had expected. His foot had barely touched the driveway when the Sawyer's front door opened, and a blanched Sylvia burst across the porch. Her hands flailed in every direction. Worry creased her forehead.

"Oh, Landon, Emma's really sick. I don't know what to do."

He jumped from the car and pushed the door shut with his foot. "Is she sleeping?" he asked, hurrying toward Sylvia.

"She's trying." Her voice quavered. "But her head and neck ache so much she has trouble getting comfortable. About the time she doses off, nausea hits, and she runs to the bathroom to vomit. Now she seems confused, like she doesn't know where she is or who I am."

Landon reached the porch, and Sylvia flung the door wide for both of them to enter.

"How long has she been sick?"

"Since around midnight last night." Sylvia ran a rumpled tissue across her face.

Eighteen hours. Longer than his symptoms had lasted. Rushing ahead of Sylvia, Landon took the stairs two at a time. The bedroom door stood ajar. A small lamp on the dresser opposite the bed only dimly lit the room.

Dressed in heart-adorned flannel pajamas, Emma lay on top of the covers. Even in the faint light, Landon could see that her cheeks glowed bright crimson. Placing a hand on her forehead, he winced at the heat. He grabbed the digital thermometer from the nightstand.

"Emma, it's me. Landon."

When she opened her eyes, they lacked their usual cocoa warmth. Instead they reminded him of a glazed chocolate doughnut, its fudgy goodness masked by a film of white. She didn't acknowledge him.

"Open your mouth, Em."

Still no response.

Sylvia now stood at the foot of the bed, wringing her hands and whimpering quietly. Landon spoke in her direction.

"Grab her purse. We're taking her to the emergency room. Can we use your SUV? It's got more room than my Camry."

"Yes. The Emergency Room. I'll get my keys." Sylvia seemed to draw strength from Landon's words. "I'll leave a note for Mort." She scuttled from the room, mumbling through her tears.

Loosening the corners of the blanket, Landon gathered it around Emma. He lifted her gently. Her head bobbled slightly. She yelped in pain.

"Hang on, Em."

Lord, she is really sick. Help her. Help me. Please.

With keys in her hand and two purse straps over one shoulder, Sylvia returned.

"Hold the door for me, please. And grab the thermometer."

"It's in my purse."

———

Reaching Mount Nittany Medical Center in State College seemed like trying to hit a moving target. The driver ahead of him resisted any speed over 45 mph. Traffic was steady in both directions, so Landon couldn't pass. Fog settled in.

Emma reclined in the passenger seat next to him. From the back seat, Sylvia administered what care she could. Her first order of business was to take Emma's temperature.

"Emma, open your mouth, sweetie."

She crooned the words several times before Emma cooperated. By the time Sylvia removed the thermometer, she was sitting on the floor of the vehicle, leaning her side against the back of the front seats.

"One hundred four point five," she whispered.

"You're sure all this happened since midnight?"

"She went to bed about ten o'clock—later than usual for a Sunday. I heard her get up at four. Before leaving for the shop, she told me she hadn't been feeling well since around midnight."

"It doesn't seem like what I had over Christmas. I was as sick as a dog, but the worst of it lasted only a few hours."

"Maybe it's just hitting her harder. She's petite. She pushes herself too much."

"I'm praying that you're right." Landon scanned the darkness and blinked back the moisture that threatened his vision. When they reached the city limits, he breathed a little more easily.

"Not long now, Em." He patted her hand and waited. She gave no response. He gulped.

In the last block before the hospital, he told Sylvia, "I'll pull up to the ER and carry her in. You park the car and meet us inside." He couldn't leave Emma now any more than he could purposefully cut off his right arm. Sylvia would have to understand.

At the emergency ramp Landon slammed the car into Park, and flung the seatbelt from his shoulder. Running through the headlights, he reached the passenger door and threw it wide.

He extended his arms to enfold Emma. Her body convulsed. She tossed from side to side, nearly pitching herself out of the vehicle. Landon planted himself in the gap and let her use his body as a backstop. Over and over, her head rose from the seat and then slammed back against it, while her body jolted as if experiencing an electric shock.

"Get help, Sylvia. Run."

CHAPTER 19 ═══════

"Sir, are you the one who brought in Emma Porter?"

"Yes. Sylvia and I."

"Sylvia?"

"Sylvia Sawyer. The lady Emma lives with."

"Is either of you her family?"

"Emma has no family nearby."

"So you are …?"

"Her boyfriend." Landon leaned forward, nearer the computer at which the woman typed. "And I need to be with Emma."

For what seemed like a lifetime, Landon had been shuffled from one person to the next, giving whatever necessary statistics he knew and trying to find out any information about her condition. Once Emma had been placed in a bed and surrounded by hospital staff, they had whisked her away. He had tried to follow.

"You can't go in there." A small nurse with a big voice had stepped in front of him, barring the way. "They'll take care of her. Someone will get you later."

Landon had given serious thought to hoisting the imperious woman over his shoulder and carrying her along with him through the doors and into the ward beyond. Now he wished he had.

"Where is her family?" The persistent voice at the desktop roused him.

"In Pittsburgh. Her dad and brother."

"Her current address?"

Rolling his eyes at the unsympathetic woman, Landon spouted off the street and city. "I need to see her."

With machine-like speed, she banged Emma's statistics into the keyboard before glancing toward him. "And when the doctors give the okay, you will." Back in automaton mode, she asked, "Does she have insurance?"

From handling Emma's accounting, Landon knew that she did and which company carried it. He'd asked Sylvia to remove the card from Emma's purse for him. Reaching into any woman's handbag seemed like entering a literal "no man's land." He slid the card across the desk.

"Great."

Again the rapid-fire tapping.

"Do you know her Social Security number?"

"No."

"Her employer?"

"She's self-employed."

At each of Landon's answers, her fingers spidered across the keys in front of her.

"Well, that's all I need for now." She punched one last button, and almost immediately a printout shot from the machine next to her. "Hang on to this for her." She handed it and Emma's insurance card to him. "Wait in the reception area until you're called or someone comes out to see you."

For a split second Landon saw commiseration in her eyes.

"Thanks for your help," she said.

He gulped and fled. As soon as he entered the waiting area, Sylvia jumped up.

"Do you know anything?"

"No, all I did was answer questions."

Sylvia wrung her hands. "I should have brought her sooner. If anything happens to …" Her sob choked off her words.

Landon put one arm across her shoulder and guided her back to the seat she'd just left. "Try not to worry."

Sliding into her chair, she sighed and looked up at Landon. "Aren't you going to sit?"

"I've been sitting. I need to walk."

"Don't go far." Panic had risen to her eyes.

He patted her shoulder. "Just up and down the hall." Fleeing from the grief in Sylvia's eyes, Landon spun toward the doorway.

A middle-aged man in hospital scrubs grabbed Landon's arm just before the two collided head-on.

"Sorry," Landon mumbled. "I wasn't watching."

"No harm done." He looked beyond Landon, raising his voice to the entire room. "Those with Emma Porter."

"Me. I am."

Sylvia sprang forward.

Landon amended his answer. "We are."

"Step into the hall with me."

At last some news.

The doctor's voice was calm and businesslike. "Ms. Porter has meningitis, an infection of the membranes surrounding the brain and spinal cord."

"Spinal meningitis!" Sylvia gasped the words.

"Yes." The doctor spoke directly to her. "It's often called that, but it actually involves both membranes."

To Landon the disease was nothing more than a term he'd heard in conversations here and there. Now he wished he'd paid more attention.

"Meningitis can cause the tissues around the brain to swell."

Glancing toward Sylvia, Landon saw her wilt into tears. He reached out and pulled her to his side.

The doctor had paused. He wasn't finished.

"Swelling interferes with blood flow and can cause complications."

"Complications?"

"Brain damage, paralysis, stroke."

The words landed like a sucker punch to Landon's midsection. "But it can be treated …" Landon begged to hear something good.

"Viral meningitis can't be treated. It often clears up on its own. For bacterial—which is what we suspect Ms. Porter has—there is treatment, but bacterial meningitis is more severe. And quite dangerous."

"There's more than one kind of meningitis?" Landon asked.

"The infection itself is meningitis. The cause of the infection is what tells us how to treat it. The first step is to ascertain the cause."

"How?"

"The severity of her symptoms and the rate of their onset point toward a bacterial cause. We're proceeding in that direction. We did a spinal tap and have taken a culture to determine the specific bacterium. We've started her on antibiotics and given her steroids for the inflammation."

"How long till you know anything for sure?"

"Twenty-four to seventy-two hours. In the meantime we hope the medications will stabilize her."

Was this good news or bad? The man's words sounded a bit encouraging, but his demeanor seemed less hopeful. "Can we see her?"

The doctor shifted his weight. "Bacterial meningitis is contagious. No more so than the common cold, but you need to be aware." He glanced at both of them before honing in on Landon. "Have you kissed her within the last two days?"

Blood surged to Landon's cheeks. "Yes."

"We'll want you on antibiotics. For right now, both of you wear masks while you're in her room. Avoid personal contact with the discharges from her nose or throat. You may see her briefly."

"Finally." Landon hoped he could wheedle his way into spending more than a few minutes with her. He tried to step around the doctor to go to Emma.

"One more thing. She's calling for her mom." His gaze held Landon's. "Where are her parents?"

"Her dad's in Pittsburgh." Landon's shoulders sagged. "But her mom—"

"Her mother passed away a couple years ago." Sylvia managed the sentence that had choked Landon.

"Get her dad here if you can. The next few hours are critical." He turned to go; then he paused. "Remember, just a few minutes."

―――――――――

Landon hadn't expected Emma to greet them with a captivating smile and a cheery hello, but when he entered the room, her lethargic condition stunned him. She was connected to tubes and monitors. Her face still blazed with fever. She didn't acknowledge their presence.

He stepped forward, feeling foolish in his "dust protector" mask. Suddenly, he realized that it should have surprised him if Emma had recognized the two of them. They had to look strange.

"Emma, can you hear me?" Her silence crushed his spirit.

Sylvia stepped up from behind him. "Emma, dear. Please, get better."

Her words conveyed exactly the right message, the one Landon's heart repeated, but his lips were too afraid to voice. Too afraid because he was forced to consider what he would do if she didn't get better.

One minute later—at least that's what it seemed like to him—a nurse entered the room.

"Time's up. Doctor's orders."

Sylvia had allowed him a few seconds alone with Emma, but the nurse seemingly had no concern for their privacy. She recorded the readings from a monitor next to the bed and checked the IV fluid levels. Then she looked sternly at him. "I'm not leaving until you're gone."

Realizing the futility of trying to sweet-talk the woman, Landon gathered his coat from the chair, bent over the bed, and whispered, "Get well. I need you."

―――――――――

Inhaling the fresher air of the hallway, Landon stood and blinked in the bright glare. He crossed to the wall in front of him and stretched his arms over his head, leaning them on the ceramic tile for support. Was it only a few hours ago that he had been planning an evening with Coach Spalding? How had the day catapulted into chaos? Stepping backward a bit, he stretched his arm and leg muscles while he let his head droop at the events of the last couple hours.

A pat on his shoulder roused him. He looked up.

"Dad! What are you …?"

"We came as soon as I got your message."

His message. Landon had forgotten all about the phone call he'd made on the way to the hospital. His dad hadn't answered, so Landon had left voice mail.

"How is she?"

Landon fought the sting in his eyes. "Not good. But at least she hasn't had any more seizures."

"Sylvia says it's bacterial meningitis."

"That's what they think."

"Were you able to reach her dad?"

"Her father!" Landon thumped his forehead with the base of his hand. "I forgot. I need her phone to get his number. It's with Sylvia. C'mon, Dad."

Landon hustled to the lounge where he found Sylvia in a teary conversation with his mother.

"Sylvia, get Emma's phone from her purse, will you?"

A few seconds later Landon took it and headed to the elevator. He'd have to go outside to make the call. "I'll be back," he said to the others.

He turned on the phone as he walked. At the hospital's front entrance, was a lighted veranda. On a nearby bench, a couple sat, deep in conversation. Landon stepped a few feet away and began looking through the list of contacts in Emma's phone. Under "Dad" he found two numbers: one for the house and one for his cell. Since it was nearly eight o'clock, Landon called the home phone.

"Hi, Sis."

The voice sounded younger and more familiar than Landon had expected. "Is this Bud?"

"Yeah, who're you?"

"It's Landon Steele. Is your dad there?"

"Why are you calling on Emma's phone? Is something wrong?"

"Bud, I need to talk to your dad. It's important."

"Let me talk to Emma."

Landon could hear the tension in Bud's voice.

"Bud, give the phone to your dad." Landon had no time for small talk.

"Dad's unavailable right now."

Unavailable. Code for *drunk* or *passed out.* Since New Year's, Emma and he had talked a few times about Bud's coping methods concerning their father's alcoholism. Of all the times for the man to give in.

"Bud, Emma's sick. She's in the hospital, and she's calling for your mom. The doctor says your dad should be here."

"How sick?" The young man's concern level had risen to nearly panicked. "What hospital?"

"Sick enough for you to load your dad into the car even if you have to carry him there. And then to drive the two of you to Mount Nittany Medical Center in State College. Do you have a GPS? Can you find the hospital?"

Not until Landon ceased spouting orders did he notice the silence at the other end.

"Did you hear what I said? Do you have a GPS?"

"I have a GPS."

Landon began to breathe more easily.

"I don't have a license. I don't even have my permit."

No license. He knew that. He and Emma had been praying for Bud to be able to drive by the time he graduated. Stupid.

"I have driven, though. With the GPS, I can find my way."

"No!" Landon couldn't bear the guilt he'd feel if anything happened to the two of them.

"Maybe my pastor or Mr. Inman could—no—that won't work, either."

"Why not?"

"Mr. Inman works nights. And Dad—doesn't like Pastor Jacobs—at all. When he came to, he'd be so mad, there's no telling what he'd do."

An idea zipped into Landon's brain. "Pack a bag for you and your dad. Plan for a few days. Your dad can let his employer know tomorrow. I'll call you back in a few minutes when I have a plan."

"What's wrong with Emma?"

"They think it's spinal meningitis."

━━━━━━

"Dad, I know it's asking a lot, but could you drive to Pittsburgh and pick up Emma's father and brother?"

Landon had explained the situation to his parents and Sylvia. His question brought stares from all three.

"I'm willing to go, but Bud doesn't know me."

"He doesn't know me either."

"But he knows who you are," Sylvia said. "He's followed Penn State for years."

"And you've talked to him." This tidbit came from Landon's mom.

Dad reentered the conversation. "How will Mr. Porter react when he finds out that a total stranger has seen him in a drunken stupor."

"Do we care what he thinks?"

His dad ignored Landon's sarcastic question.

"Maybe they could ride the bus." Landon's mind scrambled for any solution.

"A drunken man on a bus?" Dad seemed more than skeptical. "You really want to try that?"

Mom and Sylvia shook their heads.

"What about a taxi?" Sylvia asked.

Landon's dad gave a half-shake of his head. "Expensive. They charge for both directions."

"How expensive?" Landon buoyed at the idea.

"One phone call and you'll know. But I'd guess five hundred or more."

Five hundred. Outrageous. Gasoline for the round trip by car would cost about fifty.

"I'll go." Dad's eyes conveyed his desire to help. "If you're sure that's what Emma would want."

The words stunned Landon. Emma would want him to make the trip. He knew that. So did his dad. "I can't leave her."

"I wish you didn't have to—but Emma needs her family."

"Doesn't she need me, too?"

"Yes, but right now she needs them more." His dad's eyes reached a new level of earnestness. "And they need to be here. Think about her brother. All that he's dealing with. A drunken father who can't drive, no license to drive himself, a sister who's far away and sick."

Dad knew Landon well. It was almost as if he could look into Landon's heart and see the hurt he experienced for Bud.

"You can't do anything here. Driving to Pittsburgh is something you can do. Bring her family to her. But be careful. We don't need anyone else in the hospital."

"What about Emma?"

"Sylvia's here. Your mom and I can stay. We'll keep you updated." His dad placed a hand on Landon's shoulder. "What's best for Emma right now?"

Landon looked directly into his father's eyes. Then he pulled Emma's phone from his pocket. Disregarding all the restrictions concerning cell phones, he redialed the Porters on his way to the parking lot. "Bud, I'm on my way. I should be there in about two hours."

"It's snowing here."

"How bad?"

"Bad enough to cause accidents."

"I'll be careful. You be ready."

When Landon left the hospital a few minutes later, the roads were dry. The farther west he drove, the worse the conditions became. An hour and a half later, he was grateful for four-wheel drive. The roads were slick, and a few vehicles slid from lane to lane on the Interstate.

It was nearly 11:00 p.m. when Landon pulled up in front of a brick ranch house in a quiet subdivision. The sidewalk had been shoveled recently, and an outside light illuminated the way to the door.

Before Landon could ring the bell, the door flung open, and a thin, brown-haired young man stood in front of him.

"You made good time." He extended a hand to Landon.

"I have a lead foot. If the weather had cooperated, I'd have been here sooner."

Bud's eyes dilated. "Not so sure I like the idea of my sister—or me—riding with you."

The kid was direct. "I got here, didn't I?"

"Good point, I guess." Bud backed up to let Landon inside. "Dad's on the sofa. Our stuff's right here."

Landon tossed the keys to him. "Put them in the trunk. Then come back and lock up. I'll get your dad."

"You need help?"

"Nope." Landon headed for the other room. "Hurry."

Chet Porter lay on his back, sprawled across the sofa. His shoes remained on his feet, and his jacket, complete with a company logo, was still zipped. He had evidently fallen onto the couch and passed out where he landed.

He was a stout man, not obese, but sturdy. Getting him to the car might not be as easy as Landon had thought.

"At least he's ready to go." Landon bent over and pulled Chet by the upper arms until the older man's head and chest were slung over Landon's shoulder and onto his back. Then Landon stood up, hoisting the dead weight with him.

"What's goin' on?"

The slurred words were the only complaint Chet Porter raised. Seconds later he was completely limp, and Landon made his way toward the door. Bud had returned.

"How'd you wake him up?"

"I didn't."

"You just threw him over your shoulder?"

"Yep."

Bud shook his head several times while he stared. Finally he bolted into action, holding the door open for Landon and then shutting it and locking up once everyone was out. Landon waited for him to open the car door.

Once Chet was settled in the back seat, Landon climbed behind the wheel and started the engine. Bud quickly hopped in next to him, and they were moving.

Until they had cleared the traffic of the city, Bud offered little except traffic tips. "Get into the left lane up here," or "Turn right at the next light."

A few times, Landon felt like he was being watched. He ignored the stares until he was out of Pittsburgh. "What?" he asked when he again felt Bud's gaze on him.

"I didn't say anything."

"You're staring."

"Sorry."

"What's on your mind?"

"Emma, mostly. I Googled *meningitis*. It sounds bad."

"It can be."

Landon answered Bud's questions the best he could, but the guy still didn't seem quite satisfied.

"Something else?"

"Nah."

The word and the tone didn't match.

"What's bugging you?"

Bud laughed nervously. "I guess I'm surprised it's really you. You even look like yourself."

"What did you think I'd look like?" Landon had fielded this reaction before. "Let me guess. Like some overweight, out-of-shape, used-to-be athlete."

The laugh was stronger this time.

"Yeah, I guess so. Emma said you were still in shape, but you never know."

"You don't trust you sister's opinion?"

"Not when it comes to someone whose college picture still hangs on her bedroom wall."

CHAPTER 20

Forty-five minutes into the return trip, Landon felt edgy and in need of caffeine. He had driven out of the snow. Now raindrops splashed on the windshield, blurring the horizon and producing a rhythmic slosh as the tires hit the pavement.

"I'm getting off at the next exit. I'll fill the gas tank and get some coffee. You'll have a few minutes if you need anything."

Bud nodded and mumbled in agreement. Then he glanced toward the back seat.

Landon sensed the young man's concern. "Don't worry. Whatever happens, we'll work it out."

"I hope so."

"He'll understand why we had to do this."

"Maybe." Bud stared into the raindrops. "If he's thinking about more than himself."

Landon couldn't believe any father would put his own concerns above those of his sick daughter. "He'd better be. Emma needs us." He broached the question he'd been wondering about since he'd seen Chet Porter on the couch. "Will he be coherent by the time we get to the hospital?"

"Depends on how much he guzzled."

"Any way to figure that out?"

"He was home just before ten."

"Is that late?"

"Kinda early."

Out till ten o'clock drinking while his son waited alone at home. Landon's head swam at the thought. Silence engulfed them the rest of the way to the gas station. Bud offered to pump the gas while Landon went inside to use the Men's room and to find the caffeine he needed.

By the time Landon was ready, Bud had finished, and Landon paid for the gasoline. He found Emma's brother washing the windshield. He handed the kid a five-dollar bill.

"Go inside and get something. I'll take over."

"I have money."

"My treat." He nodded toward the store. "Hurry."

210

Putting the squeegee back into the water, Landon heard a thud and saw the SUV shake. He snatched the handle of the passenger side door. Chet Porter was lying face down on the floor.

The man lifted his head from the carpet and slurred, "Wha's goin on? Where am I?"

Landon felt like reaching in and hauling the guy up by the scruff of his neck. "You're in Sylvia Sawyer's car on the way to State College."

"Sylvia who? Don't know no Sylvia—in State College—don't know no Sylvia—"

"Yes, you do. Emma—remember her—your daughter—she lives with Sylvia."

"Emma?" A glimmer of recognition shot through the man's eyes. "Course I remember—"

"Good. We're on our way to see her."

"What time's it?"

"Just after midnight, Monday night."

Chet raised himself to his elbows, attempting to get up. "Gotta get to bed. Have to work tomorrow."

"You're in a—"

Before Landon could finish, the man's face flopped to the carpet. He didn't move again. Landon stood, gaping at the unconscious muddle. Then he closed the door and climbed back into the car. He was pulling up to the convenience store when Bud exited the building.

At one o'clock Landon's phone rang. He snatched it from the cubbyhole between the seats. "Hi, Dad. How's Emma?"

"Where are you?"

"About twenty minutes away. How's Emma?"

"Not so good." A long pause ensued. "The medications haven't helped much. Seizures began again about ten minutes ago."

Landon nearly slammed his phone into the steering wheel.

"The doctor asked again about her family."

The murky night became even blearier, and Landon swiped at his eyes with one hand. "Tell her to fight. Tell her I love her."

"I'll give her the first message. You can deliver the other."

Landon heard the catch in his dad's throat.

"Hurry. But be careful."

Landon prayed. Bud prayed. Chet slept. Ten minutes later the phone rang again.

"They have the seizures under control, for the moment, at least."

His dad's upbeat voice restarted Landon's heart. "Are the symptoms any better?"

"Not much."

"So she's not out of the woods?"

"Not yet, but she's fighting."

His dad's response seemed veiled. "What do you mean?"

"We'll talk in a few minutes. Bye, Son."

Landon closed the phone.

"Is she worse?"

"No." Landon relayed the news without adding any of his misgivings. "It's time to check on your dad. I'll pull over. You get out and go into the back with him. See if you can wake him up."

Entering the hospital with a half-sober man at his side was a new and highly uncomfortable situation for Landon. Emma's father looked haggard, his eyes blood shot. But he was able to walk, although not with any speed or much coordination.

Bud handled the ordeal like a champion. He talked his dad through the process of where they were and why they were here. He offered assistance when Chet needed it. Otherwise, he let his father do the best he could, neither coddling nor ignoring him.

The trip down the hallway, onto the elevator, and toward ICU seemed eternal. Finally, they neared Emma's room. No one was seated in the waiting area. Landon stuck his head inside Emma's door. His mom jumped up from her seat.

"You're here." Her voiced was garbled because of the mask she wore. "Praise the Lord." She hugged him on the way by.

His dad rose to follow her. "We'll send one of them in with you."

After donning his white-paper disease shield, Landon said, "No, Dad, not yet." He didn't take his eyes from Emma's reddened cheeks. "Tell me what you didn't say on the phone."

Dad stepped forward, laying a hand across Landon's shoulder. "Let her father and Bud come in and see her. I'll talk to you in the waiting room."

"I don't want Chet in here without me. I don't trust him."

"Chet Porter is her dad. You can't keep him away." His father's gaze locked onto Landon's and stayed there until Landon agreed. Then he glanced toward the bed. "Talk to her. I'll introduce myself and then send them in. You and I will chat down the hall."

Landon nodded. His dad left the room.

"Em, it's me, Landon. Can you hear me?" He leaned over her, longing to kiss her feverish cheek, to ease her pain. "I brought Bud and your dad. Open your eyes for them, okay? Bud's really worried."

Her eyelids fluttered briefly, but she gave no other response.

Bud's really worried. Whom was he kidding? Bud wasn't the only one floundering in anxiety. If the words "Please, get well" had raced through Landon's brain once, they'd made more than a hundred dashes through his troubled psyche. Each time, he'd followed them with, "God, help her." Looking at her now, he staggered under the realization that she looked no better than she had when he left.

"I love you." Desperately, Landon poured out his heart, begging silently for some tangible evidence that she'd heard, that she knew he was by her side.

Emma lay unfazed.

The opening door provided some small distraction from the searing pain in his chest.

"Emma, I'm here." Bud entered, scared and uncertain. His face, as blanched as the white T-shirt he wore, contrasted with his dark eyes—black holes of sadness. He wiped nervous fingers down the front of his blue jeans as he crossed to join Landon at the bedside.

"Where's your dad?"

"With your parents. He—he—can't come in."

"They won't let him?" Landon turned toward the door, muttering, "I'm getting Emma's doctor. I drove four hours because he wanted your dad here."

Bud stepped in front of Landon. "It's not the hospital."

Landon's ire toward Mount Nittany Medical slowly quelled.

"What is it, then?"

Bud's shoulders slumped, and he stared at the floor. "It's Mom." The teen's glance inched upward. "He says he can't watch anyone else in the family die."

"Die! Emma's not going to die." Landon grabbed the door and hurled himself into the hallway. What a coward Chet Porter was. Landon wished he'd dragged the man from the couch earlier and sloshed him through the snow instead of carrying him to the car. Maybe the cold and wet would have stunned some sense into the craven.

Storming into the waiting room, Landon watched his dad stand and place one hand on Chet's shoulder. From his seat, Emma's father glanced first at Landon's dad then at Landon. He slid back farther onto his chair.

"Get up and go see your daughter." Landon's words were quiet but not gentle. Chet flinched. Landon strode closer. "Walk down that hall and be the father—the man—that both Bud and Emma need."

"I can't."

"Listen to me." Bending over, Landon clamped both his hands on the arms of Chet's chair. "I carried you to the car while you were passed out." Landon saw the look of caution in his dad's eyes. He ignored it. "I can carry you down the hall if I need to."

"That's enough, Son."

Landon spun toward his father. "You're right, Dad. It is enough." Landon aimed the words in Chet's direction. "Enough time for him to quit pitying himself over the loss of his wife. To stop wallowing in booze. To start thinking about his family."

"Wait a minute." Chet's first clear words shot toward Landon. "Who are you to be lecturing me on my family? Until a few minutes ago, I didn't know you were anything other than a washed-up college linebacker."

Landon countered the verbal blow. "It's not because you couldn't have—or shouldn't have. Bud's known for weeks. He and I talked about my relationship with Emma on Christmas day."

Once again Landon's dad tried to intervene. "This isn't the time or place for this discussion."

Landon scanned the area. Not a soul was in the waiting room except the three men. His mom had evidently taken refuge somewhere else when the sparks started. "This is exactly the time and place. Emma needs him now. And she's just up the hallway." Landon was prepared to hold his position all night.

A standoff ensued. Seconds passed. Finally, Chet Porter's chin dropped, and his eyes left Landon's.

"I'll be there in a few minutes."

Could Landon trust the man to keep his word? He started to warn Chet not to renege, but his dad's eyes pleaded with him not to. Rising to his full height, Landon backed away from Chet's chair. He noticed relief on the faces of both older men. Then he headed back toward Emma.

———

Minutes turned to hours as Bud and Landon kept vigil at Emma's side. Sometimes they talked. Usually, they remained quiet. Occasionally, one or both dosed off. Each time that Emma called out for her mom, Bud would tell her how much their mother loved her. Hearing the words and his voice seemed to calm her.

After the first half-hour when there was no sign of Emma's dad, Landon thought about a repeat performance in the waiting room. But Bud's skill in dealing with his sister made Landon think she might be better off without her father. So he remained where he was.

It was nearly dawn when the door opened quietly, and Chet Porter entered. He was scruffy and disheveled but seemingly aware of the situation. Landon nudged Bud awake.

"Dad, you're here."

Landon stood and bit back the words, "It's about time." He pointed to the masks. Turning to Bud, he said, "I'll be in the waiting room."

———

Exhausted, Landon plopped into the chair next to his dozing father.

The movement roused his dad, who lifted his head from the wall behind him. "Hi. What time is it?"

"Just after six."

"How's Emma?"

"About the same, but no seizures in the last few hours."

Landon's father sat up, rubbing his eyes and stretching the kinks out of his neck. His gray hair looked as though he'd run his hands through it a number of times, but overall, he looked alert, especially for having been awake much of the night.

"Where's Mom?"

"She went home a few hours ago for a little sleep. She'll be back around 8:00."

"Did *you* get any rest?"

"Yes. Right after Chet went to see Emma."

Was his dad confused? "I wouldn't call that anything at all."

"What do you mean?"

"Chet Porter walked into Emma's room about five minutes ago."

"What?" His dad leaned toward Landon. "He left here around 2:30. You're sure he didn't go in to see her?"

"Positive. Bud and I stayed all night."

"Wonder where he went?" He paused only briefly. "You don't suppose he—"

"Found a drink?" Landon wanted to assume the worst about where Chet Porter may have been. And he would have assumed it if he hadn't seen the man enter Emma's room. "I wondered the same thing, but he looked fine a couple minutes ago."

"Good." His dad bent to pull his shoes out from under the chair and slide his feet into them. "Did Emma call out for her mom last night?"

"Yeah, a few times. Bud talked to her. That kid's amazing."

While Landon related the happenings of the night, his dad tied the shoelaces. "You pushed Chet pretty hard."

"I know." Landon shifted slightly. "I felt a little guilty later." Studying his dad, he added, "I was so mad. I wanted to deck him."

"I was afraid you might."

"Was I wrong?"

"You sure didn't score any points with him. Chet and I talked."

The skin on the back of Landon's neck tingled.

"He called you names—none of them complimentary."

Landon cast a sidelong glance at his dad.

"He was about thirty minutes into his diatribe before he found anything positive to say."

Landon had to know. "What was it?"

"He figured you knew how to deliver a blow, or he might have taken a swing at you."

"Good thing he didn't. I'd have let him have it."

"Landon."

"Dad, you saw the guy last night. You should have seen him when I got to his house. He—"

His dad raised a hand to halt him. "Let it go, Son. The man has problems, deep-seated ones that won't be resolved overnight. Let's be thankful that he's still here, and there was no violence." He paused to let the words sink in. "He's with his daughter now, and that's the most important thing."

"I guess so." The admission had stuck briefly in Landon's throat.

"He's not all bad, especially for what he's been through."

"What did he tell you?"

"About his parents, his brother and sister, and Emma's mom—whom he still misses."

"He's made it worse by drinking." Landon wasn't ready to be charitable.

"No doubt. Doesn't everyone struggle to overcome heartache?"

His dad hadn't raised his voice, but the message of his words blared. It had taken Landon over four years to win his battle—and he knew to call on the Lord for help.

"I'll let it go for now—for you and for Emma." In his peripheral vision, Landon saw a familiar figure in the hallway. He jumped up. "Doctor Finch," he called as he hurried toward the man.

"Good morning."

"Any news from Emma Porter's spinal tap?"

"Not for at least twenty-four hours." The doctor glanced at his watch. "For now the medications we've administered are helping. Slightly reduced fever. Seizures under control. No sign of other complications." Crisply, the man turned and strode down the hall.

Landon had only begun to process the word *complications* when he saw the doctor's back several feet away. "But, doctor," Landon called. He got no response.

"Let's have that talk we missed last night." Dad now stood next to Landon. "I need to find a cup of coffee." His father put a hand on Landon's elbow and propelled him forward.

"What complications, Dad?"

"No talk of complications before caffeine."

━━━━━━━━━

"Bacterial meningitis is serious in its own right, but it can cause other problems." Landon's dad pulled a folded sheet of paper from his shirt pocket and handed it across the table to his son.

Sipping his steaming coffee, Landon scorched his throat on the gulp he inhaled. He sucked in a breath of cool air and set down his cup. His eyes scanned the sheet. Then he read aloud: "Possible complications include the following:

    hydrocephalus: build up of fluid inside the skull
    encephalitis: brain swelling

brain damage: loss of memory and/or concentration, decreased
    coordination and balance,
learning difficulties
hearing loss
seizures."

Landon wanted to wad up the paper and pitch it into the nearest trash can. Brain damage. Hearing loss.

He and Emma had gone to church together on Sunday. She'd been fine. Forty-eight hours later she was fighting fever and seizures, wrestling a formidable sickness. One that could change her life forever. Or maybe even claim it. His head throbbed at the possible consequences. He rubbed the base of his palms over his eyes before looking over at his dad. "How did this happen?"

"You mean how did she contract meningitis?"

"Yeah."

"They don't know." His dad seemed almost as flummoxed as Landon was. "According to what you have in your hand, most adults who get it live in proximity to others—in dormitories or military barracks."

"That's not Emma,"

"No, but it's even possible for bacteria in a person's mouth or throat to break through the body's immune defenses."

"Why, Dad? Why Emma?"

"I don't have an answer for that either."

Exasperated, Landon blurted. "I'm trying to—" He clamped his mouth shut.

"Trying to what?"

"Trying to trust God." Avoiding the questioning look in his father's eyes, Landon swallowed a swig of his cooling coffee. "But this is hard."

Dad narrowed his gaze on Landon. "Being faithful and obedient is always hard."

His father's wisdom jolted Landon's heart.

"And it's never finished." His dad spoke with conviction. "One test leads to another."

"Why can't things be easy?"

"Because then we forget about God."

"I didn't." Landon's retort was strong and quick. "I served God during the best times. I was a witness to my teammates. I lived a clean life, set a good example.

Dad's tilting head halted Landon's litany.

"What happened at the first real test the Lord ever gave you?'

Realization smacked Landon with the force of a team bus. He stared into his coffee mug. Several seconds elapsed. "I forgot Him."

"And when people tried to help you see that God had other plans for your life?"

The emotion in Dad's voice drew Landon's gaze upward. His father was taking no joy in seeing his son's anguish. Landon exhaled loudly. "I ignored them." Landon twisted the mug handle from side to side. "But I asked forgiveness. I got help about the nightmares. I let football back in. I even considered a job in the football department."

Landon's father wasn't finished asking questions. "And when did all these things start?

"When did they start?" Landon repeated his dad's words.

Dad nodded.

Landon processed. *The football changes came because of Coach Spalding.* Landon opened his mouth. *No, I'm different because of . . .* "Emma. They started with Emma. She's the one who made me willing to change."

"Exactly." Dad nodded his assent. "Your interest in Emma forced you to think about God. She wouldn't let you shut out an entire portion of your life simply because you were angry at Him."

"See, Dad. I'm getting it. I'm closer to God. I—"

"Emma made your life good again." When Landon smiled in agreement, Dad asked yet another question. "Will you forget God this time if He removes Emma from your life?" Before Landon had time to answer, Dad spoke. "Who are you really trusting?"

Landon slumped in his chair. Tears stung his eyes. Guilt pierced his heart. Through his angst, he barely heard Dad's words. "I'll be in the waiting room on Emma's floor."

━━━━━━

For over an hour Landon wandered the area around Mount Nittany Medical. He walked on sidewalks and through parking lots, never really seeing where he was going or where he'd been. He never found a secluded place to sit and be alone.

What he did find was peace. Peace that came step by step. He confessed his pride. He submitted his life. He accepted God's plan for Emma, whatever it might be.

Was he still worried about her? Yes. Would a piece of his heart die if she did? It appeared to do so even at the thought. Would he remember God even through the trial? He determined to try.

Chilled in body but refreshed in spirit, he entered the waiting room where Dad sat reading *Time.*

Dad closed the magazine when Landon sat down next to him. He scanned Landon's face but didn't ask questions. "You seem better."

Landon nodded. "I am."

"But you need some sleep."

"Probably."

"Go home for a while."

"I'm not leaving Emma."

"You live less than ten minutes from here. We'll call you."

"I might not hear the phone."

"We know where you live." A hint of sarcasm sprinkled his dad's words. Landon couldn't help but grin.

"If you don't answer, someone will come and get you."

Landon shook his head.

"At least rest here."

"I hate the idea of strangers watching me sleep." He grimaced. "Besides, Bud and Chet have been with Emma long enough. I'll go back and take one of their places." A weary smile reached his mouth and eyes. "Snoring in front of them won't be quite as embarrassing."

The hours crept by. Doctors, nurses, and other hospital staff appeared, bringing or taking items, studying and recording statistics from monitors, asking questions or making requests, only to disappear into the nebulous areas outside Landon's world, the world he experienced from the chair nearest Emma.

He watched. He prayed. He catnapped. Sometimes Bud joined him. At others, Landon's mom occupied the chair next to him. Not until late afternoon did Emma's dad return.

Landon looked up when he walked in. Chet merely grunted and sat. Suspicion lurked in two sets of eyes. The air thickened with tension.

Landon wouldn't have bet on Mr. Porter's being sober, but he appeared to be. He leaned toward his daughter. "Wake up, baby girl. I want to see you smile."

Where had that endearment come from? Emma had never mentioned being her father's "baby girl," even though she was. Landon had thought of Chet Porter only as the drunken, absent father, not as the sober, caring dad. A twinge of guilt hit him as he remembered last night.

"You don't like me much, do you?"

Landon's head jerked up as he realized the man was speaking to him. He felt trapped. He couldn't honestly deny Chet's words, but he didn't want to boldly admit them either. He stared openly a moment, gathering his thoughts.

"I don't like what you do to yourself and your family when you drink." *Good answer. Honest and direct.*

"And you'd do better if you were in my place?"

Emma's dad understood *direct,* too, it seemed.

"I sure would try."

"And you think I haven't."

Another stab of guilt. "I didn't say that."

"Not in those words. Not this afternoon. Last night you sure meant them."

Finally, Landon could go on the offense. "You got so drunk you passed out. You put Bud in a terrible situation. You disappeared, leaving Emma for hours. And that's just last night. Doesn't seem like you're trying too hard."

"Maybe you don't know as much as you think."

Maybe. Landon's bigger problem at that moment was what he did know. He suddenly recalled a Bible verse saying something about honoring the aged and fearing God. He knew it was Old Testament law, yet he still couldn't shake the correlation it made. Honoring one's elders is expected of those who love God. *Chet Porter doesn't deserve honor.*

Before the words had exited his thoughts, Landon started. God never let anyone excuse his sin by pointing out the shortcomings of others. Landon owned responsibility for his own actions and words. He swallowed hard but spoke calmly. "I'm sure I don't."

Chet started slightly. He gazed at Landon. "Maybe I'll tell you, some—"

Dr. Finch opened the door and stepped inside. Bud was right behind him. "The results of the spinal tap are in."

CHAPTER 21 ═══════

"**W**e've isolated the bacterium. And what it's sensitive to."

"So it's treatable?" Landon asked. At the doctor's nod, he shot both fists into the air. He leaned over Emma's bed. "You hear that, honey? Help is on the way."

Dr. Finch grinned. "We'll start the specific antibiotic immediately. She'll respond quickly."

"How long till she's better?" Chet asked the question before Landon had a chance.

"Too soon to know for sure. Could be over a month till she's normal. Ten to fourteen days on the antibiotics."

"Ten to fourteen days?" Bud and Landon repeated simultaneously.

"That's a long time in the hospital." Again Chet had read Landon's mind.

"Yes, it is," Dr. Finch conceded. "She's very sick. She'll remain in ICU for the time being. Keep wearing the masks. You don't want to get this." He turned toward Landon. "You did start that antibiotic I prescribed, right?"

Landon nodded. Mom had gotten the pills while Landon drove to Pittsburgh.

"What prescription?" Chet asked.

"Bacterial meningitis is contagious." The doctor nodded toward Landon. "He needs an antibiotic to forestall the bacterium."

"What about my son and me?"

"You haven't been near her the last few days, have you?"

"No."

"The concern is for anyone who was in direct contact before onset."

Chet's gaze riveted on Landon who felt the heat of that stare. Another second passed before Chet looked back at the doctor.

"Direct contact?" he asked.

"Touching, sharing food or drinks, kissing."

Landon ignored the glare that emanated from Chet's face.

Dr. Finch cleared his throat. "I'll stop by later to check on her."

"Are you sleeping with my baby girl?"

Chet's words smacked Landon almost before the door had closed behind the doctor.

"Dad!" Bud gulped and stared. "Emma wouldn't—"

"Are you?" Chet had taken one step closer to Landon.

"No."

Chet's face resembled that of a tiger poised for attack. "You asked her though, didn't you?"

"No."

His jaw slackened only slightly. "You wanted to. Don't deny it. You want my daughter. I can see it in your eyes."

Bud stepped between Landon and Chet. "Dad, don't talk about Emma that way." He pushed his dad to widen the distance.

"I'm not talking about her. I'm talking about him." Chet Porter's extended index finger aimed at Landon's chest. "How much 'direct contact' have you two had?" He bellowed the words around Bud.

"I've held her hand. I've kissed her." Landon blurted the words in Emma's defense as much as in his own. "That's it. If you don't believe me, ask her when she wakes up. Or will you call her a liar, too?"

"Emma doesn't lie."

"On that we agree." Landon met and held Chet's gaze.

Chet blinked. He cleared his throat. Then he grabbed his coat from the back of the chair. "I'm going for a walk."

"Dad, don't." Bud snatched at his father's arm.

Chet avoided his son's eyes. "I'll be back."

Landon watched the door close. Then, ignoring Bud, he rested his head on the wall behind him and shut his bleary eyes. Would he and Chet Porter ever be able to peacefully co-exist? Why did the man seem determined to goad Landon into a squabble? Why couldn't Landon resist the challenge? How would their aversion for each other affect Emma? He pulled a chair close to Emma's bed and sat. The questions pursued each other through his mind while Landon struggled to keep pace. Finally, he gave up the chase and succumbed to sleep.

"You been here all this time, young man?"

"Wha-what?" Was someone talking to him? Landon opened his eyes. He found himself nearly face to face with Charlene, the same portly, fifty-something aide who had been in the room the evening before. She was standing. He wasn't.

"You're wearing the same clothes you had on last night. I figure you must've stayed through." She leaned back a little and surveyed his appearance. "I like the business look, honey, but even on you it fades eventually."

Landon rubbed both hands across his face, willing his muddled brain to clear. When he opened his eyes again, Charlene had moved to his left, and now stood arms akimbo, hands on her hips, head cocked at an angle.

"Didn't want to miss anything."

"You from out of town? We got lots of motels around here."

"My apartment's ten minutes away."

"Ten minutes!" Her hands flew into the air, barely missing the side of Landon's cheek. "And you're still here with those scruffy whiskers and slept-in clothes. Go home and freshen up for your lady friend. You'll want to be your dashing self when she wakes up."

Landon managed a tired grin. "My dashing self?"

"Gallant, debonair, romantic." Her eyes widened.

"I know what it means," he said with a hoarse chuckle. "I just don't feel very *dashing* at the moment."

Charlene swatted at his arm. "Just what I been saying. *Rumpled* isn't *dashing*." She refilled Emma's water pitcher. Then she wagged a finger at Landon on her way toward the door. "She deserves debonair."

Landon hid a grin behind his upraised hand as he waved. He shook his head and chuckled.

Bud stuck his head inside the room. "Has she left?"

"Who? Charlene?"

"Alias the Neatness Police." Bud sat next to Landon.

Finally awake, Landon noticed that Bud had changed clothes. "She arrested you, too, huh?"

"She told me I'd never get the ketchup out of my T-shirt if I didn't soak it soon. Dad agreed. He's compulsive about stains. Ever since the Army."

Landon surveyed his oxford. "No spots here. That's probably the only thing about me that your dad approves of."

Bud's leg jiggled up and down rapidly while he studied the linoleum. "Dad shouldn't have assumed you and Emma were—you know."

Landon saw the embarrassment in Bud's face. "No, he shouldn't have." Landon turned to face Emma's brother more directly. "But I can understand why he did."

Surprise chased the unease from Bud's face. "He knows what Emma believes."

"He wasn't questioning her. He accused me."

"He doesn't know you."

"But he understands men—knows how we think." Bud's raised eyebrows made Landon wonder if the high school senior was as naive as he seemed. "And he knows the reputation of college athletes."

Bud coughed. His knee once again began to jiggle. Maybe he understood more than Landon thought.

"I'm not surprised or angry that he asked."

"What? You sure looked ready to fight."

"He should have asked in private. And he should have believed me when I told him no."

Landon's eyes turned toward Emma, and he caressed her with his glance. "But your dad's right, I do want her, more and more each day."

"Whoa. Whoa." Bud extended his hands in Landon's direction. "Too much information. She's my sister."

Landon laughed outright. "Most women are someone's sister."

"Yeah, but not mine." He stepped to Emma's bed and then looked back at Landon. "And I don't want to think of her as anything other than that."

"Oh, come on," Landon leaned back in his chair, enjoying Bud's discomfort. "Don't tell me you don't have any friends with a sister. You know the one—two or three years younger than you and your buddy."

While Landon spoke, Bud's hands slid back and forth across the top of the bed rail, and his gaze skittered around the room.

"She hung around and stared at you when you were at his house. She was scrawny and gangly, and you two called her names and made her cry."

Bud glanced at Landon. "Yeah, we did." A sheepish grin lit his usually-too-serious face. "Stephen's mom made us apologize—lots of times."

So there was one specific girl. Landon had bumbled onto something worth pursuing. "But she kept coming back."

The grin lit Bud's eyes.

"Then one day you noticed that she wasn't scrawny anymore."

Bud was nodding. "Yeah, sort of overnight."

"That's the way it happens." Landon sat forward. "What's her name?"

"Sarah."

"Does she know you like her?"

"No—yeah—I don't know." Bud turned and leaned on the railing. "She's really popular."

"And her brother? What's he think?"

Bud stared at the ceiling before looking at Landon. "He says I'm an idiot and that I should have told her a year ago."

"Why didn't you?"

"She was only fifteen. Her parents wouldn't let her date. And I couldn't drive. What would we have done?"

"What would you have done?" Landon stepped toward Bud. "Are you kidding?" He settled both hands on the younger man's shoulders. "You would have found more reasons to visit your buddy. And stayed long enough to get a supper invitation." Landon raised a questioning eyebrow. "You would have made sure you got the seat next to hers."

Bud's face was a portrait of missed opportunity. He nodded.

"If it was her turn to wash the dishes, you would have dried. If she wanted to go for a walk, you'd have helped her with her coat." Landon squeezed Bud's tense frame. "You would have spent time getting to know each other."

Bud exhaled, and his chin drooped to his chest. "I am an idiot."

Landon nudged Bud's shoulder with his fist. "A bit dense, maybe."

"I've liked her for a long time." Optimism sparkled dimly in Bud's eyes. "She's funny and happy and kind—and really pretty."

Landon's eyes twinkled brightly. "All of that *and* someone's sister?"

"Yeah." Bud laughed softly and glanced at Emma. "I guess it's not so hard to believe."

"What's not hard to believe?" Chet Porter had entered the room just as his son spoke.

"That sisters can be wonderful," Landon answered for Bud.

"You have a sister?"

"I'm an only child."

Chet wagged his head but moved past Landon without comment. "How are you, baby girl?"

Landon watched as Emma shifted her head slightly, as if trying to dislodge the unconsciousness from her brain.

"She seems to hear me more."

Hope welled in Landon's chest. "I think so, too."

Evidently remembering the directive that allowed only two people in the room, Bud started toward the door.

Chet's words halted him. "What's the name of that redhead from school, the one that came home with Emma several times?"

"Hailey?" Landon suggested. He didn't remember that she was a redhead, but that was the name of Emma's roommate.

"No, Maggie."

"That's it. I knew you'd remember." Chet quickly left the room.

Landon turned to Bud. "Maggie?"

"A friend from the Culinary Institute."

Things didn't make sense. "I'm going to see what's up." Landon followed Chet out the door. Landon's dad was there, too.

"I'll call the school, explain Emma's illness, and ask for Maggie's address." Chet ran his hand through his disheveled hair. "It's a long shot, but it's our only shot right now."

"What are you talking about?"

"Emma's shop." Landon's dad addressed him. "She needs help."

He was right. With Emma in the hospital for nearly two weeks, she would need lots of it. Pepper would be back in classes soon and could work only part-time. Landon knew he could do the bookkeeping, and his mom and Sylvia would help where they could, but none of them had an inkling of how to create chocolates.

Chet reentered the conversation. "Maggie's from the cooking school. She and Emma are friends." He sighed loudly. "I have no idea of where she is or what she's doing, but if she can help Emma, I think she will." He paused. "I need to find a phone book and look up the school's number."

"Wait." Once again ignoring the restriction against cell phone use, Landon pulled his out phone and accessed the Internet. "What's the school's full name?"

Within a few seconds, Chet was heading outside, Landon's phone in one hand and, in the other, the school's phone number written on the back of Landon's business card.

Landon turned to his dad. "He smells like beer. Where's he been?"

"I drove him to Bellefonte to see Emma's shop. He was really impressed."

"He didn't get beer at her shop."

"No, he bought it at the distributor."

"You took him to buy beer?" Landon reached for the wall to support himself. •

"Yes. He's an alcoholic. He's under a lot of pressure. He needed a drink."

227

Landon couldn't deny his dad's words. Neither could he fathom his father's actions.

"The rest of the six-pack is in the car. I have the keys. We'll know where he is and how much he's had."

"You're enabling him."

"No. I'm helping him—and his family—during a stressful situation." His dad stepped closer. "His problems won't go away overnight. He'll need support and time. Most of all he needs the Lord. Right now he has none of them. Let's get him through this crisis. We can tackle the spiritual issues and his addiction later."

Landon opened his mouth but clamped it shut again. Chet was returning.

"I got an answering machine. Asked her to call me back at this number."

More waiting. The three men huddled in the hallway, planning a way for Heavenly Chocolates to survive without its creative genius.

Landon's dad spoke up. "I'll check with Betty and see what days she could work the rest of this week and next. Assuming that we find someone to make candy, we'll need somebody else to sell it."

"What about the little pixie girl? Can she help?"

Landon's head jerked up. He stared at Chet.

"What's wrong?" Chet addressed Landon. "Doesn't she remind you of that pixie in *Peter Pan?*"

"Y-y-yes. With lighter hair, Pepper could be Tinkerbell's double." Landon swallowed. He and Chet Porter had actually agreed on something.

Landon was still mulling over the notion when Bud hurried into the hallway. "She's calling for Landon."

His heart pounding, Landon dodged his dad and Chet. He deftly snatched the mask from Bud's outstretched hand. He was still adjusting it when he reached her bed.

"Emma?"

Her eyelids opened. She studied his face. "Landon." She lifted her hand slightly. "You're here."

Landon's knees buckled. She heard his voice. She knew his name. She recognized him, even with his safety mask. She didn't appear to have suffered any brain damage. The hope in his heart befuddled his brain. "You're awake," he finally managed, grasping her fingers.

"So are you."

He grinned at her statement of the obvious, but his smile froze. The simple had become the profound. For the first time in over four years he was awake. Despite hours of stress induced insomnia, his mind, his soul, and his emotions were vividly alert to God and His plans.

He squeezed her soft hand. "Mostly because of you."

Puzzlement etched her face.

"Meeting you woke me up—to football, to acceptance, to God—to love."

She smiled weakly. "That's so sweet."

Her lashes fluttered, and Landon knew sleep would reclaim her soon.

He was scruffy and disheveled. She was ill and in a hospital. Still, there couldn't be a better time. He cleared his throat. When her gaze turned upward, he said, "I love you."

Weakly she whispered, "I love you, too." A momentary gleam lit her weary eyes. "You won't fall asleep again even after I do, will you?"

"I'm awake for good." It was a vow he would keep.

Addendum

In November of 2011, former Penn State football coach Jerry Sandusky was arrested on multiple counts of sexual abuse against young boys whom he was supposedly mentoring. Two days later, Penn State's vice-president and athletic director were both charged with lying to the grand jury concerning the Sandusky case. On November 9, 2011, long-time football coach Joe Paterno, along with the PSU president, was fired. Paterno's termination sparked outrage and riots among the student body.

The next year (2012) brought other landmarks. Joe Paterno died from lung cancer in January. In June, Sandusky was convicted of multiple counts of sexual abuse, and in July, FBI Director, Louis Freeh, issued a report against the university citing its culpability in the Sandusky situation. Less than two weeks later, the NCAA handed out unprecedented sanctions against Penn State. The penalties included, but were not limited to, a $60 million fine, suspension from four years of Bowl Game eligibility and the slashing of 111 Paterno victories to move him from the number one position of coaching wins to number seven.

In late July, the Commonwealth of Pennsylvania filed an anti-trust lawsuit against the NCAA, mostly concerning how the fine moneys would be spent. The NCAA later filed a counter suit. The outcomes of both are pending.

I have changed the timing of the initial events from November to January and have omitted all names of those accused except for the legendary coach, Joe Paterno. I have tried to present facts without rushing to judgment.

CPSIA information can be obtained at www.ICGtesting.com
Printed in the USA
BVOW08s1135080913

330532BV00001B/2/P